MOON FLOWER

VAMPIRES
of
LOS ANGELES

HEATHER EWEN-FOSTER

For Terry
I will never cease to find inspiration in you.

Ancient Greek Terminology

archon (AR - kawn), *n.*:
pl. archontes (ar - KAWN - tes)
Ruler, commander, chief, captain. An elected officer serving
in a formal vampire government called a *politeia*.

basileus (bas - ill - AI - oos), *n.*:
pl. basileis (bas - ill - AI - ees)
King, lord, master. Usually a term reserved for hereditary
kings.

basileia (bas - ill - AI - uh), *n.*:
pl. basileiai (bas - ill - AI - eye)
Monarchy, kingdom, dominion.

basilissa (bas - ill - IH - suh), *n.*:
pl. basilissai (bas - ill - IH - seye)
Queen, mistress.

dikastes (dee - kas - TAYS), *n.*:
pl. dikastai (dee - kas - TEYE)
Constituent member of a *dikasterion*; juror or judge who
hears cases during a trial.

dikasterion (dee - kas - TAIR - ee - ahn), *n.*:
pl. dikasteria
A tribunal or court of justice.

hetaireia (het - eye - RAY - uh), *n.*:
pl. hetaireiai (het - eye - RAY - eye)
A coven, companionship, association, or brother/sisterhood.
A community of vampires are only considered a *hetaireia*
if they are ruled by a formal governing body, a *politeia*.

koinon (KOY - nawn), *n.*:
pl. koina (KOY - naw)
A vampire community. An ancient term predating vampire
government that refers to a primitive organization of
vampires. Los Angeles is considered a Koinon rather
than an Hetaireia because it has no formal vampire
government in place.

krisis (KREE - sis), *n.*:
pl. kriseis (KREE - says)
A trial, dispute, or judgment.

mater (maw - TAIR), *n.*:
pl. matres (maw - TRES)
Mother. The female sire of a vampire.

neoi (nay - OY), *pl. n.*:
New / young ones. The younger members of a vampire
community or coven.

nomos (NOH - mohs), *n.*:
pl. nomoi (NOH - moy)
Law, custom, ordinance. Taken here to mean the
Constitutional Law of a governing *politeia*.

oligarchia (all - ih - GAR - kee - uh), *n.*:
pl. oligarchiai (all - ih - GAR - kee - eye)
An oligarchy, or government in the hands of a few people
or families. Los Angeles functions as a "benevolent
oligarchy" under the watchful eyes of the Stoicheia,
who as a collective look out for the well-being of the
koinon. But since there is no Constitutional Law in
place, they lack any coercive control over the members
of the *koinon*.

pater (paw - TAIR), *n.*:
pl. patres (paw - TRES)
Father. The male sire of a vampire.

phygas (feye - GAWS), *n.*:
pl. phygades (feye - GAW - des)
Exile, runaway, fugitive, banished person, or refugee.
Name for the elders of the Los Angeles community
who are called "Exiles" because none of them are from
Los Angeles.

politeia (paw - li - TAY - uh), *n.*:
pl. politeiai (paw - li - TAY - eye)
Republic or commonwealth. The formal vampire
government. Only with a *politeia* in place can a vampire
community be considered a proper *hetaireia*.

stoicheion (stoy - KAY - awn), *n.*:
pl. stoicheia (stoy - KAY - uh)
An elemental who has control of one of the four basic
elements, earth, wind, fire, and water. This is a unique

ability not all vampires possess. All Los Angeles Phygades are *stoicheia*, though not all *stoicheia* are Phygades; there are rare examples of them living outside of Los Angeles.

Synedrion (sih - NAY - dree - awn), *n.*:
The International Vampire Council. A representative body consisting of the king or queen (*basileus* or *basilissa*) from every city in the world with a *politeia* in place. Meets once a year.

THE BIRTH

Terror. Pain. Then darkness.

This is how it starts.

The only link to the world around you is the sound of your own heartbeat pounding in your ears. Your hearing seems to be the only sense still functioning, while sight, smell, touch, and taste seem oddly suspended.

You vaguely realize something is wrong with that pounding. You become aware that your pulse is slowing, beat by beat, which rapidly absorbs all of your attention.

Soon, far sooner than should be possible, you have reached that critical point where that little muscle—the strongest in the human body—struggles to keep you from crossing the threshold dividing the world of life from what awaits you at death.

But something else is terribly wrong: there is no warm light to dissolve into, there are no familiar faces waiting to usher you into paradise. There is only darkness and a failing heart that tries to pump what is no longer there. The terror within you surges as you realize that, should your heart fail, this great, dark oblivion of nothingness will become permanent. And all that is you—your very essence of self—will be gone.

And your heart, most assuredly, is failing.

It is at this crucial moment, when time seems to stand still, that you are offered a choice—a choice that is really no choice at all since the basic animal instinct to stay alive now dominates higher forms of reason.

You do not hesitate. You embrace the offer with a ferocity that speaks to the predatory nature once so close to the surface in humanity, though long since buried by generations of social, sedentary living and the trappings of "civilization."

Then comes the oblivion, but not the one you expected—not the one which serves as the fate of everyone else. You are in limbo, with no beginning and no ending. No up and no down. But your sense of self is mercifully intact. You are still you.

Here, in this mental womb, you remain for days until—if you are one of the lucky ones—you open your eyes for the first time to a world utterly transformed. And, as you lay there staring into the brilliant colors of the night, you slowly realize that nothing will ever be the same.

This, dear readers, is what we call The Birth.

My name is Sonia.

I am Vampire.

CHAPTER 1

I T'S THE HOUR BEFORE midnight. For humans in Hollywood, it's the electric hour, the time when that last fortifying snort of cocaine hits the bloodstream before they head out the door for a night of revelry. Heartbeats accelerate, body oils, sweat, and sex hormones intensify, and the vampires of Los Angeles close their eyes and lose themselves in rapture over the intoxicating waves of humanity.

My story begins during the electric hour on a Wednesday. I'm sitting in my favorite coffee shop, settling in for the next couple of hours. I realize that, at first glance, this establishment has little to recommend it to someone such as me. I'm two centuries old and change, and I no longer consume human food or beverages.

But as with everything in L.A., it's about location, location, location.

Situated on the north side of the infamous Strip, Pete's sits across the street from the Viper Room, just east of the Key Club, the Rainbow, the Roxy, and the Whiskey.

During the day it caters to the usual assortment of business professionals and tourists. By the time the sun goes down, this place attracts an entirely different and far more eclectic clientele, making it an obvious choice for my purposes.

Obviously, I don't come for the coffee.

You see, the key to vampire survival is adaptability. At some point during the first century of our vampire lives, we must all make the choice to either modernize and join the mainstream or die. Naturally, most of us choose to live, but it becomes more difficult as time goes by. I often wonder how the ancient ones manage to cope in the Greek *Hetaireia*, the oldest coven in the world. I keep up with the times and follow the shifts in technology, fashion, and politics, as well as the more subtle shifts in language, philosophy, and gender relations. I accomplish this by spending significant amounts of time among humans.

It's vampire anthropology 101, really. I'm 183 years removed from my human lifetime, which I spent primarily on a farm just outside of Sydney, Australia. I was turned just before my 30th birthday in the year 1840. Though I am still young compared to ancient standards, much has changed in the world since my human years, and I have been forced to change right along with it.

Keeping up with the humans is doubly important in L.A., where the vampire existence can largely be a solitary one. If you aren't careful, it's all too easy to fall into the habits of a recluse, habits that call attention to you first as an eccentric, later as a monster. Before you know it, the neighbors have become frightened because you've lost track of time and haven't changed residences in fifty years. And not even the finest plastic surgeons of Beverly Hills can keep you looking young for *that* long.

This sort of thing winds you up on the cover of the tabloids. And despite what everyone likes to claim, people do actually read those things. Hell, *I* read those things. And tabloids are just one step away from *Extra*, which is, in turn, just one step away from *Entertainment Tonight*. Then comes the 8 o'clock news, and that's about the time the Feds take notice. Before you know it, you find yourself shackled in some government lab under a mountain somewhere. No one wants that. Just ask the aliens.

Does the government know about us? Some do. I'm assuming we are one of those nasty little secrets the President learns about upon taking office. The upper echelons of the FBI know about us, same goes for the CIA. Currently, they all ignore us, and we like it that way. Humans pose a danger. It is always best to remember that. They are cattle, yes. But a stampeding herd will wipe anything off the Earth. I don't care how old you are.

So, I try to work in some 'human time' every night. My chosen venue is this coffee shop. I like it because of the interesting nightlife it attracts from the nearby clubs. While I recognize a few regulars, most of the faces change from night to night.

Looking down at my lap, I scan the room through my lashes, noting the usual assortment of tattoos, facial piercings, and spiked hair. In one corner sits a group of Goths, and in another a collection of junkies. Every night, same story, different faces.

Then the door opens with its customary jingle. I look down at my watch: 11:15 pm. Right on time.

I keep my head down as the newcomer makes his way across the room to the counter. I slowly separate his scent signature from the others in the room. God, how I love his scent. Sure enough, I identify the unique layers of phero-mone laced with the day's worth of body oils and faint traces of sweat making up his unique body chemistry. His name is Alex—Alex Chevalier—and I don't need to look up at him to see his face: it's perfectly preserved in my mind's eye. Even as I relate this story, I see the stormy gray of his eyes, turned down a little at the outer corners, and framed by a thick fringe of long, curling lashes, and the dark brown of his wavy hair—cut too long for Wall Street, but too short for the rockers here on the Sunset Strip. His body is lean and athletic, his skin golden brown and sprinkled with small freckles around his eyes and collar bone. I know his name from his brief conver-sations with the baristas, and that he's recently moved here from San Francisco. He's a photo-journalist, unmarried, no girlfriend, and he has a dog named Fluffy.

Alex gets his coffee—always a large fair-trade French roast—and comes to sit down less than five feet away from me. If I look up at him now, I might catch him looking at me before turning to the *National Geographic* he has brought with him.

But I don't look up.

Now don't get me wrong, my pleasure is strictly voyeuristic. Some vampires do have relationships with humans. My friend Sunny has many, many relationships with humans, if you can call them that. But I have a very strict policy for dating humans—I don't. As simple as that. With one significant exception, I've never made love with a human. As far as Alex knows, I don't exist, and will never exist for him. That's the plan, anyway.

Nevertheless, when he takes a seat so close to me, a little

shiver runs up my spine. A faint smile graces my lips. Oh, my, at such close proximity, I smell him all the better—nothing wrong with that. But as I sit here, wallowing in the scented waves of body heat pulsing off his skin to the beat of his heart, a new smell abruptly eclipses Alex.

Pungent. Sour. Oily.

Drug users don't smell very good, especially if they habitually use stimulants. Stimulants make their bodies excrete too much sweat and oil, while rotting out their gums and other soft tissues. I put down the paperback I'm pretending to read and look up at my new friend.

"Hey, Gorgeous," he says, leering.

I have acquired an admirer from the group of junkies in the far corner. Towering over me, he looks like Machine Gun Kelly, but this version is missing several teeth. And his two full sleeves of tattoos are violent and pornographic.

Lovely.

Now, it's not like I haven't had to deal with this sort of attention in the past. I'm considered rather attractive, with long blonde hair, opal green eyes, and body proportions that never go out of style. But my methods for dealing with such advances are not anything I care to exhibit in such a public venue, and certainly not so close to Alex.

"I said, 'hey, Gorgeous.'" When he breathes on me, I almost gag. This guy is rotting on the inside, and sure enough his elevated and erratic pulse suggests he has something much stronger than caffeine in his system. As his heartbeat continues to accelerate, I know whatever drug it is, he snorted it or injected it recently.

"You're really pretty," he says. "I want you to sit on my face."

I ignore him, but this won't work for long. Stimulants have a tendency to bolster the user's determination. And this guy looks determined. He poses no threat to me. If so inclined, I can easily pick him up and hurl him through the front window. Or I can snap his neck, or tear out his throat. I am an apex predator, and he constitutes nothing more than an irritant.

Unfortunately, he's an irritant who has now caught Alex's full attention.

Shit. The last thing I need is a rescuer.

The junkie says again where he would like me to sit, and this time he adds a few other explicit and creative suggestions. I heave a sigh. This is not going well. I sense a subtle shift in Alex's body chemistry. He's getting mad.

So, I do what I have to do. I look up at the fool and smile. Then I shift partially through The Change. My eyes shift to an iridescent green, my pupils slit like a cat's, and my fangs partially descend. We call it 'The Look.' All vampires can do it. And my doctor friend Neichia theorizes that we excrete a sort of 'predator' chemical that goes straight to humans' limbic systems, putting their bodies into a state of panic.

Normally it's extremely effective, but this guy doesn't flinch. The drugs must have created communication problems between his limbic system and olfactory senses. Grabbing me by the arm, he hauls me out of my chair and spins me around. If I hadn't been partway through the change, I'd have seen it coming. But the look comes at a cost, holding me in an unnatural limbo, disorienting me.

With his arm now in a strangle-hold across my throat, he presses me tightly against his body and the cold point of a blade touches the small of my back. My assailant applies pressure, and the wound grows warm. Blood trickles down my back and into my jeans, ruining one of my favorite blouses.

"You look scary when you're mad," he growls, his breath hot and damp in my ear. "But we're gonna go have ourselves some fun now. I'm gonna wipe that look right off your face."

He tightens his stranglehold on me, and, leaning forward, licks up the side of my face in one slow drag. Bingo. I can now clearly detect the drug in his saliva, and it's PCP for the win, laced with enough heroin to take out an African elephant. He's almost certainly delusional and has a superhuman resistance to pain, which gives him superhuman strength. Makes no difference to me. I can rip off his arms if I want to.

But I'm not worried about me.

Looking around at the alarmed faces in the silent coffee shop, I know that unless I do something, my assailant is going to hurt someone. And that something is going to burn me with these humans and this establishment for good. They're about to get an eyeful of something they're never supposed to see.

Bloody hell. I've landed myself in a nice predicament.

Alex slowly gets to his feet, mirrored by a college kid in the corner. I can see the latter's date frantically dialing a number on her phone. Can I wait this out until the cops arrive?

I don't think so.

Sure enough, Alex takes a step towards us.

CHAPTER 2

"LET HER GO." ALEX's voice is soft, but commanding. He takes another step forward.

The junkie transfers the blade from my back to my neck. "Come any closer, boy, and I'm gonna cut her and then I'm gonna gut you." He turns his attention back to me. "You don't want me to cut you, now do you, girlie? You don't want me to hurt you?"

Alex stands within this asshole's reach. I dutifully shake my head. No, I don't want the junkie to hurt me. Then I roll my eyes theatrically at Alex in a silent plea for him to back off.

It works. Raising his hands, Alex takes a step back. "Come on, man," he says. "Let her go. You don't really want to do this."

Alex is wrong on this count. The junkie definitely wants to do this, and is having an excellent time of it. But Alex is almost out of reach. He needs to take one more step backwards, and he'll be in the clear. I try to look even more terrified.

Alex responds and steps back.

But now I have another problem.

The college kid in the corner has circled around behind us, and he's edging his way closer, positioning himself for a surprise attack.

Time to act.

I bring my hand up lightning fast, crushing my assailant's wrist. Howling, he drops the knife as I spin around, still holding onto his wrecked wrist. I pull his arm out of its socket while shoving my knee hard into his groin. Someone on PCP might disregard a broken wrist and bruised testicles, but it's hard to put up much of a fight when one of your arms is no longer functional.

Falling to his knees, the junkie clutches his dislocated arm, screaming. He's lucky. Had I pulled any harder, I'd have torn all the soft tissues connecting his arm to his body, causing an injury that would have plagued him for the rest of his life. As it stands, he only needs a doctor to put the arm back into the socket. The crushed wrist needs surgery, but I'm not perfect. Especially since what I really want to do is bite him. Bite him hard. Tear out his throat. And watch him bleed out. I want it so badly, I can taste it. Then I realize I *do* taste blood—my own—flowing from a gash in my lower lip courtesy of fully descended fangs.

Shit. I've gone through The Change.

By the time Alex rushes forward to grab the knife, I'm halfway out the door. I catch a quick glimpse of him looking around in confusion before I let the door close behind me. None of the other patrons see me leave. If they had, it would have been a blur. One minute I'm there, the next I'm gone. Vanished. A ghost image caught on their visual cortex.

My car is parked in front of the tattoo shop next door. For the first time since moving to Los Angeles, I regret having scored such a choice parking spot. My car is distinctive. Anyone can clearly see it from the coffee shop's door. I hear the scream of sirens growing louder as they close in.

Fluorescent lights and neon tubing make the tattoo shop look cheerful. And business is good. Through the open door, I see a handful of customers milling around, though none of them pay me any attention. I'm not so lucky with the two sitting out front in plastic chairs, smoking and watching the people walk by. I keep my head down, avoiding eye contact, but one of them is feeling friendly, despite the sirens and commotion.

"Hey, baby," he says. "I like your car." A beautiful Asian dragon tattoo coils up his right arm, its orange, red, green, and gold scales luminous in the tattoo shop's glow.

"Thanks." I throw a glance over my shoulder. No one has followed me. The sirens are getting closer.

"What year is it?"

"'81." I don't want to look like I'm fleeing. This guy would be able to ID me in any lineup. I can hear four distinct sirens barreling down Sunset Boulevard in our direction. Does one of them have a canine unit? Can't tell. The tattooed guys' smoke is messing with my senses. But dogs are bad news—they can track.

"That's the Magnum P. I. Ferrari, isn't it?" Tattoo Man asks.

I answer in the affirmative as I slide into the driver's seat, but Tattoo Man's attention has finally been diverted to the four cop cars screeching up to the coffee shop, two in the front, and two down the side alley. One of them does have a canine unit. Shit. Time to go.

I fire up the engine and risk an illegal U-turn just as

the cops enter the coffee shop with weapons drawn, one of them hanging onto the harness of a wolfish looking brute that looks like he wants to eat someone. Once I'm eastbound, I relax a little. I'm pretty sure no one from the coffee shop will be able to trace me by name.

But as I cross La Cienega, passing the Comedy Store and then the House of Blues, I consider if I can still be traced through the car. By the time I pass the customary line of limousines parked outside the ivy-covered street entrance to the Chateau Marmont, I've convinced myself that this is unlikely. From this point on, though, I'll be prudent and park farther away from businesses I plan to visit more than once.

Soon the character of Sunset begins to shift, motels replacing exclusive boutique hotels, strip clubs replacing the music clubs, and billboards advertising AIDS awareness groups replacing the massive posters for Guess jeans and Calvin Klein perfume. The giant Guitar Center Hollywood marks the completion of the transformation as fast-food chains, gas stations, and liquor stores come to dominate the Boulevard.

I've now passed safely out of West Hollywood and into Hollywood proper without a hint of a flashing light behind me. But a sad note of regret tinges my relief. I will not see Alex anymore. Almost as soon as his face pops into my mind, however, I dismiss it. He is a human. Nothing more. Humans come and humans go. That is the nature of their existence.

By the time I ease up to the red light at Sunset and La Brea, I'm relaxed enough to let my thoughts drift. I muse over what I shall do for the rest of the night. I have tentative plans with Neichia to come over for bloody marys around two, and I have a sneaking suspicion Sunny will be staying at my place for the next few days—seems I remember him telling me about a party he planned to throw. This means I'll be plus one houseguest for at least a week. By then all the partyers will have been removed from his Malibu compound and the cleaning crew will have scoured the place top to bottom to eradicate the human smell.

As I wait for the light to change, absently reflecting on Sunny and his legendary parties, I smell something familiar.

Alex.

I smell Alex, more than a mile from where I'd left him. He has to be in a car, somewhere very close by. I look to my left and see a cream-colored Bentley convertible full of twenty-somethings. They look very rich and very bored. Alex is not among them.

Turning to my right, I jump at Alex's unexpected proximity. There he is alright, pulled up next to me in a black, beautifully-restored, 1970s Cougar. Sitting bolt upright in the driver's seat, he's gripping the steering wheel at ten and two. His window is down, and Led Zeppelin's Kashmire filters through his stereo. Despite the mellow beat of the music, he seems agitated, as he scans the traffic ahead of us. Shocked to see him outside the familiar context of the coffee shop, I stare. Maybe he feels the weight of my gaze. He turns to glance at me, then does a double take, recognizing me. His body responds, positively electrified. With a sinking feeling, I realize he was probably scanning the traffic ahead in search of me.

Damn. I hadn't gotten away cleanly after all.

In a frantic motion he signals me to roll down my

window. I shake my head and turn away, but he honks his horn. I turn only enough to see him gesturing for me to pull over into a parking lot just ahead.

This is too much. Too damn much. If I don't ditch him, he'll follow me home. He'd been too close to me when that junkie forced me to defend myself. While it likely wasn't entirely clear to the rest of the coffee shop patrons what exactly happened, Alex had gotten an eyeful. Other vampires would probably just kill him. Or turn him into a familiar. Not me. Instead, I plan to use this car for what Ferrari intended, driving like Mario Andretti chased by devils until I shake him. And then I will lay low and stay out of WeHo for a while.

The light changes green. I pop the clutch and hit the gas. Hard.

Something is wrong. The truck is coming too fast. I'm not going to make it. He's running the light. My best hope is to floor the gas pedal and pray he just clips me behind the door. The impact crushes my passenger door, and my head smashes into my side window with enough force to spider-web it. Then, the world goes crazy. At first, I think it's just the head injury, but the forces pushing and pulling on my body tell me my car is rolling for what seems like ages. I have the clarity to hope my neck isn't broken. The spinal column is complex and a broken neck takes a long time to heal, even for a vampire.

The car stops, and I am hanging upside down. I see a pool of blood forming on the ceiling from a head wound. Must have been one hell of a crack on the head, but my neck is not broken. I can't say the same for my right leg. It doesn't hurt, but my femur is warm and tingly.

As I hang there and take stock of my physical condition, my driver's side window bursts open and a frantic hand reaches through to unlock the door. The owner of the hand fumbles at first with the 1980's push lock, then grabs the handle and nearly pulls the wrecked door off its hinges. The hand comes back with a large, utilitarian-looking knife and starts sawing away at my seat belt. I watch all of this with detached interest until I fall and clunk my head when the seat belt gives way.

The hands return, hook themselves under my armpits, and start to tug me out of the car. But I can't exit the vehicle just yet. Blood trickles down the side of my face. I still feel the warm pull of deep healing along my femur bone. It would look very bad for me to be pulled from the car with extensive injuries, then miraculously heal myself in front of a crowd of humans.

I slap at the hands and push them away. The determined hands redouble their efforts. The guy is strong, but no match for me. I shove the hands back so hard, I knock whomever they belong to on his arse outside the door.

"Stop fighting me, lady! I have to get you out of there!"

The hands come back, determined to yank me free, so I scratch one of them and shove again.

"God dammit!" the male roars. "Stop fighting!"

The hands come back. I prepare to scratch again, but they yank back before I can get them. The head injury must be affecting my speed. After a brief pause, a face appears in the window. I know that face. With exaggerated calm, the face speaks and tells me the gas tank has ruptured and he needs to get me out of the car.

Well, that changes things. All at once, the acrid smell

of gasoline overwhelms me. How the hell did I miss that? I start scrambling to free myself from the car. Vampires can burn for quite a while before they die, but surviving an explosion would be even more difficult to explain away than a healed femur bone.

The hands reappear and again hook under my armpits. I start shoving with my legs to disentangle myself from under the steering wheel column. With the combined effort of his pulling and my pushing, I'm free. I shoot to my feet with speed not quite human. His face briefly shows surprise before he grabs my arm. We both run to a safer distance. Making it over to the barrier formed by two motorcycle cops, we turn just in time to see my little Ferrari ignite.

For the first time it registers that my rescuer is none other than Alex. His expression full of concern, he studies the crusted blood on my face and the wet clots still clinging to my hair. He makes a move to lift the bloody mess away, no doubt under sway of that masculine need to assess the damage. But I'm healed now. I catch him easily by the wrist.

"I'm fine," I say. "And you're a photographer. Not a doctor."

He looks surprised, and I almost kick myself. I'm not supposed to know that. Maybe my concussion hasn't fully healed after all.

"You need to go to the hospital." He takes my arm and pulls me toward the paramedics, now busy treating the bloody truck driver—a kid who looks all of seventeen—for a broken nose.

I want to break his neck. I loved that Ferrari.

I can't allow the paramedics to examine me, and I certainly can't allow them to take me to the hospital.

I pull my arm out of Alex's grip. "No hospital."

He looks back at me. His initial lack of comprehension melts into patient understanding. Speaking slowly, he tells me I probably have a concussion and will need some stitches.

I can't tell him my injuries have healed. Instead, I say, "I'm not hurt."

His eyebrows come together in a frown, and he cocks his head. "I have some first aid training. Can I please examine your wound? Then we can decide if you need to go to the hospital."

"No," I say. "I'm fine."

I know what he would see—white, unbroken skin without even the hint of a bruise.

He gives me a searching look, but only for a moment. Then he nods, and turns to watch the firefighters deal with my poor, dead car. After a few seconds, he shifts his gaze back to me and smiles.

"My name is Alex, and I think you are Sonia?"

Surprised, I nod. Still smiling, he turns back to watch the firefighters.

And so I meet Alex Chevalier.

CHAPTER 3

At half-past three, Alex and I pull up to my little
Spanish colonial in Whitley Heights. He'd stayed
with me during the aftermath of my accident,
giving a witness statement to the police and promising to
appear in court, should it come to that. Finally, as the tow
truck drivers moved in to clear the wreckage, Alex asked me
if I would like him to take me home.

After standing for hours under the lights of Sunset,
under the steady scrutiny of the looky-loos, the police, and
ultimately the paramedics, who had to determine I wasn't
drunk or on drugs, I didn't think twice about allowing him
to see where I lived. Unthinkable only hours earlier.

We sit there for a few seconds, the menacing rumble of
his muscle car breaking the stillness of the quiet street. He's
looking at me, waiting for my cue. Do I invite him in? What
the hell? I've broken every other vampire rule tonight. Might
as well make it a clean sweep. Besides, I can't ignore the things
that Mr. Alex Chevalier has seen tonight, way
too much for the collective security of
the Los Angeles vampire community,
the *Koinon*.

Alex's reactions are odd, to say the least. I've never screwed up this badly in front of a human before, but I imagine the human in question would be pretty freaked out. Alex has seen me crush a man's wrist and pull his arm from its socket. Alex has seen me move with supernatural speed. He has even seen me emerge unscathed from a car wreck that would likely kill an ordinary human.

And Alex doesn't seem freaked out *at all*.

And he isn't hiding it, either. I can smell the pheromones linked to anxiety and fear, but Alex smells like a happy, healthy, non-threatened human enjoying the remnants of a moderate caffeine buzz.

There is more to Alex than meets the eye, and I need to find out what that is.

I smile at him. "Would you like to come in?"

"Sure." He cuts the car's motor, as if it's the most normal invitation in the world.

I swing open the heavy door and scramble to gracefully extract myself from the low-slung seat. Once free from the car, I swing the heavy door shut and listen to the sound reverberate up and down the deserted street. My neighbors are behind closed doors and windows, all safely tucked away in their beds.

No witnesses so far, but there'll still be the car to dispose of.

Passing through the front gate, I lead the way through my little courtyard to the massive mission-style front door. My movements are slow and deliberate. I've lost some blood, and truth be told, I'm hurting more from my injuries than I normally would. I need to feed and I need to sleep.

As I enter into the standard negotiations with the door's

intractable locks, Alex follows behind me, taking an equally leisurely route, commenting on the fountain's Moorish inspired tilework and the large bougainvillea dropping its red petals into the water. I contribute to our chitchat, telling him that the bougainvillea tree is the oldest in the neighborhood, and the honeysuckle vines clinging to the courtyard walls attract hummingbirds early in the morning.

Nice and polite. So far, so good.

However, my composure leaves me the moment I step through my door. I clap my hand over my nose and mouth as the ripe aroma of sex, four or five hours after the fact, hits me full in the face like a brick wall.

Oh, God.

Sunny is here. I forgot I was expecting him tonight.

But where the hell is the McLaren?

He must have come in a Lyft.

Damn. Damn. Damn.

"Um, is everything okay?" Behind me, Alex's voice sounds uncertain.

No wonder. I have stopped dead in the doorway, hunched over with my hand over my mouth. Straightening up, I wrench my hand away from my face and take in deep breaths to acclimatize faster to the smell. Sunny, mercifully, is somewhere downstairs—probably in the bedroom. With any luck, he's exhausted himself with his marathon of sex and debauchery and is passed out cold.

If I decide Alex is a threat and needs to be eliminated, I must do it on my terms. I need to be sure. Sunny is a predator by nature, and he wouldn't think twice about taking Alex out. But my conscience will haunt me unless I know for certain that Alex has to go.

Regaining some shreds of composure, I remember to flick on the lights. I dump my purse onto the chair next to the door and move into the kitchen, putting the kettle on.

The last time I'd been able to drink a human beverage was in the mid-sixties. I remember it clearly because Harold Holt had just been sworn in as Australia's seventeenth Prime Minister. But Sunny was turned in the year 1997, and will still be able to drink things other than blood for many years to come. He has a secret penchant for herbal tea, so I keep the house well stocked since he makes his extended stays so often.

Meanwhile, Alex has moved to the living room and is checking out my little library on the bookshelves to either side of the fireplace. Interesting. Most who gain admittance into my little sanctuary go straight to the large picture window overlooking the lights of the city.

As I join him, Alex pulls a small volume off the shelves.

"You've got very eclectic tastes," he observes. "What did you think of this one?"

He holds out a collection of three Raymond Chandler detective novels, featuring the irascible, heavy drinking, heavy smoking, woman-slapping detective Marlowe, noir anti-hero par excellence. As fans of hardboiled detective fiction know, Chandler's stories are all set in Los Angeles. When I first moved to L.A. in the late seventies, I eagerly read through these, hoping to get a feel for the place.

Chandler did not disappoint. My favorite line of Marlowe's is from *The Big Sleep*: "It seemed like a nice neighborhood to have bad habits in." That, in a nutshell, is a fair description of every neighborhood in Los Angeles from Los Feliz westward through to the Pacific Palisades on the coast. People have many bad habits around these parts, and we vampires can hear and smell most of them.

"I love that one." I pull another book off the shelf with almost identical binding, and I hold it out for Alex to see. "I've also got this volume of his short stories, but I think Chandler's novels are really his strong point."

"I used to love these stories when I was a kid," he says, almost to himself, "but my favorites are the Sam Spade stories, *The Maltese Falcon* and *The Thin Man*. Growing up in San Francisco, those were the ones to read. But I also liked the Los Angeles stories. Do you have any Cain here?"

"I've got *Double Indemnity* and *The Postman Always Rings Twice* somewhere around here," I say. "They're pretty good, too, but I prefer Chandler. Marlowe just seems more romantic to me somehow. Chandler's work has an elegance I find lacking in Cain."

"Yeah," he agrees. "Chandler's definitely got that whole short, direct tough-guy writing style down, and he's got that thing about the weather."

I draw a blank. "The weather?"

"Yeah, you know, the winds—the hot winds—I can't remember what they're called right now. You know what I mean?"

I nod. "The Santa Ana winds, the dreaded Santa Anas of Southern California."

Just then the kettle whistle blows, and I excuse myself to go pour his tea. Realizing I should also appear to be drinking something, I take another tea cup down and randomly select a bag for myself out of the assortment box.

When I return with both cups, I find him sitting in the

large brown leather loveseat next to the fireplace, looking at the very old framed photograph I keep on the mantelpiece.

"So, the Santa Anas," he says, without looking up. "Are they really that bad?"

"Ha. I can tell you're new to Southern California. They don't have quite the debilitating effect on me that Chandler claims for most." I set a tea cup down on the table next to him, and take a seat on the sofa. "I seem to remember hearing something once about the crime rate going up during Santa Anas. Supposedly, Emergency Rooms are busier because that's when all the crazies come out. You can definitely tell when one is blowing—no doubt in your mind."

He looks up at me questioningly. I can see under the light that his eyes have very dark bands of jade in them. I wonder what they would look like if he wore something dark green, like a cozy dark green sweater.

"Well," I continue, "they make you sneeze—I sneeze a lot during Santa Anas. They also tend to start fires in the canyons, and when the fires get big, all the smoke and ash they create makes you sneeze even more. The winds are particularly bad for those with allergies, but since I don't have allergies, they don't bother me as much."

"Hmmm," he says, studying the photograph more closely. I wish he'd put the bloody thing down. But, then again, with him looking down like that I can see the contrast between his long, dark lashes and the delicate skin just under his eyes. And from the way the light shines on his skin, it glows seductively. The heat in me grows, and my teeth throb as they become more pointed and sharp.

God, I'm hungry.

Alarmed, I shoot out of my chair and look frantically

around for something with which to occupy myself. Then, just as abruptly, I sit down again. This is utterly ridiculous. You'd think I hadn't been near a human man in fifty years! And why the hell is he studying that damn photograph? I fight not to tell him to put it down or, better yet, snatch it out of his hands. But I don't trust myself to get that close to him.

My head is throbbing from my wound and my need to feed. I have my blood supply locked in my room downstairs, but all I have on hand is bovine blood from the slaughter-houses. Good God, what I'd give for fresh human blood. And Alex is such a tempting source.

"Not long ago," I begin desperately, "I read a short story about fires in Malibu caused by the Santa Ana winds..." Alex puts the photograph down on the side table and politely returns his attention to me. Okay... one mission accomplished. "—the author lived in Malibu and she claimed that during the fires, horses would go up in flames and people would shoot them on the beaches."

Too macabre? Probably. But he'd put the photograph of Owen down.

Alex's face contorts into a look of disgust. "The horses caught *fire* and so they *shot* them on the *beach*?"

I nod.

"Well, that's the most horrible thing I've heard in a while." He pauses a minute and appears deep in thought. "If they were on fire, then how did they get them down to the beach?"

"I don't know—I guess maybe she meant after the fire crews put out the fires, someone brought the burned horses down to the beach, where they were shot. And I'm not sure why they couldn't just shoot them where they stood, instead of dragging the poor things down to the beach. But, honestly, the mental image I got was of flaming horses running around on the beach with people shooting at them."

Then I do a bad thing: I crack a smile. I don't mean to, and I don't really think it's funny. But at that particular moment, the image of flaming horses running around in Malibu seems a bit comical.

He smiles, too. Then he gives a small whuffle of a laugh. Before long he's crescendoed into full laughter. After a few moments, he regains control of himself and looks at me very seriously. "That's horrible."

"Yes." I tamp my smile down, and we both regard each other with serious faces. He cracks first and soon becomes helpless once more in the grips of laughter. And I, too, find myself chuckling. It has been a very long time since I've laughed.

Eventually we laugh ourselves into exhaustion and sit there numbly shaking our heads. I wonder what the hell is wrong with me. I love horses, I really do! Probably more than most, considering I lived on a farm for almost a hundred years.

But I know what this is. This is the release of the tension that has been simmering just below the surface since the accident. I've been acutely aware of it, adding to the already stressful evening. And it seems Alex has felt it, too.

I'm also acutely aware of a problem… a big problem. I'm getting to know Alex better than I should. I like him. But there is something off about him. The more time I spend with him, the more I feel it. He's not reacting the way a normal human should. Boiled down to the essentials,

I must find out what kind of threat he poses to my community. And I need to keep my distance in case I must eliminate him.

So far, I'm failing spectacularly on both counts.

But my survival and the survival of my *Koinon* are far more important than any animal attraction for Alex.

Don't get attached, my Stoicheía mentor Rafael once advised. *Never get attached. They are cattle. They are food. They are sex. But they are nothing more.*

By the time Rafael had shared this little nugget of vampire wisdom, I had a 50-year marriage to a human under my belt. And I am determined never to allow another human that close to me again.

And honestly, who even knows if this attraction is real? I'm in desperate need of blood. It could very well be Roger, my portly UPS driver, sitting in that loveseat and I'd be getting off on his pheromone cocktail, thinking I see stars in his eyes.

The sound of movement downstairs yanks me out of my thoughts.

Damn! I completely forgot about Sunny!

And it sounds like he's awake.

Shit.

CHAPTER 4

ALEX HAS REGAINED HIS composure, but I only half listen as he tells me about his move from San Francisco.

"Don't get me wrong," he says. "I love the Bay Area, and it will always be my home. My sisters still live up there, so I'll go back for the holidays and things like that, but I really needed to try somewhere new."

What the hell is Sunny doing down there? It sounds, of all things, like he is rummaging through my closet. But why?

"I've already lived in New York, where I did my undergrad, and Chicago, my post grad, so I figured Los Angeles would be the next big place to live."

I nod to let him know I'm listening. The rummaging noises are becoming louder and louder. I start to worry Alex might be able to hear them. Not that it matters. Now that Sunny is awake, he's not going to let Alex out the door without getting a look at him first. I brace myself for the inevitable.

"L.A. seemed like the logical choice since it's still just a car drive away from my sisters."

30

I can hear the screeching of hangers being shoved up and down their rails as Sunny pursues his mystery quest.

"With my work, I can live anywhere, so that's always a plus. What do you do?"

The sound below has stopped.

Brace for it.

"Sonia?"

Any moment.

"Sonia?"

"Y—Yes?" I blink at Alex. "Yes, I'm sorry—did you ask me something?"

"No problem." He smiles. "I asked you what you do."

"Oh," I reply, responding again to the smile. "I carve gemstones."

Alex's face lights up. He opens his mouth to respond, but Sunny's arrival cuts him off. And when I say he "arrives," I mean it literally. The bastard doesn't take the stairs at human speed, but rather zooms up them so fast, it looks like he's appeared in my living room out of thin air. It's a neat trick. I've seen it a million times.

But Alex hasn't. At just about the time I feel the air stir behind me, poor Alex nearly jumps out of his skin. I can see by the shock on his face that I'd better turn around. I hope to God Sunny isn't naked. We've already had our "no naked Sunny in Sonia's house" talk many times. I pray he's not feeling rebellious. I plaster a congenial smile onto my face and pivot around.

And there he is: Sunshine the vampire, standing at the top of my stairs, larger than life with a big, toothy grin on his face. Too toothy for my taste. His fangs are partially out.

"Hello!" he booms, smiling like an idiot. I'm going to kill him.

While the Powers that Be have technically answered my little prayer, they haven't answered it by much. Sunny stands in his powerful glory like a muscular golden Adonis, clothed only in my black silk kimono robe and the biggest pair of fuzzy slippers I've ever seen. Leopard print fuzzy slippers. And my kimono just barely covers his necessities.

As I stare at him and struggle to think of something to say, Sunny glances at me, his brilliant blue eyes flashing with humor, before he covers the distance between himself and Alex in three large strides. For a moment, I fear what Sunny might do. By the looks of Alex, so does he. Alex has no idea he's in any real danger. He probably figures he's caught up in a "one too many roosters in the hen house" scenario. And Sunny is, by far, the bigger rooster. I, on the other hand, know better, and that leads me to question my judgment of Sunny's intentions and wonder if I have, indeed, placed Alex in danger. Now don't get me wrong. If Alex has to go, he has to go. I'd just like to make that decision myself. I don't need a hungry Sunny making the decision for me. Alex deserves better.

Fortunately, Sunny soon puts both our fears to rest. Towering over Alex, who is still seated on the love seat, Sunny thrusts his large hand into Alex's face.

"Howdy, partner, I'm Sunny."

Sunny is neither a Texan, nor a cowboy. The southern twang to his speech is new. Brand new, only a few weeks new. He's been working on a Country album, and he's picked up the accent, as he always does. I have my theories. Even before he was turned, Sonny had a remarkable ear, perfect pitch. Hence, the tendency, sometimes regrettable, to pick up languages and accents like a second skin. I fear we're in regrettable territory. Until Sunny finishes with this album, this bona fide native of Los Angeles is going to sound like a ridiculous parody of a cowboy. In all other respects, he is one of the most direct and non-affected personalities you are likely to meet. His legendary charm captivates humans and vampires alike, and he wears his unshakable self-confidence as easily as he wears my kimono. These qualities, coupled with the face of a Michelangelo David and the lean, muscular physique of a Hemsworth, ensures that he dominates any space he chooses to occupy.

Sunny is irresistible. And deadly. Despite numerous requests from the *oligarchia* to cease and desist, Sunny still hunts human prey almost every night. He needs human blood in order to keep up his colossal strength. No bovine blood for Sunny. And no store-bought blood, either. He likes it straight from the source, warmed by a beating heart.

For these reasons my fears for Alex linger, though thankfully my inner vampire doesn't surface. That would be a fight I couldn't win. Not many vampires come to mind, who could take Sunny on in a fight without some serious help from several others. Even the very oldest among the *Stoicheía*, our elders, would think twice before tangling with him. Yet Sunny's strength has nothing to do with age. He is a bit of an enigma in the vampire world.

He and Alex seem to be getting along well enough. Sunny has occupied the seat next to Alex, sitting uncomfortably close to him in his little kimono as he questions him about Fluffy. Sunny has a human fondness for dogs, and could no doubt smell the "Fluffster" on Alex's clothes. As I re-engage with the conversation, Alex rattles off the various charms of the Fluffster and tells Sunny about the pound in the rough part of San Francisco where he'd found the dog. For his part, Sunny shows avid interest in the adoption process and the general availability of pit bulls in Northern California. I happen to know (though am not supposed to tell this to anybody) that Sunny donates about half his fortune to charity, and he moonlights as a baby cuddler in the NICU at UCLA over in Westwood.

Though Alex has relaxed somewhat, he's still pretty nervous. In the last ten minutes, his body chemistry has shifted, and he smells agitated. Sure enough, as their conversation about Fluffy peters out, Alex jumps on the opportunity. He leans back in the rendition of a fatigued stretch, complete with an exaggerated yawn, then checks his watch and relays surprise. "Oh, my," his expression reads, "is that really the time?"

What he says is, "I think I should get going." He sends me an apologetic look as he gets to his feet. "It's getting late, and I don't want to keep you up all night."

Then his eyebrows draw together in concern, "You must be exhausted!" he exclaims. "I can't believe I forgot. You've probably been dying to get me out of here." Alex shakes his head. "You've had quite a night!"

Sunny watches this performance with undisguised interest. I accept the reality that I can't hide my accident from him indefinitely. First, I have to somehow account for the missing car. There are likely going to be other repercussions. The *Stoicheía* have eyes everywhere. Still, I wish Alex hadn't opened his big mouth in front of Sunny.

I say I'll show Alex out—he's quick to move, obviously

eager to leave now. As I open the door for him, I thank him for all of his help. He says something along the lines of "it was the least I could do," and then he kisses me on the cheek. Liquid fire bursts through the side of my face and something dangerous erupts deep down inside of me. I vaguely hear him tell me he will see me tomorrow night, and then I gently close the door behind him.

"No, you won't," I murmur at the door.

Sunny stirs behind me. I pivot to face him and see a delighted expression on his face. He's silent at first. I assume he's trying to decide how best to launch his attack. He starts with a surprisingly subtle tactic.

"Where's the Ferrari?" Obviously, he would have heard me drive up in it.

I kill a few seconds, staring at him, and then shrug. Might as well just come out with it. He'll learn all about it eventually, anyway.

I casually walk past him, back into the living room. "I had a little accident, and I totaled the car."

"A caaaaaar accident?" he asks, following on my heels. He draws out the vowel sound in an obnoxious parody of concern. Then, more seriously. "How did that happen?"

It's a fair question. Between our heightened sensory perception and the practical need to avoid situations that call attention to ourselves, car accidents are not part of the vampire life. This is held so strongly amongst our kind, some of the older members of our *Koinon* don't even own cars and rely entirely on public transport and hired cars. I personally think this is stupid, since a vampire in a car driven by a human is far more likely to have an accident than when we drive ourselves. But the old ones are often intractable eccentrics, suspicious of the automobile as a quintessentially bourgeois invention, the mascot of the industrial revolution. In fact, hatred of the automobile is one of the few things the Old World aristocrats, socialists, and revolutionaries agree upon.

Sunny is not one of those vampires, though he does hire cars for the practical reason that great amounts of alcohol sometimes flow through his bloodstream. Though it takes a much larger dose of alcohol to inebriate a vampire, a field sobriety test using any sort of digital breathalyzer will read the same for a vampire as it does for a human. Sunny could spend his evening drowning in enough whisky to kill a 300-pound human strongman and barely feel buzzed, but the good old breathalyzer will claim he has enough alcohol in his system to cause kidney failure. And jails are just as dangerous a place for vampires as hospitals.

Sunny gently grabs me by the shoulders, then turns me to face him. "Seriously, Sonia. What happened?"

So, I tell him the whole story, almost. I only leave out Alex's role in flustering me at the stop light. In fact, I don't mention Alex at all except for the part about pulling me out of the car. I need a rational explanation as to why I invited him into my home.

Sunny's quick mind digests this information and doubles down on the Alex issue. "So, you just met this Alex guy tonight?"

I'm tempted to lie, but Sunny will taste it.

"No. I've seen him at the coffee shop on Sunset."

"Is he a regular?"

I sigh and slump my shoulders. I feel like a naughty child caught red-handed.

"Yes." I groan. "And to answer your next question, I've been going to that coffee shop for about four weeks. He started coming in three weeks ago."

Sunny steeples his fingers and ponders this information for a moment. The look on his face reminds me of that statue, "The Thinker." Then I snort, imagining the statue's muscular physique wrapped in a black silk kimono.

"So you like him." It's a declaration, not a question.

"I don't date humans," I remind him. "You know that."

"Yes, but I don't really understand." Sunny picks up the old photograph Alex had been studying earlier. He holds it up for me to see. "Does it have anything to do with him?" he asks. "Because if it does, you've got to let that go—he wouldn't want you to live out the rest of your life alone."

"No," I answer stiffly. "It has nothing to do with him. Humans are like children. How could I possibly have any kind of a meaningful relationship with someone who has lived only a fraction of the number of years I have? What the hell would we talk about?"

Sunny nods. "Is that how you see me? Do you see me as a child?"

I can't help but laugh. "Of *course,* I see you as a child! You were born only fifty years ago!" Then, more seriously, "Gechina turned you in 1997. I turned vampire in *1840*. I am 157 years older than you!"

He stares at me blankly.

I try a different tactic. "In the words of Captain Kirk," I say with mock solemnity, "I was out saving the galaxy while your grandfather was in diapers."

Still nothing. I probably shouldn't have mentioned Gechina. Or, could be he hasn't seen *Star Trek Generations*.

"Look," I say, reasonably, "I do see you as a bit of a child sometimes, but that is part of the reason why I like you—you can call it your 'boyish charm' if it makes you feel any better."

"But there are some things," I go on, "that you and I simply can't talk about because the world we live in now is still your world—you haven't had to adjust to anything except maybe the generational shifts in popular music. You don't know what it's like to force yourself to accept changes that are not always for the better."

Sonny arches a brow, but says nothing.

Exasperated, I start my explanation. "Automobiles, telephones, television sets, World Wars, the development of nuclear warfare, computers, music television, AIDS, genocide, cell phones, iPods, iPhones, YouTube, A.I., social media, pandemics."

No response.

"I've lived from a time when using the word 'Fuck' would get you publicly whipped, and now I hear eleven-year-old schoolgirls dropping F-bombs on TikTok."

Nothing.

"I've gone from a time when a woman had to wear her ridiculous, voluminous underwear while taking a *bath* in her *own private bathroom*, to a time when women wear thong bikinis to the grocery store!"

This seems to spark something.

"I had to become accustomed to washing my hair every day, to shaving first my legs, then other parts of my body, and now I'm supposed to have it *all* waxed off! And then it just grows right back within a day because I'm a damn vampire!"

"Are you finished?"

"Not quite. You still have your birth name, Sunny. Your hippie parents are still alive. You still get to talk to them. You haven't even had to change identities yet. You were born Sunny Michaels, and you still are Sunny Michaels. The Relocator doesn't even have an account for you yet."

"And that," he says, "is the only valid argument you've made. All the other things are superficial. People don't change—mankind sucks and always has sucked. Mass murderers today aren't doing anything sicker than what's been done by the same mass-murdering motherfuckers in the past. Genocide is nothing new. Nothing is really new!"

Sunny isn't done. "What kind of conversations do you want to have with people about those things, anyway? Nuclear warfare isn't exactly my favorite thing to philosophize about. And I have lived through some of those things. But who cares? What *matters* is the *people*, and the *people* never change. Human nature is just as bad as it's always been. Just read the Bible. Or anything about the Romans. Those Romans were some sick fuckers."

I stare at him, shocked.

Finally, Sunny finishes spilling what's on his mind. "You should give this Alex guy a shot. He obviously digs you—go have fun with him. Owen would want you to do that rather than live your life always alone."

Sunny reaches over his head and stretches, managing a fair imitation of the elaborate one Alex had performed for me earlier. When Sunny stretches, though, the short kimono no longer covers his unmentionables. I laugh. It isn't as if I, or most of my neighbors for that matter, haven't seen it all before. Sunny had been known, on more than one occasion, to bring in the trash bins wearing only the "cock sock" Flea gave him as a gift.

"I'm going to go out for a while," he announces.

Then he is gone. My eyes track him to the stairs, but I lose him once he turns on the speed to go back downstairs.

I go to the old photograph of Owen that stands on my side table. I sit down where Alex and Sunny had just been, and stare at the grim-faced man looking terribly uncomfortable in a stiff suit that appears too small for him. People didn't smile in photographs in those days, and it seems strange to see such a serious look on a face far more accustomed to laughter. I smile to myself as I remember his great, booming guffaws, and the way his eyes would tear up sometimes when something struck him as particularly funny.

Sunny is correct. I do avoid humans because of Owen, though not for the reason he thinks. I agree that Owen would not like to see me living this way. But I'll have to wait another century before I can properly explain my reasons to Sunny. He hasn't lived enough life yet to understand what it's like to love a human, to marry and share your life. He doesn't realize how rapidly time goes by in a human lifespan—what seems like a blink of an eye for us takes its toll on the human body as decades speed by.

Sunny doesn't comprehend the helplessness, pain, and eventual loss of dignity that accompanies the progress of old age. And then your human is gone forever, and you are left only with dust, wondering what happened to that personality that you once loved so ardently. Where do they go? Do they still exist? It all seems so terribly unfair. You wonder why God brings life into the world in the first place, if only to extinguish it so completely after such a short period of time. You find yourself asking, what's the point?

The old hurt spreads through my belly as I remember. With a sigh I get up from the chair and pause a moment longer to wish my husband a good night. Then I turn off the light and wander to my office with the dim intention of getting some work done. I have a new shipment of raw opal from Australia to sort through, and the black doublets I cut last night need to be polished and set. Even as my mind is now thankfully distracted by these mundane thoughts, I note Alex's lingering scent in my living room.

CHAPTER 5

THAT DAY, I DREAM of Australia.

I am sitting shotgun next to Owen on his old wagon pulled by his two draft horses, Jack and Jill. We sit in silence at a high point in the road between Owen's farm and town, overlooking the expanse of scraggy bush and red soil of the Outback, made all the redder by the fading rays of the setting sun. Even at this time of day I feel the heat saturated in my long, brown cotton dress and petticoats. The hint of a cool breeze kisses my face, and sweat collects at the nape of my neck before it trickles down my spine.

It is beautiful.

"I spoke to Sir Bourke's man yesterday," Owen begins, "he says your seven years will be served next month."

I don't say anything, but I begin to fidget with the buttons of the ruffled cuff at my wrist. I know my seven year sentence working on Owen's farm will soon be up. But I don't know exactly what that means for me. I will never go back to England, even if I could afford passage. That miserable island holds nothing for me but pain. Australia is my home. Owen's farm is my home. But, now what? Where will I go? I feel panic settle into the pit of my stomach.

"I reckon December to be a fine month for a wedding," he tells me. "What do you think?"

I look at him in confusion. He appears so earnest; no hint of the laughter that usually dances in those pale blue eyes. His reddish brows are drawn together as he channels all his concentration onto my face. I look away from him, still confused. Who is getting married? In the distance a small wallaby takes a break in its perambulations to stop and take a good look at us. Probably wonders what we are doing just sitting here. I wonder the same.

"Well?" he asks, urgency in his voice, "What do you think?"

"Whether December is a good month for a wedding?" I answer, my voice trailing off into uncertainty. With my sentence up next month, I have more important things to worry about than somebody getting married.

"No, dammit!" he says in exasperation, "Moira, I'm asking you to be my wife!"

I look at him in shock while he gingerly pulls a small velvet bag out of his shirt pocket. It is worn with age. Dumping the contents carefully into the palm of his calloused hand, I see he holds a small gold ring.

"It belonged to my mother," he says softly, handing it to me.

Understanding finally dawning on me, I look up into his face and see naked hope. By that look alone, I know he loves me.

"Moira," he says to me, his beautiful Welsh accents thick and rough with emotion, "will you do me the honor of becoming my wife?"

When I wake, it takes me a moment to remember where I am. No longer in Australia. And judging by the snoring sounds nearby, I have company. I roll over to find Sunny passed out next to me. He is wearing the pink velvet sleep mask I thought I'd lost several months back, and a pair of cashmere pajama pants. The pajama pants are the condition for him being allowed to sleep in my bed with me. It is, he claims, the only bed in my house he can sleep in. I've even gone so far as to put another bed, identical down to the very make and size of the mattress, in one of the guest bedrooms upstairs, but Sunny refuses to try it. In the end he wore me down, as he always does. I made him promise to wear pajamas. And to tell you the truth, it's kind of nice to wake up with someone next to you, even if they snore.

I roll onto my back and fumble for the alarm clock. The bright green digital numbers read 7:03pm. We've slept in. Just then Sunny makes a little contented noise, and I see his fangs are out—he is having a pleasant dream—so I decide not to wake him. I roll out of bed, find my slippers with my feet, and make my way over to the full-size refrigerator I keep next to the bed. Rummaging around until I find a bag of bovine blood due to expire the next day, I grab my pink fluffy robe on my way out the door, closing it quietly behind me.

Once upstairs, I pour my bag of blood into my favorite coffee mug and pop it into the microwave. While it warms, I retrieve the paper. The expected summons awaits me on the doorstep in the form of a little note in crisp, white personal stationary, with the monogram B M A embossed in elegant script on the envelope. The letters stand for Bianca Andreuola Medici, one of the biggest pain in the ass *Stoicheia* living in Los Angeles.

I pick up the summons and the paper and bring them inside. Both, however, can wait until I've attended to my thirst. When the microwave chimes, I pull out my bovine blood, give it a little stir, then carry it into the living room where I stand by the window. Slowly savoring my breakfast, I watch the sky lose its purple hues as the Hollywood lights brighten, twilight transitioning to the dark of night. Those few stars I can still see over the brilliance of the city lights twinkle faintly in the sky, their distant fires no match for the immediate intensity of the metropolis.

In the Australia of my human lifetime, and for many years of my vampire life, the sky would come alive at night with light and movement. In those days, there were nights you could count as many as twenty shooting stars in the space of an hour. But that world is long gone, claimed many years ago by the urban sprawl of Sydney.

I feel the nourishment of the blood slowly spread through my body. It is nothing compared to the strength and vitality human blood would give me, but human blood is not so easy to come by in this day and age. Humans today have a tendency to notice when large numbers of people start disappearing. Not that you necessarily have to kill a human during the feeding process, but leaving bite marks on living bodies creates a whole new set of problems. Besides, I grew accustomed to bovine blood long ago, and I decided my diminished strength was a fair trade-off for the security it allows.

Turning away from the window, I notice something sitting on the side table next to the couch: an iPhone, and it doesn't belong to me. It must be either Alex's or Sunny's; both sat next to that table last night. Bringing the screen up, I see the name "Alex Chevalier" superimposed upon the photo of a surly-faced, white pit bull with only one eye. This must be the infamous Fluffy. I set the phone back down. That is a problem for later.

With a sigh, I turn to the summons. I look longingly at the newspaper, sorely tempted to ignore the elegant white envelope lying next to it. But I cannot ignore a summons from Bianca. Not from a *Stoicheía* of her age and stature. Why Bianca elected herself to be the watchdog of the *Koinon* is beyond me, but watchdog she is.

So, upon finding the summons from Bianca on my doorstep, I know she isn't requesting a social call—I am in trouble, and I have a pretty good idea why. Like I said, vampires don't get into car accidents. A single car accident can threaten the security of the entire *Koinon*. And *Stoicheía* have eyes and ears everywhere.

Tearing open the little envelope with my finger nail, I remove a thick white card engraved with a simple "M." The short message inside reads: *"Dear Sonia, I request the pleasure of your company this evening at 8:30pm. Until then, Bianca."* The perfectly formed black letters bespeak elegance and power, the only expression of individuality the subtle flourish of the "B" in the signature. This little note, hand-written no doubt with an antique fountain pen, comingles Old World charm with Corporate Executive Officer efficiency.

I glance at the clock on the microwave: 7:38.

Dammit. The drive from Hollywood to Beverly Hills takes at least twenty minutes. I am going to be late.

CHAPTER 6

SURE ENOUGH, I AM fifteen minutes late when the Lyft pulls up to the gate of Bianca's Beverly Hills estate. The driver stops the car so I can announce my arrival to the little security box. Hearing the high-pitched sound of a tiny motor, I look up to see a small camera adjust its position to catch my face. We sit for a few moments while Bianca's private security personnel confirm my identity.

Once given official clearance, the large gates begin to move, groaning heavily under their own weight. It takes a few seconds for the colossal ironwork, decorated with an elaborate "M," to break inward far enough for us to pass through. Then we drive up the long, winding driveway, lined alternately with palm trees and softly glowing lights. Soon we catch the first glimpse of Bianca's residence, illuminated dramatically by a series of floodlights mounted along the base of the villa's Italian frontage. Eventually the drive terminates in a large circle with a vast fountain, dominated by a marble reproduction of *Laocoön and his Sons* at its center.

"Nice statue," my driver remarks, side-eyeing the trio, and more particularly, the two massive sea serpents strangling them to death.

According to legend, the sea god Poseidon sent the serpents to stop Laocoön from warning the Trojans about the Greek warriors lurking in the belly of the Trojan horse.

The statue, the faces of Laocoön and his sons twisted in the agony of death, is grisly enough during the day. Now, in the dark of night, with the floodlights on, the dramatic play of light and shadow make it absolutely ghastly.

Bianca's way of welcoming her visitors: a work of art that sends a message. Don't fuck with me.

As the Lyft circles the fountain, coming to a stop directly in front of Bianca's villa, a figure jogs down one of the staircases and hurries over to my door. Short and portly, he wears a pair of belted khakis and a blue and white striped polo shirt. The round dome of his balding head, coupled with his too small wire-rimmed glasses, give him an owlish look. His name is Simon. He is a familiar and works as Bianca's human secretary.

Yanking open my door, he apologizes breathlessly for making me wait, though I doubt it was more than five seconds. He must have been posted out front to greet me when I arrived. Poor guy probably just left his post to use the facilities. But I can tell he is genuinely nervous, so I smile warmly at him as I exit the car. While he tells the Lyft driver to wait, I use that time to admire the house.

Neichia told me once that Bianca's home is no mere approximation of a Mediterranean palace. Supposedly, the architect modeled it after one of the Medici villas in Tuscany. True or not, the place certainly looks Italian. The house itself is three stories high, the ground floor hidden by a series of arched enclaves called loggia. The villa's floodlights, placed to leave the interiors of these little spaces in shadow, make them look dark and a little dangerous. All sorts of nasty things could skulk in those loggia.

The main entrance is on the second floor, hidden from view by a wide columned porch with its triangular roof. I think of it as a mini-Parthenon. From each end of the porch, two staircases descend, curving inward like the pincers of a pincher bug, so that they almost meet together on the ground floor in front of the loggia. Balustrades and intricate iron work matching the estate's front gates wrap around the perimeter of the second floor, and a large clock and bell top off the villa's flat roof.

Very Italian. Very Renaissance. And very impressive.

With the Lyft driver dutifully waiting, Simon motions me to follow him. We proceed up the right side of the pincer staircase. In his haste, Simon had left one side of the great front doors open, and he hurriedly ushers me through, moving aside to follow me in. As I step inside, my eyes and nose immediately start to burn: sulfur. Bianca's element is fire.

That's the funny thing about our Elders: *Stoicheia* means "elements" in Ancient Greek. Our elders all control one of the four elements: air, earth, water, and fire. No one knows exactly why, or why this seems to be a phenomenon unique to the Los Angeles elders. There are a lot of things we don't know about the *Stoicheia*, not the least what they are doing here in Los Angeles in the first place. Vampires their age generally don't like to leave their lands of origin. And none of the Los Angeles *Stoicheia* are native to North America

I remove my jacket. Bianca's place is always about fifteen

degrees hotter inside than outside, even with the central air. The deeper I go into the villa, the worse it will get. We power straight across the vast, brilliantly colored, mosaic floor of the receiving hall to a set of tall, carved doors.

As I pause so Simon can open the next door for me with a rushed flourish, I glance up and catch a glimpse of the hall's frescoed ceiling, the mythical figures painted in the same vivid colors as the floor design. I wonder if, like the exterior, this too has a fading duplicate that draws tourists somewhere in Tuscany.

In the next room, I find myself transported from an Italian Renaissance villa to an eighteenth-century French *salon*. *This* room most certainly does *not* have a fading duplicate, at least not anywhere in Italy. It's pure Versailles.

Simon bids me make myself comfortable, then softly closes the door behind me. I'm late, so I'm certain I'll be cooling my heels for a while before Bianca graces me with her presence. I didn't bring a book with me, so I have nothing to do but look around the room as I wait.

This room stretches the full length of the palace's western wing. The room is ablaze with light, thousands of tiny lit candles in the wall sconces, floor-mounted candelabras, and, of course, the massive three-tiered crystal chandelier in the center. I am essentially a creature of the night, so all of this light is hard on my eyes. If Bianca's element weren't fire, she'd have a hard time with it, too.

I eye the room's *piece de resistance*—the imposing portrait hanging over the marble mantelpiece. There she is, the mistress of the house herself, in an elaborate Marie-Antoinette-style dress in pale pink brocade, with the extremely low-cut bodice fashionable in the late-eighteenth century.

It must have been painted during her *salonnière* days in Paris just before the Revolution. It's said that she ran the most fashionable and exclusive salon of the day, attracting the brightest and most beautiful from throughout Europe. In many ways it was a natural role for her to play, engaging many of the same social and cultural talents she'd developed during her earlier, human days as the premier courtesan of sixteenth-century Florence.

Everything considered, the portrait is a fairly good likeness of Bianca. The artist managed to catch the smoldering black eyes, her arched, aristocratic brows, and the famous Medici nose. Bianca is supposedly the illegitimate daughter of Cosimo de Medici, the "godfather" of Renaissance Florence. Many discount this rumor, thinking it much like saying you're the long-lost direct descendent of Richard the Lionheart or Henry VIII. But I think there might be something to Bianca's claim. Once I found a portrait of Cosimo in a large book on Renaissance art, and it is difficult to ignore the family resemblance. In any case, Bianca has held on to the Medici name, despite the general rule to change our names every fifty years.

I select a seat among a modern grouping of French antique furniture arranged near the fireplace. A silver tea set sits steaming on a low satinwood table between two *fauteuils* and a long *canapé*. Bianca knows perfectly well I can no longer drink human beverages, but, then again, the tea set's purpose has nothing to do with serving me tea. It's there to remind me of my place in the pecking order. Bianca is a *Stoicheía*, centuries removed from the days when she could still consume things other than blood, but I am not. Her message is clear: Compared to her, I am practically human. It also tells me that I am too insignificant for her to keep track of my exact age. Total bullshit. Bianca keeps track of everything.

Easing myself gently onto the gold silk damask of one of the *fauteuils*, I have no doubt my course jeans are rubbing up against a piece of furniture older than I am. Gradually becoming more confident that the dainty cabriole legs of the chair are not going to snap under my weight, I lean back into the generous seat designed to accommodate hoopskirts and petticoats.

Bianca, surprisingly, doesn't make me wait long. Suddenly the wall between the fireplace and the large Louis XVth commode opens, not five feet from where I sit. It is only natural that a Renaissance palace should have secret passageways, but it still makes me jump. Feeling foolish, I jump a second time when Bianca abruptly appears across from me, her face set in a condescending expression of gracious welcome. I'm blasted with the taste of ashes in my mouth, tinged with the tang of Black Opium perfume.

"Sonia, so good of you to come," Bianca purrs in faint Italian accents. The Tuscan undercurrent in the shape of her words is also total bullshit. Bianca would have lost her accent eons ago. I lost most of mine after only about a hundred years. "I'm so sorry to have kept you waiting." She smiles at me, displaying a row of preternaturally white teeth. No hint of friendly emotion touches the glittering blackness of her eyes.

Carradhy, comes my Maker's whisper.

Witch.

She seats herself in a graceful movement, too sudden to be human, and arranges her long limbs in an elegant rendition of repose. The air shimmers around her, like heat rising off the asphalt during a heatwave. The temperature of the room has gone up another ten degrees since her arrival. I peel off my second layer, down to my lace chemise.

As usual, Bianca wears unrelieved black Armani. Her long jet black hair is swept up into an immaculate twist. The double strand of white pearls around her long, white neck, their subtle luminescence nearly matching the tone of her skin, is her only ornamentation. I shift in my seat. At least I'm wearing decent shoes, my new black lace Blahnik Manolos that set me back a cool $800. They give me some comfort.

"I'm sorry to hear you've been in an automobile accident," she begins. Never one to beat around the bush, Bianca no doubt reserves her social pleasantries for those of more exalted status. "Would you be so kind as to describe for me what happened? It must have been absolutely dreadful."

I have my story prepared, having spent much of the Lyft ride rehearsing it. My primary goal is to keep Alex out of it as much as possible, pride being my main motivation. Too embarrassed to admit I'd crashed my car because of a good looking *human,* I made a few key changes to my story. Unfortunately, this leaves one or two glaring holes in my account, but with a little luck, Bianca won't care enough to pursue them. Surely, her goal is to reprimand me for careless behavior.

So I relate the bare bones of the accident, leaving out two key facts: that the car rolled twice, and that I'd been injured. Those unfortunate details might need to come out eventually, but I'm not about to offer them up voluntarily. My heavily-edited version takes all of twenty seconds to relate. Then I wait to see if she presses me for more details. She does.

"*Dio Santo!*" She speaks as she exhales. I practically choke from another blast of ashes in my mouth. "So terrible, indeed!" She pauses, as if taking a moment to absorb the particulars of my Spartan account. I feel pretty sure about what she will ask me next; we are at the first hole in my story.

"But tell me," she begins, "how did you not see that the truck was running the red light?"

Bingo.

A fair question. Some of us possess psychic abilities, which tend to develop and become stronger with age. I personally have no psychic powers, but my highly developed sensory perception affords me a type of presentiment. To humans, all vampires might seem psychic, though in actual fact this is because we pick up sensory information before they do. Bianca is asking me why I didn't see or hear the truck coming. Why did I gun the green light so recklessly? The answer, of course, is Alex; an answer I'm not about to provide. I don't want him on the *Stoicheía* radar. Bad things tend to happen to humans on the *Stoicheía* radar. But in cat-and-mouse games such as these, half-truths are often the best way to go.

"I was distracted." I have to admit that one.

"*Really?* By what, if you don't mind my asking?" Again, a fair question. Not easy to distract a vampire. Focus tends to accompany age.

"I was distracted by a human I had just seen in the coffee shop." So far, so good. We're still within the realm of truth. But now it's time to get creative. "He was in the car behind me. He accosted me and threatened me in the coffee shop, and then it appears he followed me." I plan to blame my "distraction" on the junkie.

"*Dio Mio!*" she gasps, rather unconvincingly. She pretends to consider the ramifications of this new information. What she's really wondering, I'm sure, is under what circumstances would I have felt threatened by a human? After all, vampires have no natural predators. We are at the very top of the food chain. Literally. We've reached the second big hole in my story, and Bianca probably realizes I'm hiding something from her. I begin to fidget with my bracelet.

As I try to figure out a way out of this little hole, I notice her expression has changed slightly. She's tilted her head to the side, her eyes now somewhat opaque. She's listening for something. I also listen, but hear nothing. But I almost, just barely, pick up a new smell, just eating at the edges of the sulfur choking out the oxygen in the room. Stale, rancid earth, almost like what you'd smell in a graveyard. An Earth *Stoicheía*? I'd never smelled one that stank quite like this.

After a moment, she nods, as if only to herself, before her gaze is back on me. The little flames from the candelabra on the mantelpiece are reflected in her eyes.

Then things get a little weird.

"I'm afraid something has come up," she informs me, "but before you leave I would like a few things cleared up." She's all business now. "Who is the man who pulled you from the car?"

I feel the shock register on my face, too surprised even to feel dismayed that my ruse is up. *Stoicheía* have their ways of finding things out, all vampires know that. When I received the summons, it came as no surprise to me that

Bianca had become aware of my accident less than 24 hours after it occurred. Sunny certainly hadn't told her. He has no loyalty to any of the *Stoicheía*. Even if she had asked him directly, he still wouldn't have told her. But this question is a little too detailed for my comfort. Had somebody been watching in the crowd last night?

"He was just a bystander," I answer. "I think he was driving the car next to me."

"Had you ever seen him before? Did you know him from somewhere?"

More shock. What are these questions? Where is she going with this? I take a few seconds to think through my next move. Clearly she has acquired detailed information about the accident, but how much does she know?

"Yes," I say. "I had seen him before. He frequents the same coffee shop I do. I'd seen him there for about three weeks."

"Did he ever come over to talk to you?"

"Why?"

Bianca's cold black eyes grow colder. "Answer the question."

"No," I reply, "he's never spoken to me. I only noticed him because he is one of the few regulars in that coffee shop at that hour. The first time we spoke was after the accident."

Bianca is quiet for a moment. I continue to fidget.

"Were you injured?" she asks, finally. "You have no airbags in your car, and I'm told the damage was extensive. Did you have any detectable injuries?"

I'm sweating through my chemise now. I swear to God, it's getting hotter. And we are on dangerous ground. Alex. Have I just put him in danger?

"No," I lie. "I was not injured. No one saw me injured. The paramedics even checked me out, and there were no visible wounds on my body." If she knows about me totaling my car and being pulled out of the wreckage by Alex, she would know about the paramedics. And, much as I hate to admit it, Bianca is good. And I'm not worried about the paramedics' safety.

But my answer fails to convince. Bianca presses the point further: "Not even when you exited the car?"

"Nope." Dammit. The feel of ashes grows in my mouth, and I know she is tasting my lie.

Bianca quiets for a moment, and I assume she's preparing more questions. Then I realize that she is listening again. But I still can't detect any unusual sounds. Naturally, because of her age her auditory powers are greater than mine, so I quickly forget about the mystery sounds. And the weird graveyard stench has receded. Besides, I'm far more concerned about where this line of questioning is going. What she says next comes as an enormous relief.

"I'm sorry," she says, "but we'll have to continue this conversation another time. Something has come up requiring my immediate attention."

Hallelujah.

Before relief settles in, she adds, "I don't think you should return to that coffee shop, and I would like you to discontinue your association with that human. You know the one I mean."

Behind me, I hear the door open and Simon steps into the room. Bianca stands, nods to me, then vanishes. She moves so quickly, I can't track her movements. Not even the air stirs from where she had been standing.

From behind, Simon says, "If you'll follow me." Not forgetting the fragile rococo legs of the chair, I carefully stand. Convinced my shift in weight will not cause the furniture to crumble to dust, I clear the room briskly and follow Simon out the door.

CHAPTER 7

I'M PISSED. AND WHEN I'm pissed, I work.

After the Lyft drops me off, I find something on my doorstep. Daisies. And they have a note. *Left my phone at your house. I'm thinking jazz at the Biltmore, Saturday night. Pick you up at 8?*

Hmm. This has possibilities. I head straight for my office, toss the daisies on my desk, and strip down to my panties. I need all of these sweaty clothes off of me. They smell like sulfur, even my bra. Blech.

My current project is a rare black seam opal from Mintabie, discovered in a dealer's stock by one of my Australian agents. The stone is destined either for a bracelet I've been working on for a few years, or a solitaire ring, depending on how the cutting and shaping process goes. I'm hoping for the bracelet since that would sell for about $100,000 once finished. It's been a while since I've sold anything that big, and I've got bills to pay.

I began the preliminary work on the stone the night before, orienting it and tracing the line of fire. Now, picking up the dry stone from my work tray, I slip on my *Opti*VISOR and hold it under my special 100 watt bulb, inspecting it carefully for cracks. While I look for opaque lines marring the brilliant fire line and dark potch, Bianca's face swims up in my mind.

Who the *hell* does she think she is? She has no authority over me, no power to order me around. She is influential, yes. But Los Angeles is an oligarchy. Sure, we younger vamps in the *Neoi* population like to listen to the *Stoicheia*, but they have no coercive powers over us. Bianca is no queen. Alex is my personal business. And Bianca can fuck off.

My stone has no discernable cracks, so I slip off the *Opti*VISOR and wheel my chair over to the grinder. Holding the stone to the medium wheel, I slowly begin to grind away at the black potch covering the top of the fire layer. Water flows over the stone and my fingers, keeping both cool, and a new plan begins to solidify in my mind—a plan that has been percolating in my subconscious since my conversation with Sunny: I am going to develop a friendship with Alex. Ha. It seems my stereotypical Australian problem with authority trumps my problem with humans.

At least with Alex.

Emphasis here is on the word *friendship*. Alex and I will be *friends*. I have already decided not to return to the coffee shop. That resolution had been made on my own terms before my audience with Bianca.

Pulling the stone back from the grinder, I bring it again under the light to inspect. I'm now at the tricky phase of the pre-shaping. I've exposed the fire line so that its colors refract brightly under the light. I could continue to grind, with the possibility that the fire would continue to become brighter, but long experience tells me that I'm in danger of grinding away fire if I continue. So, flipping the opal over, I grind away some of the potch to adjust the stone's thickness, and then rough out the bottom for the dop stick. I grab a towel to thoroughly dry the opal.

Friends, indeed.

I grab a dop stick from my tray and absently begin to heat the wax on the tip over my alcohol lamp. Then, as I position the dripping stick onto the back of the opal, shaping the wax with my fingers and checking to make sure the fire line is at a 90 degree angle to the dop stick, I allow myself a private smile.

Friends with benefits? Tempting.

I quickly dunk the dop stick into the grinder's water tray to cool it down, return it to my work tray and switch off the overhead lamp.

CHAPTER 8

S ATURDAY NIGHT COMES SOONER than expected. Going out on a date with a human, even a *friendly* date, takes some preparation. There are backstories to establish, childhoods to invent, and family to revivify. One small outing requires a sophisticated matrix of lies to be created, rehearsed, and remembered.

I do none of this.

Most of my preparation goes into the careful planning of my outfit for the big night. This is L.A. If you're going to go out on a Saturday night, you've got to look good, especially if you're a celebrity, but even *more* especially if you're a vampire. It's just how we roll.

I settle on a vintage Valentino pencil skirt in crimson satin, a fitted black cashmere sweater with cap sleeves, and black Prada heels with an ankle strap. Looking at the finished ensemble in my full-length mirror, I decide something is missing. I wiggle out of the skirt to add a pair of black fishnet thigh-highs with a 1940s style line down the back. I finish the outfit off with a pair of heavy, black onyx earrings. In keeping with the '40s theme, I roll the front of my hair, then pull it back rockabilly style into black beaded hair clips, and let the rest fall in natural waves down my back. A black beaded clutch ties my accessories together. Finally, I am ready to hear some jazz.

I appear in the living room just as Alex knocks on the front door. Sunny glances up from his guitar and does a double take when he sees me. I had not mentioned my little date. I only look this good when he's dragging me out to a party or a club.

Plastering a relaxed smile on my face, I open the door for Alex. All thoughts about how good *I* look vanish. Seems I'm not the only one who put some thought into their outfit. Giving him an appreciative look up and down, I see that Alex has traded in his usual uniform of faded jeans and long-sleeve henley for a slim fitting black-ruffled tuxedo shirt tucked into a hip-hugging pair of black trousers, creased sharply down the front and belted with a large western buckle. To keep things casual, the top three buttons of his shirt are open, revealing his perfectly shaped, sun kissed collar bone. He completes the look with a butter-soft black leather sports coat.

"You look beautiful." His lips curved up playfully at the corners.

"As do you." He's giving Sunny a run for his money.

As I turn back towards the kitchen to grab my purse, I notice Sunny has closed his mouth and is now watching me with a peculiar look on his face. Ignoring him, I pull the door firmly shut behind me. Whatever Sunny has to say to me will have to wait till tomorrow. He'll be safely entrenched in a VIP booth at Basque by the time I get home. But if he plans to give me any crap over this, the hypocrite had better think again.

"Well," Alex says once we're settled in the car, "I'm glad you decided to go out with me. I was prepared to look pretty stupid if you'd answered your door in your flannel pajamas and bathrobe. Without my phone, it was kind of a shot in the dark."

I laugh, then pull his phone from my purse. "It was a bold move," I say, handing it over. "But if I'd decided not to come, I would have had Sunny send you away. You wouldn't have to see me in my pajamas."

"Oh, that would have been *much* better. Now I'm *really* glad you accepted."

I chuckle as he makes his way through the complicated network of little streets towards the Hollywood Freeway. He has his radio set to the classic rock station, and The Cult's *Firewoman* blazes through the speakers. The trip from Hollywood to downtown Los Angeles on a Saturday night doesn't take too long—fifteen, maybe twenty minutes without traffic and allowing that nothing is going on at the Staples Center. After negotiating the Cougar onto the freeway and into one of the faster-moving lanes, Alex breaks the silence.

"Your friend Sunny isn't by chance Sunny Michaels, the music producer, is he?"

For a moment, I'm surprised. To me, Sunny is just Sunny the vampire—I keep forgetting he still has a public persona.

"Yes," I reply, "he's the same Sunny Michaels."

Alex whistles through his teeth, impressed. He has every right to be. Sunny is currently the most famous and sought-after music producer in L.A., probably in the world. Working with Sunny equals Grammys, and everybody in the music biz knows it. What everybody *doesn't* know is *why*. But it makes sense really, if you think about it. Sunny's super-enhanced auditory abilities enable him to hear things regular human ears can't, so he can produce beautiful music with a richness of tonal color, harmonic depths, and melodic variations that simply surpasses anything humans produce. The sounds Sunny coaxes out of the music is something vampires can sink their teeth into, pun absolutely intended, and for humans… well, it takes their hearts and minds somewhere they never thought possible. At least that's what the critics in *Rolling Stone* say.

But this situation cannot endure forever. At some point Sunny will have to give it up. His clients will inevitably start noticing that he's not aging. I figure he can carry on like this for another decade or so, but no longer. I think it's probably why he's begun developing his song-writing chops, knowing he doesn't need a public persona to write songs. He can create in the privacy of his own home with minimal contact with the outside world.

"So how did you meet him?" Alex asks. "Since you're not Rihanna or Lady Gaga, I don't suppose you'd have much professional interaction with big time music producers."

Hmmm. Was Alex fishing around to see if Sunny and I have a more personal history than just friendship? He sounds so nonchalant, I can't tell. But, ulterior motive or no, we have already reached the first problem question, and I have no canned answer for this. It never crossed my mind I'd have to talk about *Sunny's* background! Obviously, I can't tell Alex I know Sunny because of the one *huge* thing we have in common.

"I met him before he became a full time producer." This is strictly true, so far so good. "I first met him when he was still just a musician who produced a little on the side. He used to play lead guitar in a band called 'Black Ocean.' They played a lot on the Strip."

"What made him stop playing?"

The Los Angeles *Koinon* made him stop playing, mainly the *Stoicheía*. Once he became a vampire, performing on stage was out of the question. They made him quit, an order he eventually came to understand and agree with, though at the time it outraged him. *That* was when we actually met. The *Stoicheía* selected me, for whatever reason, to talk him down. Strangely enough, it worked. Sunny listened, and we became good friends.

"He injured his hand," I lie. "He couldn't play the way he used to, so he transitioned into a behind the scenes role."

It seems Alex wants to ask more questions about Sunny, but we exit the freeway at Temple and he needs to concentrate more on where we're going. I keep forgetting he isn't a local. Once we pull up to the modern porte-cochere of the old 1920s hotel, Alex hands his keys to the valet and we proceed towards the main entrance under the massive red brick towers.

Our destination is the Cognac Room, a dark, intimate little lounge whose atmosphere hearkens back to the days of men in double-breasted suits and women with tightly rolled hair and European cigarettes dropping ash carelessly from the ends of their long ivory holders. As we pass through the doorway into the crowded room, I notice through my temporary sensory overload that every pair of female eyes has settled appreciatively on Alex. But I'm not ruffled; same thing happens when I go anywhere with Sunny.

The jazz trio—a guitar, wind player, and a drummer—are

set up at the far end of the room. The wind player has his flute out and is playing a playful, sexy rendition of *The Girl from Ipanema* over the mellow chords of the guitarist's jazz box and the drummer's soft bossa beat. Most of the seats are full, but Alex locates a pair with a table towards the back in a dark corner. This suits me. It's quieter in the back, so we can have a conversation.

Once seated, the waitress promptly pays us a visit and I motion for Alex to order first. My strategy is to order the same thing he does and then dump my drink into his at regular intervals when his head is turned, or into the potted plant next to me. After hearing the bar's specialties, he orders a Black Dahlia martini, so I order the same. The waitress, an attractive thirty-something, is gone mere seconds before she returns with our drinks. I see her wink at Alex and smirk. She's probably written her number on the underside of the napkin she's placing under his drink. Again, same thing happens whenever I go anywhere with Sunny.

Alex, for his part, seems so oblivious, I suspect it's more practiced than genuine. As I steal a glance at him while he settles in for the evening, I can imagine he's had plenty of opportunity to practice being oblivious to female admiration. But as he takes off his jacket, the warm, musky scent of his body washes over me in a tempting wave and his body chemistry—the unique blend of his pheromones at that moment—offer me intimate information. I know right then and there, from his scent, that he wants me. And yes, it is *me* and not the waitress. Those pheromones have been building up for some time. Even as he sits there rolling up the cuffs of his sleeves, I know the most private cravings of his body. My teeth began to throb while I breathe him in… deeply. My own body responds to his with dangerous needs of its own.

The only source of light in our little corner is the small votive candle on the table between us, valiantly flickering away in its little glass jar. While he watches the musicians, I watch him. The darkness had made his pupils grow so large, they seemed to have consumed his irises, creating dark liquid pools a romantic might call fathomless. In the background, the guitar has begun playing the seductive opening bars to one of my favorite songs, *At Last*.

"So…" He turns his attention to me suddenly, yanking me out of my reverie. Damn, he's going to get the first question in. My second strategy for the night is to try to get him to do most of the talking. The less talking I do, the fewer the number of lies I will need to remember later.

But then he pauses, as if forgetting what he had planned to say. He looks at my face closely, turning his head slightly to the side as he studies my features. I look down and begin to fidget with my martini.

"You're making me uncomfortable," I say finally.

He immediately snaps out of it.

"Sorry." He gives himself a little shake. "I'm a photographer, so I'm used to staring at people through lenses. I tend to forget they don't like it when I do it without a camera."

"It's fine," I say, "but what were you staring at?"

"There's something about you." He turns his head slightly to the side again. "Something I've seen before. You remind me of someone, and I'm trying to figure out exactly why. It's not your face—I'm good with faces. It's something else, a quality, or maybe an aura."

"You're doing it again," I inform him.

I keep my voice neutral, but his scrutiny unnerves me. I have a pretty good idea what is going on. He's noticing that I'm not human. As a photographer, he studies life and humanity in all its different permutations. Now, he is picking up on the fact that I don't quite fit in. Not a good sign.

"Whoops." He snaps out of it again, giving himself another little shake. "Sorry. Again. I won't do it any more tonight, I promise."

"It's fine," I say again. I dismiss my unease. Even if he's picking up on my differences, he has no basis with which to compare my vampirism. Unless he knows all about vampires' existence and has met one before…

"So," he begins again.

To interrupt him, I blurt, "Tell me about your work. How long have you been a photographer?"

"I'm sorry," he says, "but I can barely hear you over the music." He stands and repositions his chair right next to me. Then he settles down again and leans back, crossing one long leg over the other and casually drapes his left arm over the back of my chair.

Perfect. Just exactly what I need—Alex sitting *closer* to me. It is hard enough just being in the same room with him. Now he's all but touching me! And, worst of all, my body is sending out all the indicators that it *wants* to be touched. The dull throbbing in my teeth intensifies, and Alex is no longer the only one broadcasting a libidinous scent signature. Thank God he can't pick up on the signals *I*'m putting out!

"Sorry," he says again, "I think you were asking me something about photography?"

"Yes. I asked you how long you've been a photographer."

He takes a sip from his martini. "Well, I first got into photography when I was twelve. My father gave me a little Nikon point and shoot for my birthday, and that started it all. I took photography as an elective in high school, won a few prizes at the local county fair, took some more classes in college, but didn't major in art or anything. By the time I graduated, I realized I wanted to be a photojournalist, so I went to journalism school at the University of Chicago."

I smirk. "That's a very canned answer, Alex. I can tell you've been asked that before."

"Ha." Alex looks down, and I get the sense that I've embarrassed him. "Standard first date answer. Sorry."

"So, do you work for the *Los Angeles Times* now?" I ask. "Is that what brought you to L.A.?"

"No, no. I'm not on staff at the *Times*, though I do contract work for them, and for *Time Magazine* and *National Geographic*. I'm a *Black Star* photographer, though you probably haven't heard of them."

"But what made you go into journalism?" I pretend to sip my martini. "It seems like you'd make more money in fashion or commercial photography."

"Yes, I could," he agrees. "There's a lot more money to be made in fashion, commercial, or even medical photography. But I like how you can tell a story with only one image, how you can catch all the drama and emotion of an event like a fire or an election or a riot with a single shot." His intensity increases as he continues. "My parents are French, and my mother's English was never good enough for her to read newspaper articles, but she could tell what was going on. And that's how she read the paper, by reading the pictures. It's powerful to think that, with just the right shot, the photographer can make the reporter's article superfluous.

"But," he says before I jump in with another question. "Now it's your turn. The other night you mentioned gemstones. Do you import them? Do you work for a jeweler?"

I sigh. The tricky bugger snuck that one in! Fortunately, he's chosen a topic I can more or less talk about safely while maintaining some semblance of the truth.

"I work mainly with Australian opal," I tell him. "I cut and polish raw opal and either sell the finished stones to jewelers or make them into jewelry myself. Sometimes I carve some of the larger, less valuable pieces into figurines. I've been working on a small chess set carved out of boulder opal for quite some time now." Half a century to be exact.

"Wow." His mouth turns down at the corners, impressed. "That's certainly unique. Where did you learn how to carve opal? Do they have schools for that sort of thing?"

"No school," I answer. "I just picked it up here and there." A hundred years alone in the Outback is plenty of time to become proficient at just about anything you set your mind to.

"Well, you must be pretty good if you can make a living at it. Do you make frequent trips to Australia to buy the raw opal?"

I shake my head. "No. I just have the best pieces sent directly to me from several mines."

"That's a pretty sweet deal. How'd you work that out?"

I take another pretend sip of my martini. "The pretty sweet deal only works because I have interests in several mines, mainly Lightning Ridge in New South Wales, and Coober Pedy and Mintabie in South Australia. I have a long-standing arrangement with several miners in Queensland, who kindly allow my agents first pick of their parcels."

Alex's eyebrows climb. "Ha. It sounds like something out of a Modesty Blaise novel. She carved gemstones, too, didn't she?"

"Why yes, Mr. Chevalier, she did," I say, pleased. "You know your 1970s feminist spy literature. How extraordinary!"

He shrugs and takes another sip of his martini. I make a mental note to dump some of mine into the plant next to me at the next opportunity.

"But unlike Modesty," I tell him, "I'm not a jewel thief."

"But you are Australian, aren't you? I can hear an accent sometimes when you talk. Very faint, but definitely there."

I carefully choose my next words. I'm going to need to move some decades around. "I'm from Sydney. But I moved to the U.S. during the '90s, so my accent isn't what it used to be. But tell me more about photography. What sort of work have you done for *National Geographic*?"

I manage to get the topic of conversation off of me and onto safer things, like six-month sojourns in North Africa living with the Bedouin and visiting refugee camps. Or any number of the exotic adventures he describes over the second round of martinis. Fortunately, his travels and life-style are interesting enough to steer clear of any backstory I haven't yet invented for myself. I'd be utterly screwed if Alex Chevalier was something more ordinary, like an accountant. But, then again, if that were true, I probably wouldn't be sitting here ignoring jazz with him in the first place.

The time passes quickly, and after a couple of hours we find ourselves back in the Cougar, passing through Los Feliz on the 101. Alex clears his throat, and I can tell he's about to ask another question. I beat him to the punch.

"So, tell me about Fluffy," I say. "We can start with how you came up with that silly name for what appears to be a very unfluffy dog." He glances my way a moment before looking back at the road, so I clarify. "You have a photo of him as your screensaver,"

Alex lifts a shoulder in a shrug. "I got Fluffy at the pound, and that's the name he came with. I figure they named him Fluffy for one of two reasons: either a ridiculous attempt to make him seem more adoptable, or someone had a really bad sense of humor."

"Then why didn't you rename him?"

"Well, Fluffy's had a hard life," he tells me. "His story is actually pretty sad. I didn't want to put him through the stress of learning a new name. He already answered to Fluffy, so I kept it."

I shift in my seat, so that I'm facing him. "What's his story?"

"You really want to hear it?" He gives me a skeptical glance, but I nod.

"Alright," he says, "but don't say I didn't warn you. According to the people at the pound, the police took Fluffy in a raid on a house where pit bulls were bred, trained, and fought."

"Oh," I say, thinking I understand. "I see. He was a fighter. That explains how he lost his eye."

Alex hesitates, then glances at me. "Not exactly. Are you sure you really want to hear this?"

"Yes." I'm intrigued. What worse fate could Fluffy have suffered than being a fighting dog?

"The thing is," Alex says carefully, "the Fluffster just hasn't got much fight in him. He looks scary as hell, and he's pretty big, which is probably why those assholes picked him out to be a fighter in the first place. But he didn't fight, or at least he didn't fight very well. That's what we assume anyway, and I can tell you from experience that he gets along with pretty much anything. Except cats. So his previous owners had a big pit bull that was basically useless to them. So, they filed his teeth down and turned him into a bait dog." He looks over at me again, apology written all over his face.

"What," I ask, horrified understanding coming slowly, "is a bait dog?"

Alex's jaw clenches, and it takes him a second to get himself under control. "They'd tie him down in the center of the pit," he says in a low voice, "and let the fighting dogs have a go at him to keep their blood lust up for the fights. We know this because that's where the police found him. Tied down in the middle of a muddy pit. He was so encrusted in blood and mud, they couldn't tell what color he was. They had to take him out on a stretcher."

"Christ." I imagine poor Fluffy. It's a myth, taken from common folklore, that vampires and dogs are natural enemies. True, we are sometimes wary of them because they can track us. But those are working dogs. Police dogs. Military dogs. As far as pet dogs, we like them very much. Vampires like to keep pets just as much as humans. And for the record, we're no more likely to feed off our animals than a human is to eat his golden retriever. Fluffy's story breaks my heart. I'm familiar with dog fighting. It's common in Australia, but this is the first I've heard of "bait dogs."

Alex breathes in deeply through his nose, then out through his mouth. His agitated pulse slows a bit and, when he speaks, he sounds resigned. "When I got him, he was covered in scars and mange from head to toe. He didn't have much in the way of fur. He didn't even have whiskers. His fur came back pretty quickly, but it took about two years for the whiskers to return."

I nod slowly, my heart hurting over the plight of the Fluffster. Humans really can be rotten sons of bitches sometimes. Then something dawns on me. "If he looked that bad at the pound, then why did you pick him to adopt? Surely by the looks of him, you wouldn't have thought he was good 'pet' material?"

Alex clears his throat and opens his mouth as if to speak, but hesitates. I wait until he finally says, "I went down there looking for a yellow lab or something like that. They had plenty of those, a whole pen of them. Fluffy's pen was next to theirs. He was all by himself, probably to protect the other dogs in case he 'snapped.'" Alex pauses. A couple of seconds tick by. "One of the pound employees told me it was his last day there—they were going to put him down the next day if someone didn't adopt him. Too many dogs out there, and they needed the space. So I took him home."

"Alex." Without thinking, I reach out to touch his arm. I feel the power of his vitality just beneath the thin layers of shirt and leather jacket. Something tells me to pull my hand back, but I don't. I like him. I'm really starting to like him.

He turns to look at me, and he smiles. I wonder if he feels the connection too.

Eyes back to the road, Alex slows the car down in order to take the Cahuenga Boulevard exit. I continue to watch his profile. I'm surprised that someone as sexy and alluring as Alex Chevalier could turn out to have a beautiful heart. Not such a common find here in the City of Angels.

Too soon, Alex pulls his Cougar up to the front of my house. He pops the button on his seatbelt, exits the car, and jogs over to my side so he can open my door for me. Electricity shoots up my arm as his hand touches mine.

I let him help me out, but then snatch my hand back. I feel a little knot of panic in the pit of my stomach as he follows me to my gate, and as we stand facing each other at my front door. He's probably trying to get a read on me to decide if I want to be kissed. The little knot of panic in my stomach explodes, and I jerk backwards involuntarily, stepping painfully into the stucco wall behind me. Alex swoops in on me as I desperately avert my face. He plants a chaste peck on my cheek. But for just a moment, his body is intimately close to mine. That—coupled with my raging libido—is all it takes. The smell of his blood floods my senses while his heartbeat thunders in my ears, deafening me to all other sounds.

I am suddenly *hungry*. My teeth pulse and throb as my canines and side incisors thicken and sharpen while I go through the change. Keeping my head down to hide my luminescent eyes, I turn away from him and yank open my front door, calling a maniacally cheerful "good-night" to him over my shoulder as I slam the door in his face.

I stand still for a few moments, my back pressed against the door, panting slightly and listening. Seconds pass before I hear his quiet footsteps as he makes his way back across my courtyard. The gate creaks as he closes and latches it. Alex's car roars back to life, and with my back still pressed against my door, I listen to the engine rumble off down my street.

I breathe a noisy sigh of relief. That had been close. *Too* close. Owen was the last human I kissed, over a hundred years ago, and I'm clearly out of practice. Though it's more than Alex's proximity that drop-kicked me through the change; I want Alex, really, truly *want* him. In both senses of the word. If Alex had kissed me on the mouth, I might have torn him to shreds.

Maybe this whole friendship plan isn't such a good idea. Putting Alex in danger just so I can have the satisfaction of pissing off Bianca seems pretty self-centered. I can definitely find safer ways to stick it to the man, or, in this case, woman. In fact, pissing off Bianca isn't difficult. With a little effort and a smidge of creativity, I can come up with all kinds of interesting ways to make Bianca unhappy with me. Hell, just *breathing* makes her unhappy with me.

Only problem is, I like Alex. I really do. Spending time with him is fun. If I can communicate to him that we're just going to be friends, this might still work. Plus, spending more time with him would help me with my control, and I clearly need to work on that.

I sigh again and dump my purse on the bag chair. I walk into the kitchen and am suddenly face to face with Sunny. He'd told me he was going to a nightclub, so I didn't think he'd still be home. But here he is, with a ludicrous grin on his face, and his fangs as fully extended as mine. He closes his eyes and gently inclines his head towards me, inhaling deeply. His stupid, smug grin grows even bigger.

Bastard.

CHAPTER 9

I DREAM OF AUSTRALIA AGAIN.

It had been a long and difficult day. The common room is deserted, the only sign of life the cheerful little flame burning in the gas lamp on the wooden table. It is just as well. Too tired for dinner and too tired for company, I make my way down the hall to my little closet of a room next to Owen's. I open the door, and let out a startled yelp: a figure is standing next to the bed. Another frightened yelp follows close on its heels when the long, white, ghostly apparition fails to evaporate the way all good ghosts are supposed to, once discovered.

As I stand with my heart thundering in my throat, I catch the barest hint of a shimmer. But dammit, this is Australia. This is no country to be frightened by silly ghosts, you have to be tougher than that. So I grit my teeth and open the door wider to shed some more light on the thing, and I discover that it isn't a ghost after all, but something far stranger: a dress hanging from a wire on the door of my wardrobe.

Puzzled, I step back out to the common room to light my bedside candle from the gas lamp's flame, then return to my room to approach the dress warily. The closer

I get, the more strange and beautiful it becomes. I've never seen anything like it. It isn't a dress, but rather a gown of thick, heavy, ivory satin covered with a pure white lace overlay ending in two wide lace flounces at the bottom. With a rounded neckline and lace, puff sleeves, it is tied back at the waist with a wide ivory satin sash. A wide rectangle of exquisite hand-made lace, matching the lace pattern of the gown's double lace flounces, hangs from the corner of the wardrobe. Laid out on my bed are long, ivory satin gloves and matching slippers.

"Do you like it?"

I whirl around to face Owen, who stands with his arms crossed across his chest, leaning in the doorway with a little smile dancing in his eyes.

"Wherever did you get such a thing?" I demand, my voice trailing off in wonder.

I still can't believe he intends for me to wear the gown, gloves and slippers. It seems amazing and yet dangerous somehow, like opening the door to find a lion cub sitting in your bed. As cute as the baby might be initially, it means the mother lioness is nearby. If Owen has stolen these things, it will be a cut and dried hanging offense. But whom in all of New South Wales could he have stolen it from? It is a gown fit for the consort of a King.

"Do you remember I told you my father died a few years ago?" he asks.

"Yes."

"Well, he left me some money. A lot of money. My sister has been keeping it for me until I'd be able to come back to England to claim it."

"Okay...but I don't understand what that has to do with—"

"Moira," he interrupts, his voice pitched low with emotion. "I didn't want to go back to England. I knew you'd never come with me, and I didn't want to be away from you for that long. And I don't really need the money."

"I still don't understand—"

"I asked my sister to buy the dress. Her husband's employer helped her. It's from Paris."

"But how?" I demand. "You only asked me to marry you three weeks ago. It would have taken at least nine months to get here!"

His smile deepens. "Actually, it took almost twice that long."

I stare at him, my mouth dropping open in shock. He gazes back at me with laughter dancing in his eyes, waiting for comprehension to set in.

"But what if I'd said no?" A hint of outrage creeps into my voice.

He laughs and pulls me towards him, resting his chin on the top of my head as I lean against his chest.

"I was hoping you would say yes."

When I wake, a smile lingers on my face.

Dammit. Alex. What the hell am I going to do about Alex?

Later that night, I find myself at my friend Neichia's house. She lives in Brentwood, an old, affluent West Side suburb, made famous in the 1990s by the Nicole Simpson and Ron Goldman murders.

Her house is one of those "glass box" modular types that became popular in Southern California in the '50s and '60s. The architect designed the single story of this particular house in an "L" shape around a swimming pool, its overall structure sectioned into cubes making up the individual rooms. The floor to ceiling glass wall on the side of the house facing the pool serves as the building's outstanding feature, with the two rooms on each end of the L shape—the master bedroom and the kitchen—having two walls of solid glass. It's the sort of house that, for privacy's sake, could only stand in the middle of an acre or so of land.

Beyond the swimming pool, a field of purple Mexican heather stretches out to the property's limit, divided down the middle by a footstone path. The path leads to a second structure, not original to the 1959 property, which at first looks like a guest house almost equal in size to the main house. Then you notice it has no windows and its single door is made out of a heavy slab of stainless steel with an impressive-looking keypad next to it. This building is Neichia's laboratory. She values her privacy when working, as well she should since that work encompasses many diverse interests, including the study of vampires and vampirism. Most of what we know about the scientific side of vampirism has come from Neichia's studies.

We are in the backyard. Neichia sits on a lounge chair, next to her pool, sipping from a tall, frosted glass. I stand a little ways away, off from a target about ten paces away from me. I heft the bowie knife in my hand, feeling its lopsided weight distribution in favor of the blade. Most would say a bowie knife is unfavorable for throwing at a target, but it's all I've ever known. I close my eyes and listen to the subtle symphony of the night: the fluttering of the garden moths hovering over the opened moonflowers, the grunting noises of a skunk family rooting around for insects beyond the property line, and the rustling of the breeze through the trees, jacarandas in the front yard and eucalyptus in the back.

Suddenly, Neichia's crisp British accent cuts through my romantic musings. "So, I hear you've found a man," she says. Then, when I don't respond immediately, she adds, "I also hear Bianca tried to scare you away from him."

I grip the Bowie's handle with my thumb, pointer finger, and middle finger. My ring finger and pinkie rest gently on the handle. Testing my grip, I draw my arm back slowly, feeling the weight of the knife, then snap my throwing arm forward in an even, smooth arc, releasing the handle at the very moment my hand starts its downward curve. I am rewarded with a solid thunk in the target.

Once again, it is pointless to try and figure out how vampires get their information. They have their ways, and the older the vampire, the more ways they seem to have. And Neichia, at four centuries and change, is the oldest vampire of my acquaintance that I can also call a friend. She is not, however, considered a *Stoicheía*, though why this should be the case, I don't know.

"I'm not so sure you could call Alex 'my man'," I say as I march over to the target. "Though I did go out on a date with him last night, and I did have a good time with him."

"Oh, he's your man alright. You might not know it yet, and he almost certainly doesn't, but I can see it and so can any vampire who knows you well. Something about you has changed; you seem *enhanced* somehow."

Neichia is quiet for a moment, stirring the contents of her bloody drink with the little stalk of celery she added just for fun.

"How long have you known him?" she asks.

It is an interesting question, since surely she knows about his role in my car accident. If she knows about Alex, I have to assume her mysterious informants have told her the same details Bianca seemed to know. But I am not dealing with Bianca here, I am dealing with my friend—totally different circumstances. Nevertheless, I decide to err on the side of caution.

"I met him, as I'm sure you already know, on the night of my accident. He's the one who pulled me from the car," I say, wrenching my blade from the post.

Neichia gives her drink another little swish. "I didn't ask when you met him," she says. "I asked you how long you've *known* him."

"Alright then: three weeks. He started coming to the coffee shop regularly three weeks before the accident. I noticed him right away."

Neichia nods and takes a sip of her drink. Then she leans back into her chair and stretches her long, pale legs, uncrossing then re-crossing them the other way.

"It was about three weeks ago that I first noticed the change in you," she muses. "I thought at the time that you had finally decided to let Sunny in your bed, and no, I'm not talking about sleeping. But even I can be wrong from time to time. What does he do?"

She asks an innocent-enough question, but the answer to it could have some potentially negative ramifications for me if I wished to see him again. Photographers, especially *news* photographers, could pose a significant threat to our *Koinon*. Still, I decide to be honest.

"He's a photographer—a photojournalist." I move away from the post ten paces, and prepare to throw again. "He does some work for the *Times*, and he's done quite a bit of magazine work."

"Hmmm," she says. "You know of course that any involvement with a journalist could be dangerous."

"Yes," I reply stiffly, hefting the knife once more so that I grip the handle properly. "I know. There are security issues to take into consideration. I've been careful and will continue to be careful in the future." The operative term here is *future*; I don't want her to get any ideas about trying to warn me off of him.

"But," I draw back once more, careful to keep my elbow pointed straight upwards at a level that is even with my head, then I snap my throwing arm forward. "Something makes me feel like it won't be an issue—" I am satisfied with another solid thunk in my target. "I don't know how to put it," I tell her. "There is something about him—something different, though I can't say exactly what."

Neichia nods. "Well, I suppose this possible 'security issue,' as you call it, must be why Bianca wants you to stay away from him: she doesn't like the whole journalist angle."

I had actually come to the same conclusion myself, but then this would mean that Bianca actually knew what Alex did for a living before I did. How could Bianca know things about Alex before me? I say as much to Neichia, and she agrees with me in the sort of vague way she has.

Then she stretches her arms over her head languorously in the beginnings of a full stretch, traveling from her fingertips down through her body and legs to the tips of her pointed toes. After holding this pose for a few seconds, she relaxes her legs and pulls her shoulders back in order to crack the vertebrae in the center of her back. She settles back into the cushions of her lounge, and finishes the last drops of her drink.

"So, you plan to see him again," she says suddenly.

I do not hesitate. "Yes."

"What do you tell him when he asks you questions about your life?"

"Well." I wrench the blade once more from the post. "So far I've managed to avoid most of those questions—the other night I kept him talking mostly about himself."

"You won't be able to avoid them forever," she informs me. "At some point you are going to have to come up with plausible answers to his questions—answers he will believe and you will remember."

I begin to feel a little irritated. I did not come here for a lecture. I have been a vampire long enough to know about the necessity of plausible lying. This may have been the first human friendship that I've pursued since moving here to Los Angeles, but I have been living in the human world successfully for quite a while now.

I think Neichia senses my irritation because she doesn't push the subject any further. She sits in the dark, swishing her celery stick in an empty glass.

"You know you are quite good at that." She motions towards the target.

I don't answer. I know I am good at it. Not everyone can throw a bowie knife. Its size makes it less than ideal. But I'd certainly had the time to practice. Owen taught me how to do it, back when I was still human. He also taught me other things with the knife. And I'd certainly had the opportunity to put them to the test. The Outback was a dangerous place, back in the nineteenth century.

I listen again for the little skunk family, but they have passed beyond the range of my hearing, so I content myself with gazing up at the stars.

"I have a favor I need to ask you," Neichia says, breaking into my reverie.

"Sure, anything." I sheath the knife, and place it next to my untouched drink on the little table next to Neichia's chaise lounge.

"I'm sure it's nothing," she says. "But I'd like to go check, just to make sure."

"What is it?"

"I haven't heard from Fiona in over two months. When you were supposed to come over last week, I was going to ask if you've heard anything from her. But now it's been over eight weeks, which is unusual."

Fiona is a pretty Irish vampire who came to Los Angeles sometime in the 1980s. I get along with her well enough, but Neichia counts Fiona among her closest friends. The fact that no one's heard from her in over two months is unusual, but not anything to cause alarm. Not yet.

"Do you want to go check on her?" I ask. "Let's go now—it's starting to get late, and we may want to take some time to look around."

Fiona's house is just a few blocks away, so we decide to walk. I am not overly concerned and am sure we'll discover a rational explanation for Fiona's radio silence. I don't say this out loud, but I think she's likely angry with Neichia, who I know to be temperamental at times. In Fiona's case, all that red hair really does indicate a fiery temper. Besides, what could possibly have gone wrong? A vampire's only natural enemy is another vampire. The problems with blood feuds that supposedly plague the rest of the vampire world are unknown here in the City of Angels. Most of us are so solitary, and we don't care much about others. Except for Bianca, who cares enough to make up for the rest of us.

When we arrive at Fiona's I quickly check myself mentally and adopt an appropriately somber frame of mind—we are here for serious business. Despite my personal feelings on the matter, Neichia is worried. A friend is unaccounted for, and we need to make sure everything is alright.

Fiona's house is built along the same lines as the famed Witch's House in Beverly Hills, complete with exaggerated gables, thatched roof, and the rounded eaves of a four-teenth-century domicile. It occurs to me that Neichia and I stand before Fiona's home much as Hansel and Gretel had stood before the witch's gingerbread cottage.

"Cheerful," I observe wryly.

Walking up to the front door, we find it unlocked. Natural enough if someone was home, but it appears no one is there. I admit this isn't a good sign. Once inside, I'm struck by a sense of hollow emptiness—as if the house has been devoid of life for some time. A strange odor, earthy, like freshly churned soil mixed with the unmistakable, cloying stench of decay, overwhelms me. I'm reminded of the stench of old European graveyards during the hot days of summer. And underneath that stink, I can detect the tangy, coppery smell of blood. A lot of blood. I begin to take our mission more seriously.

The house is dark, and not just because it lacks lights. Dark, richly carved woods dominate the house's interior.

The staircase before us is carved from a rich, dark mahogany, with two matching banisters, the middle of each step worn down from decades of use. A massive mantelpiece made of the same mahogany dominates the living room off to the right, and dark hardwood floors and heavy, rustic timbres brace the ceiling. Even the cream-colored plaster seems muted by the dark hues.

Neither Neichia nor I wish to stay here any longer than necessary, so a wordless agreement passes between us to split up. As she heads up the stairs, which creak with every step, I continue searching downstairs. Fiona's preference for sparse furnishings is apparent in a single, small sofa in front of the fireplace. A covered grand piano in the far corner is the only other piece in the sitting room. The dining room/library fares little better, although several bookcases display everything from tattered paperback romances to leather-bound editions of nineteenth and twentieth-century classics. I quickly dismiss the two front rooms, because these are Fiona's public spaces and probably don't contain what I'm looking for. I need to find her blood supply.

I don't need to look far. Located directly behind the dining room/library, the kitchen is tiny with little in the way of modern amenities, other than a small microwave plugged in next to an itty-bitty stove. Opening the tiny 1930s-sized refrigerator, I look through Fiona's visible blood supply. Blood bags—whether from the slaughterhouse, the hospital, the Red Cross, or a private blood bank—always have expiration dates on them. That provides us with a timeline. Sure enough, half of her supply is out of code. Her oldest bags of blood expired ten weeks ago.

From the kitchen, I stumble unexpectedly upon the

master bedroom suite. As I move to the center of the room, noting the unmade bed, the smell of blood becomes stronger. Along with the smell of rot.

I call for Neichia.

I go first to Fiona's large walk-in closets rather than the bathroom, where the blood smell seems to be strongest. As I slowly open each door, a little light automatically switches on. Inside, I find a full set of designer luggage, and no bags appear to be missing. I see no obvious gaps in the multiple rows of hangers.

Next, I turn to the master bathroom. The rotten, coppery smell grows stronger as I approach, as does a strange humming sound. As I get closer, the foulness of the odor overwhelms me.

Then it hits me—the sound is flies—lots of flies. The smell is unmistakable. Rotting blood. Where is Neichia? Should I ask her to take a look at the bathroom with me?

I chide myself for being gutless. Whatever is on the other side of the door cannot hurt me.

I push open the door and behold the most beautiful bathroom suite I have ever seen. Feng Shui meets Trump Towers.

And it is covered in blood.

Lots and lots of blood.

Blood covers the antique vanity; blood covers the smart toilet; blood splatters spread across the side of the whirlpool tub; blood spray smears the shower door; and blood covers almost three-quarters of the floor.

Christ. How can there be so much blood?

On the counter, next to the sink sits a coffee cup half full of coagulated blood. This appears to be attracting most of the flies. The blood almost everywhere else has long since dried to a brownish black crust.

On the floor, next to the sink, is the body.

Fiona.

She lies naked, twisted, her body contorted into an unnatural position—telling me her back must be broken. Her jaws yawn wide, and her fangs are out. With her teeth elongated like that, she looks like a tiger yawning. Except she isn't yawning. She's dead. And she's been dead long enough that her extremities are starting to decompose into dust. That is the way of dead vampires. Our body remains uncorrupted for a remarkable length of time, but eventually we return to dust.

Dust to dust.

Her throat has been ripped out. She has bled out. How the fuck did that happen? Vampires do not bleed out. Our biology makes it impossible. We heal too quickly.

Christ.

Am I frightened? I don't know. Do I even know how to be afraid anymore? It has been such a long time since something has truly threatened me. But I'm perplexed. A vampire's only natural enemy is another vampire. And sure, we do kill each other upon occasion… but not like this. This is downright unnatural.

I hear a sound and turn to see Neichia at the bedroom door. She pauses only for a moment, determining I am indeed in this room. She comes to me with such speed, she looks like a DVD scanning forward. When she stops, she grips my arm, her eyes signaling fear and urgency.

"We need to get out of here." She looks over my shoulder into the bathroom and repeats, "We need to get out of here. Right now."

The graveyard stench has grown heavier, the cloying sweetness of decay so beautifully rich in the air, I could sink my teeth into it.

But no, I'm not afraid. I'm intrigued. I gesture at the body, as if to say, "Don't you want to look?" But she responds by pulling forcefully on my arm, hurting me as she drags me towards the bedroom door.

"Okay, okay! Fine, I'm coming!" I cry in exasperation. "Stop yanking me. I'm coming!"

Once outside the house, Neichia takes a few deep breaths and composes herself. The cemetery smell lingers in the air, its sweetness at war with the thick, rich scent of Fiona's moonflowers climbing a trellis next to the door.

We have not yet found the source of that smell.

"Jesus, Neichia! What the hell happened in there?" I rub my wounded arm. I'm not sure whether I mean Fiona's body in the bathroom or Neichia's sudden freak-out. Then I see Neichia's fangs are fully descended and her eyes glow.

Many things can make a vampire inadvertently go through the change, salient among them being immediate mortal danger.

Yet I'm still not frightened, but why? Why didn't I go through the change?

I repeat my question, noting that Neichia's fangs are slowly retracting. I no longer detect the cemetery stink. But looking into the fading glow of her vampire eyes, I catch a brief glimpse of what it means to have lived in this world for four centuries: wisdom, pain…

…and fear.

She blinks and looks away. "We are in danger. We're all in terrible danger."

CHAPTER 10

THE NEXT NIGHT, I decide to cancel my plans with Alex. It works out beautifully that he's leaving for San Francisco the next morning to tie up some loose ends. I need some time alone to process what happened at Fiona's.

Sunny has returned to Malibu, and every night I find myself checking the locks on all my doors before I settle into my work. I'm still not afraid, but it seems the prudent thing to do. Fiona was Neichia's friend, not mine. I didn't know her well, so do not mourn her loss. As callous as it sounds, vampires are used to death. The death of a vampire is unusual, but not unheard of. And always it comes violently, at the hands of another vampire. I cannot account for her loss of blood. It remains a mystery, but Fiona must have pissed off the wrong vampire. I can think of no other explanation.

Before Alex leaves, we make plans via text for the Saturday after his return to go see one of his friends play at the Kibitz Room of Canters. I invite Sunny along to play chaperone. Alex tested the limits of my self-control by attempting to kiss me—there can be no more of that. Sunny's presence will, I hope, keep our libidos firmly in check.

In the meantime, I agree to attend a party with Sunny. Though not usually a party-goer—in fact, I hate parties—I find it difficult to resist Sunny when he lays on the charm.

The party is hosted by a 150-year-old American vampire named Ely, at the Gable and Lombard Penthouse of the Roosevelt Hotel. It's a beautiful, multi-storied space composed of dark, rich woods, cream-colored upholsteries, and the copious use of mirrors and floor-to-ceiling arched windows to create the illusion of endless space.

As Sunny and I step through the door, I see that Ely has redecorated. The central focus of the living room is a circular arrangement of cream upholstered sofas and armchairs. A rosewood coffee table serves as the focal point, and next to all the sofas and armchairs are side tables made completely of mirrors. Stretching from wall to wall is a plush, geometric carpet of muted colors. The polished rosewood bar is off to the right, with several matching rosewood pub tables, and to the left is the spiral staircase with beautiful ironwork leading up to bedrooms on the second floor.

Ely has about thirty or so vampires in attendance, all of them the most bright and beautiful of the Los Angeles *Koinon*, dressed to the teeth in typical Hollywood vampire splendor. Eat your heart out, Paris Fashion Week. They are gathered in small groups around the pub tables and the bar, or sprawled on the sofas holding champagne glasses of Cristal champagne mixed with blood.

Sunny and I scan the crowd for familiar faces. I'm surprised at the number of friends I see, far more than I had anticipated. Maybe this evening won't be so bad after all.

As I relax my posture a little, our host descends upon us with arms outstretched in a gesture of welcome. Giving his slim figure a once over as he advances, a smile comes to my lips. It's been a while since I've seen Ely, but his tight herringbone trousers, white dress shirt, skinny tie, and cashmere cardigan fashionably patched at the elbows tells me he still has that Rat Pack thing going on that he hasn't been able to shake since the early 2000s.

Tipping his fedora back at a jaunty angle so he can kiss me, he welcomes us magnanimously to his humble abode. He winks at me knowingly, sliding his hands down to rest elegantly on his hips. "For what I'm paying, though, I hope you won't find it *too* humble."

Sunny doesn't bother to respond, but heads for the bar as Ely links his arm through mine. "You know, baby," he says, walking me into the living room, "it has been way *too long*! Why don't you come out anymore? I never see you *anywhere*."

Like Sunny, I don't bother to respond. I just allow Ely to carry on in his stylized dialect until he deposits me on one of the sofas. Then, making his apologies that he is needed elsewhere, he vanishes and a few moments later I hear him greeting his newest arrivals in the same extravagant tones.

I find myself alone for barely thirty seconds before Sunny reappears, holding two glasses. I sniff the one he hands to me. Mixing alcohol with blood is theoretically supposed to make it go down easier for those of us old enough to have problems with human beverages. Even though the blood is human, I'm unwilling to trust my sensitive digestive system to Ely's bartender. This is far too elegant a party for me to have issues in the bathroom. They'd be talking about it for months.

Nevertheless, I'm grateful to have a drink to hold while I mingle with the other guests. So I thank Sunny, who doesn't hear me. Following his gaze across the room, I see he's found his quarry for the evening: Etoile, the pretty French vampire with long, platinum blonde hair. She's standing alone in the corner next to the bar, in between two torchieres with dramatic sculptural uplighters. The light shining on her golden head makes her look angelic. Etoile's solitude, and her attempts to blend in with the muted frescoed wall behind her, is significant. We rarely see her without Etienne, the slightly effeminate vampire (at least according to Sunny) with whom she left France two decades ago. She's wearing a modest brown sweater dress, which blends wonderfully with the Earthy tones of the room, but does nothing to camouflage her amazing curves. Poor Etoile. She could wear a pilgrim's getup, and still look like a pinup from the forties.

Seeing Sunny's reaction to her, I give him a shove in her direction. He's always had a thing for the wallflowers. "Go," I say. "Come find me later."

"Huh?" He blinks at me. "I'm sorry, what did you say?"

"You'd better get over there now. We don't know where Etienne is. He could come back to her any minute."

Sunny's eyes clear a little, once more showing signs of intelligence, though it is definitely horny intelligence.

"Thanks, babe," he says, kissing me quickly on the cheek. Then, after a few steps towards Etoile, he stops and looks over his shoulder at me. "You know," he says, winking, "it's only because I can't have you." And then he is gone. Moments later, I hear Etoile's warm laughter fill up her corner of the room. The game is afoot.

Alone now, I look around for some of those friendly faces I'd noted upon arrival. Fortunately, I don't have to look far. My friend Jolene is standing at a table over by the bar, talking to the vampires Alastair and Leslie, both of whom I'm on friendly terms with. I approach them just in time to hear Jolene tell the other two, "I don't know, she just seems to have vanished."

Despite barging in on their conversation, the three vampires seem pleased to see me. That often happens when you don't go out much.

"I hate to be rude," I begin once we have gone through the pleasantries, "but I overheard you say something about someone being missing." I set my champagne glass down on the tall pub table.

"Yes," Jolene answers. "I was just telling Alastair and Leslie that I haven't heard from Rachel in about a month."

Rachel? Not Fiona?

Then, as the three of us listen, Jolene describes the details surrounding Rachel's disappearance. It sounds eerily familiar. When Jolene reaches the point in which she went to investigate Rachel's house, I find myself holding my breath. Here, Jolene's story diverges from mine. Signs of a struggle were the only indications of foul play Jolene discovered. She found some overturned furniture, but no bloody massacre. Rachel is just gone, leaving behind no trace other than a refrigerator full of expired blood and a tossed living room.

It occurs to me then to tell my story about Fiona, but something stops me. For now the evidence of Fiona's untimely end needs to be kept between Neichia and myself, although I cannot say why. Neichia said that she would "take care of things," and I assumed that included cleaning up the crime scene as well as emptying the house of any vampire traces.

I don't need to tell you just how bad it would have been if any human had come across Fiona's house in the condition Neichia and I found it. I also assumed that meant she would contact the *Stoicheía* to inform them of our discoveries. They have not made Fiona's demise public, so for now I won't either. Besides, I don't want to alarm Jolene any further. She already suspects foul play and doesn't need Fiona's story to make her suspicions worse.

As Jolene finishes recounting the strange stillness of Rachel's vacant house, a plump little vampire named Beverley joins our group, listening intently to the end of Jolene's tale. Beverley, it turns out, has a story of her own. As she sips her bloody champagne, we learn that her friend Natalie has been missing for several weeks. We listen to her account of a disappeared friend and an empty house.

Once again, there is no mention of blood. Both Rachel and Natalie have disappeared without leaving any trace of themselves behind. But the real bombshell comes when Beverley tells us that, based on other conversations she's had that evening, two more vampires, Garret and Dean, are also missing.

A heavy silence hangs in the air. Alastair sets his drink down. "So," he starts, then a significant pause. "Rachel, Natalie, Garret, and Dean have mysteriously disappeared from their homes without a trace." He then holds up his hand when Jolene looks about to interrupt him. "*And* none of them left of their own free will. Am I correct?"

The ladies nod. I don't move.

"I don't buy it," he says flatly. "Who exactly is supposed to have taken them? What possible force could have overcome them? Other than another vampire?"

Lesley speaks for the first time. "That's what we're trying to figure out. Haven't you been listening?" Her eyes flash a warning.

He grimaces as he pulls on his shirt collar. "I *have* been listening. To every word. But we're jumping to conclusions by assuming foul play. How do we know the four of them haven't just gone somewhere together? We have no evidence to the contrary."

I can see the points of his fangs starting to show. This is really upsetting him.

"What about the expired blood?" Jolene demands. "No vampire would leave that in their fridge. It's disgusting, not to say dangerous. What happens if a neighbor comes snooping because of the smell?"

"It would have to smell pretty bad for human neighbors to notice." Alastair points out. "Maybe they're all just slobs." He does have a point about the smell, but I find it hard to believe that they all share the same gross housekeeping habits. I sniff the beginnings of a conspiracy. I sense the tension escalating, and now see the points of Jolene's fangs, while Alastair still pulls at his collar like it's choking him.

"You are being an idiot," Jolene snaps. "Something is going on, something has happened to them!" She inhales deeply, and lets the air out in a long, shuddering breath. Her fangs are fully descended.

"Fine." Alastair stretches the word in a deceptively civil tone while bearing his elongated canines. "Then I repeat my earlier question: Who or what has supposedly taken them? What force would have the power to kidnap four vampires?" He takes our collective silence to indicate his victory. "You see? Nothing. Nothing could have kidnapped them!"

"What about murder?" I ask quietly.

And so I throw gasoline onto the fire.

All four turn to face me, eyes round with shock. Alastair now yanks at his collar until the top button pops off, his face and neck a blotchy red. Jolene keeps her features carefully immobile, lips closed tightly over her fangs. She doesn't want to threaten me.

Lesley speaks first. "Murder?" She says the word slowly, rolling it off of her tongue as though grasping the full magnitude of it. "You think they've been killed? By what? What could have killed them? And why?"

The time has come for me to tell them about Fiona and the evidence of a massacre in her bathroom. But even as I look into their expectant faces, taking in the disbelief mirrored in each set of eyes, something tells me not to. Something tells me it isn't safe.

"I'm disappointed in you, Sonia," Alastair says. "I had figured you would be on my side in this. But you're worse than the rest of them." He turns to look at me full in the face. "The only thing that can kill a vampire is another vampire."

Sure, a vampire taking out another vampire isn't unheard of. But more than one smells like feud. And Los Angeles has never seen a feud before.

Alistair's lips have curled back from his teeth while he waits for me to respond, and I'm certain he's scared. So scared, he's panting, now tearing at the second button on his shirt.

He takes a step towards me. "Take it back."

Bewildered, I stand my ground. "Take what back, Alastair?" I say his name sharply, attempting to bring him back from wherever the fear has taken him.

He takes another step. "Take it back! All of it! *Now!*" He snarls, threatening me with his fangs.

He's making no sense. I don't move or speak, but he towers over me. Hot, angry breath stinking of soured champagne blasts into my face. But I smell no blood on his breath. He's drinking his alcohol straight. He must be younger than me, perhaps by as much as a century.

If we fight, I will win.

He takes another step, his body now crowding into mine. Thank god my strappy heels have some traction when I dig them into the plush carpet, refusing to be bullied backwards.

Now I'm angry. The vampire in me responds, and I go through a partial change. My pupils narrow into slits, my deadly points sharpen and elongate.

Alastair's face is a mask of fury, the shape of his mouth contorted like one of those old tragedy masks from the theater. Music swings in the background, but the din of voices has quieted. I sense all eyes on me.

"I will tell you once more…" he begins, spittle oozing out of the corners of his mouth. But, before he goes on, his eyes widen as something drags him abruptly backwards and away from me. Sunny stands behind him, and holding him by the back of the neck he easily lifts Alastair off of the ground. Alastair struggles, swinging his feet back and forth wildly to find purchase while he kicks at Sunny.

"Stop struggling, man," Sunny growls. "You're only going to hurt yourself."

Alastair continues to flail around, still trying to kick at Sunny behind him. He knocks over the pub table my champagne sits on. The glass bounces off the plush carpet, and booze and blood splash across the geometric patterns. Sunny allows Alastair to carry on like this for a few moments, but finally gives him a good, hard shake. I hear the bones in Alastair's neck break. His body quiets and his head now sits at an odd angle on his hunched shoulders.

But Sunny has not seriously injured Alastair, whose neck will be fully healed within an hour. Alastair must relax his body for the healing to take place, and that space of time should allow him to calm the hell down and rethink whatever it is that makes him want to fight me.

Sunny sets Alastair's feet on the ground, and walks him to one of the couches, still holding him by the back of the neck. He sits him down and whispers something in Alastair's ear, gives him a hard clap on the back, and comes over to join me.

"I could have handled him myself, you know." I'm trying to decide if I'm pissed at him for interfering. I set the table to rights, and pick up my empty wine glass.

"I know," he replies cheerfully, taking my wineglass from me and setting it on the bar. "But you could have torn your dress. And I like that dress."

Sunny's smile is impossible to resist. Designed to charm the anger out of women, it has a 100% success rate. It works now.

"Really, Sonia," he continues, once my features have softened into a smile, "I can't take you anywhere. I bring you to a party and you're ready to brawl. What the hell did you say to poor Alastair? I don't think he's ever been in a fight in his life."

When I don't dignify his question with an answer, he continues on, warming up to his subject. "Have your reclusive ways finally turned you into an Australian hillbilly? Somehow I think that Australian hillbillies must be worse than American ones. Is there somewhere I can send you, some sort of hillbilly rehab that will socialize you again?"

I shake my head. "Go back to Etoile. You're making her jealous."

"No, my lovely Sonia, *you* are making her jealous. But now that I'm satisfied you're not going to bite anyone, I think I will return to the beautiful Etoile. I think I'd just about talked her into joining me in one of the bedrooms before you started picking fights."

I open my mouth to say something obnoxious, but he's gone before I can get the words out. I will talk to him about Alastair on the way home. Maybe. I'm still not clear what just happened. What in hell made Alastair go violent? That jerk is supposed to be a friend of mine!

CHAPTER 11

SUDDENLY, FATIGUE HITS. I want to go home. But Sunny and Etoile have disappeared, and my friend's reputation for being a thorough lover tells me I'll be here for a while. Scanning the room, I find another cluster of friendly faces in the corner opposite to where I stand. Maybe this time no one will try to fight me.

I'm about half-way across the room, when yet another vampire invades my personal space and impedes my progress. This time, it's Constanzo, a relatively new arrival from Italy I don't know very well. But, taking in his handsome features set in a slightly amused, mildly flirtatious expression, I don't interpret him as a threat. I take a step back so I can see him better, noting that, like Bianca, he favors immaculate black Armani. I think about asking him if black Armani is some sort of national uniform, but, in light of my little altercation with Alastair, I decide not to risk antagonizing him.

"Fear can do extraordinary things to those not accustomed to it." He speaks softly, his words shaped by his thick Italian accent. His sing-song cadence, characteristic of Italians speaking English as a second language, is far more pronounced than Bianca's. His dark eyes twinkle with amusement and a hint of malice.

"I beg your pardon?" I ask, not quite following his meaning. It is easy to get lost in his hypnotic eyes. They are a brilliant and beautiful bluish green, the colors shifting and moving almost like a kaleidoscope.

"Your friend Alastair," he replies. "You're wondering why he attacked you. He's afraid, though he doesn't understand it in that way. He wants to strike out at the one who has made him so afraid. What did you say to him?"

Constanzo's face is so close to mine, he dominates my entire field of vision. The way he repeats the word "afraid" pulses in my mind, like a set of waves crashing on a beach. Even after he stops speaking, I hear *afraid* echo over and over in my head. What had I said to Alastair to make him so *afraid?* Looking up into Constanzo's beautiful eyes, I want to tell him everything—everything I know he wants to hear. I feel light and airy, gently set loose in the wind like a kite, with Constanzo holding my string.

"But you have also known fear recently," he says. "I can smell it. What has made you so *afraid?* Is that what you told Alastair to make him *afraid?*"

There was that word again.

I drift along on the eddies of Constanzo's thrall, that one little word pulsing through my mind: *Afraid. Afraid. Afraid.*

"You have a secret," he whispers. "Did you tell Alastair your secret? Is that what made him so *afraid?*"

I don't answer, but the hairs on the back of my neck rise, goosebumps cover my arms. A warning alarm goes off in

my head. The pulsing *afraid* becomes replaced with *danger.*
Danger. Danger. Danger.

"I want you to tell me your secret," Constanzo whispers.
"Tell me what it is that you know." Constanzo smiles down
at me, looking so beautiful and so innocent. But something
is wrong. I can feel it now. That little cord that Constanzo
is holding onto—it's thrall. Dammit, the bastard really *does*
have me in thrall. I shake my head like a dog, and take a
step back. We are standing in the middle of the room. Is
he going to follow me backwards? But this time he doesn't
come after me. That would have been too threatening for
the magic he is trying to work on me at that moment.

Carradhy. The warning whispers again in my mind. It
is the voice of my Maker, whispering to me across time and
space from the Eora Nation. *Carradhy.* Cleverman.

As I gain perspective, I see it in Constanzo's eyes more
clearly than before. I see hunger. Hunger for…something.
He's willing to do anything to satisfy that hunger. Anything
at all.

"I'm not sure what I said to him." I've regained my
composure and speak evenly. "I said many things. I don't
know which one set him off."

Constanzo tastes my lie. I feel it. But he can do nothing
about it. The spell is broken, and we are in the middle of a
party. I step purposely around him and continue my progress to the other end of the room. It takes me a while to
shake off the effects of his spell, and as I walk away the
weight of his eyes bore into my back.

I make headway across the room, but become aware the
atmosphere of the party has changed. The anxiety I detected
in the undertones of voices now dominates and flavors the

conversations with new colors. I come to learn that Rachel, Natalie, Garrett, and Dean aren't the only missing vampires.

For the rest of the party, I move from group to group, careful to avoid both Alastair and Constanzo, gathering up the names of the missing. By the time Sunny reappears, showing signs of restlessness that signals the need to feed, I have put together a list of seventeen missing vampires, plus Fiona. Most residences have been checked for evidence of foul play, though nothing conclusive has been found. I don't mention Fiona. In no other case has any trace of the vampire been left behind, and in no other case has any vampire been missing for as long as Fiona. She, apparently, is the first and most violent case.

When Sunny and I finally leave, a heavy mood has settled on Ely's party guests. I wonder if perhaps I am not the only one collecting names. What began as a series of strange coincidences has developed into the awful truth of seventeen names. Why are these particular vampires being targeted? And what can be done about it? We have no formal government, no police force. Los Angeles is the Wild West of the Vampire World. All we have is the loose rule of the *Oligarchia*, the Elders, and all they really do is just watch us.

Constanzo is correct about fear. It does extraordinary things to those not accustomed to it. But mere fear didn't make Alastair attack me at the party. No, it was far more personal than that. On the ride home, Sunny tells me that Alastair's paramour, Svetlana, has not been heard from in several weeks. I can only imagine what went through Alastair's mind when he heard about other vampires going missing. On some level he must have come to the same conclusion I did. Vampires, even young ones, are powerful.

Kidnapping one and keeping him or her captive would be difficult enough; it would be downright impossible for the numbers of confirmed missing. The only logical conclusion is that they must be dead. Something is killing off the vampires of Los Angeles.

After Sunny drops me off at my house, and returns to Malibu, I lock the door behind me, switch on some lights.

I think of Neichia; what was it she said to me at Fiona's house?

We are in danger. We're all in terrible danger

I need to call Neichia.

CHAPTER 12

N EICHIA DOESN'T CALL ME back until early Saturday evening, when I'm heading out the door with
Alex. I pick up only to tell her I'll call her back
later. She agrees that we have many things to talk about.

Despite Wednesday's developments, and my preoccu-
pation over the safety of my *Koinon*, I begin the evening
in a good mood. I've never been to the Kibitz Room, so I
wasn't exactly sure what to wear. But since it's always better
to be overdressed than underdressed, I planned my wardrobe as though Sunny was dragging me out to Privilege
or the Cabana Club. I settled on butter-soft leather pants
that fit me like a glove, a peacock blue silk halter that ties
around my neck and waist, leaving my back bare, three-
inch leopard print Gucci heels, and my second best pair of
opal earrings. I pulled my hair up into a high ponytail, then
grabbed a black pashmina in case it gets chilly. Finally, I feel
ready for whatever the night will bring.

Alex pulls up as I'm admiring myself in my
full length mirror. I hurry up the steps
to the front door and swing it wide
so he can get the full effect of my

efforts all at once. Once I lay eyes on him, though, I forget all about myself. Alex's outfit is simple and perfect: faded jeans with the beginnings of a tear on the left knee and a soft, long-sleeve henley in a dark teal that clings to his lean body. The color brings out the teal undertones of his eyes, making them a perfect match to his shirt. Those eyes widen when he sees me in my full, tarted-up glory, and I am gratified to feel his pulse quicken slightly.

But then things get a little weird. As we pass through my courtyard, he places his hand on the small of my back in one of those masculine gestures that is both intimate and possessive. But the second he touches the bare skin of my back, he suddenly yanks it back as if burned.

Once in the car, he carefully negotiates the Cougar's heavy body through the twists and turns of my neighborhood's narrow streets with a dexterity that comes with practice. As before he is silent while driving the old Hollywood streets, but when he keeps up the silence after we make it out of Whitley Heights and turn south onto Highland, I become irritated. After a few blocks, I decide to pick up the slack.

"How was San Francisco?" I ask.

"It was fine." He shrugs, staring ahead out the window. "Same as always."

Silence.

I turn so that I'm facing him. I know he can see me out of the corner of his eye. "What did you do while you were there?"

"Nothing much." He pauses as he turns west onto Sunset. He still refuses to look at me. "The usual stuff with family."

"Did you see any friends?" At this point, I am annoyed. Sure, he's good looking, and I'm attracted to his body chemistry, but Jesus Christ, I'm over two centuries old, and I have better things to do with my time than be ignored by a human man.

"No," he says flatly, "no friends."

After a few more blocks, Alex turns left onto Fairfax and heads south down into the Fairfax district. The longer he stares ahead into the traffic, giving me the silent treatment, the angrier I get. By the time Canter's large neon sign comes into view, I've already called a Lyft. Yes, he's attracted to me, but there's also something else—something significant. He's hiding something. I can taste it off him. Deception has a distinct flavor. And deception doesn't interest me.

As we near Canter's, it becomes clear we won't find parking on Fairfax, and Canter's lot has a large "FULL" sign blocking its entrance. Without comment, Alex silently passes our destination, turns right, then right again onto a residential street one block west of the deli. The parking here is limited as well, no doubt spilling over from the residents in the apartment buildings lining both sides of the street. Alex manages to find a spot just large enough for his car about half a block north of Beverly. For most, it would have been a parallel parking nightmare, but Alex eases the large body of his muscle car into the spot expertly, with very little need to adjust. Despite being pissed at him, I'm impressed.

Once he cuts the power, I prepare to get out of the car and stomp off towards my Lyft, Gucci heels be damned. But he put his hand on my thigh, not in a suggestive way, but rather a light touch telling me to stay put for a second. Then, he sighs and shakes his head.

"I know what you are," he says quietly.

I frown. "I'm sorry?"

"I know you're not human," he says. "I don't know what you call yourself, but I've seen your kind before and I know you are one of them."

Shock blasts me full in the face. *One of them.*

I swallow hard. I can't say anything stupid. I can't give anything away. *Shit. Am I going to have to kill Alex?*

"What would you call me?" I finally ask.

He looks me straight in the eye. "I would call you a vampire."

A second wave of shock hits me. *Jesus Christ. How could he possibly know that?*

I don't say anything. I can't. He's a journalist. I might have to kill him for the safety of my *Koinon*. For real. Holy fuck.

I can't deny the part of my nature that's slightly turned on by the idea. He's right. I'm a vampire, and I feed on death. But I never thought it would've been Alex. But now, certain things are starting to make sense. Oh my God, he must have known all along. Finally, I ask him as much. It's really all I can do.

"How long have you known?" I ask.

"For a while. On some level, before we met. At the coffee shop. I could tell you were different. There is something about you similar to the others I've known. I can't tell you exactly what it is. But I've known for a while."

I frown. This seems impossible. "What others have you known?"

"I spent time in Africa with a tribe that counted about fifteen vampires in its population. They lived openly, so

I got to know their kind well. I even allowed one of the women to feed from me."

"*What?*" This repulses me. I cannot say why, but it does. It is the way of our kind. We do not share humans. "Alex, you are someone else's familiar!"

I open my car door. "I'm leaving. I've called a Lyft. They'll be at Canters in five minutes. I have to go."

"Sonia! Wait," he calls after me.

But no. No, no, no. He's been fed on by another vampire. That changes things. He belongs to her. We don't share humans. Good God, Alex is a familiar. He is *her* familiar. Wherever she is. He belongs to her.

I slam the car door shut behind me, and start my march. I'm not even thinking of killing Alex now, I am so thoroughly repulsed by him. I turn down a side street at the end of the block that crosses Fairfax, but then notice a gap in the buildings up ahead. I pause to peer down the dark alley and see the busy traffic of Fairfax on the other side. But this looks like a particularly mucky alley. My shoes will be better off going around, but dammit, my Lyft is waiting and won't wait forever. I start picking my way through the muck, noting briefly that Alex is not following me.

Smart human.

The alleyway runs the length of a city block along an east-west axis, between four buildings. The two buildings on the western side are apartments, and looking up I see small windows and old fashioned rusted fire-escapes like the ones you see in New York City apartment buildings. The two buildings on the eastern side of the alley, fronting Fairfax, are businesses. Both the residential and commercial buildings are flush against each other, but have a small gap between them large enough for a man to fit. The gap is exactly the sort of nasty little place a mugger could hide and jump out at an unsuspecting walker. But I doubt this alley sees enough traffic to encourage would-be muggers. Judging by the amount of refuse strewn across the ground, this place could easily qualify as one of Frost's proverbial roads not taken.

"Sonia! Wait!"

Alex is following me now. Idiot. This alley is the perfect place to kill him.

I hop lightly over a puddle of urine—I guess that somebody has indeed passed through here relatively recently.

I'm just about to tell Alex to fuck off, when a shadowy figure steps out of the gap between the buildings in front of us, blocking our way. I barely have enough time to register that it's Sunny. I'd forgotten he was coming tonight. He growls menacingly.

"Sonia," his voice is very low, too low for Alex to hear, "*GET OUT!*" He stands about fifteen feet ahead of us, feet planted wide, body rigid.

Looking closely at his face, I can see he's gone through the change. His eyes glow a preternatural green in the dark, and his fangs are fully descended.

Then I go rapidly through the change.

I don't even have time to fight it. I feel it in the sharpening of my night vision, as my pupils contract to slits and my eyes turn a glowing green like a black cat's. My fingernails thicken and sharpen into lethal talons. Likewise, my four lateral incisors sharpen into points, while my fangs grow out quickly to their full, deadly length.

This can only mean one thing: I am in immediate mortal danger.

CHAPTER 13

I N DANGER FROM WHAT? From Sunny? Alex can't see who is standing in front of us, but he can see the glowing eyes. He bristles at my side, but doesn't call out a challenge as most guys would. Nevertheless, tension runs through his body. I smell his testosterone levels increase. He's in a fight or flight response to danger, and he's chosen to fight.

Ever so slowly, I take a step in front of Alex. Then I smell it, the overwhelming stench of graveyard, the rot of decomposing bodies breaking down into moist soil. I see it. It descends fast from the top of the building. It's a large, black shape with edges I can't make out. I see Sunny crouching, arms outstretched, throwing his head back in an unearthly, predatory scream.

Instinctively, I shove Alex out of the way a little too hard and dimly register the dull crack of his head on the brick. But testosterone now pumps through my body as well, and I kick off my heels, yawning widely to dislocate my jaw like a snake and display my fanged teeth. I slash my lower lip with my canines and taste my own blood, sending myself into a blood lusting rage.

The creature, whatever it is, lands between us, facing towards Sunny. It advances upon him. I almost feel disappointment, knowing that Sunny will kill it before I have a go at it. I'm not a fighter by nature, but when push comes to shove, I can shove with the best of them.

Sunny meets the thing's advance with his handsome features twisted into a mask of terrifying fury. He brings it in just close enough that it could touch him, then leaps straight up about ten feet, and lands neatly behind the thing, swiping viciously at the back of the creature's unprotected neck with his claws, attempting to sever its spinal cord. The creature shrieks and whirls around, its clawed hand lashing out for Sunny's throat. Sunny jumps back easily, just out of reach, taunting it.

They circle around, facing each other like snarling dogs. I see the thing's horrible face. Not a creature. A monster—a monster with the face and body of a decomposing corpse. The swollen face, green and black marbled skin, protruding eyes, and lips curled back away from teeth and gums in a grimace displays jagged teeth and two long, unmistakable vampire fangs. Around its nose and mouth, the skin is blistering and peeling off in sheets. Clumps of hair fall away from its head. The body, clothed in a black shroud, is massive and bloated, and the creature stinks of putrefied innards.

I have never seen nor heard of anything so awful.

If it is a type of vampire, as its fangs suggest, that makes it all the more difficult to kill. Sunny knows this as surely as I do.

Sunny forms a double fist with both hands and lunges forward to bring them crashing down on the creature's head, attempting to drive the spinal column into the brain. This move won't kill it, but any brain injury will be more difficult to heal and could possibly incapacitate it long enough for us to take its head off.

Damn, if only I had my knife. But a Bowie knife is hard to hide in skimpy clothing. Shit. I might have to rethink my wardrobe

The creature ducks easily to one side, evading Sunny's blow. It grabs one of Sunny's arms, sinking its fangs into his flesh. Sonny screams as the thing feeds off him. The creature's movements are a blur of motion, its speed possibly surpassing our own.

This is bad.

Sunny slams both his arm and the creature attached to it against the alley wall. Stunned from the force of the blow, the creature releases Sunny and falls to the ground, bits of brick crumbling down on top of it. Sunny takes advantage of its momentary disorientation by lunging in to smash the thing's head against the wall with his bone-crushing strength. However, as soon as Sunny gets close enough, the creature grabs hold of his arm once again and flings him against the opposite wall. Sunny plunges head-first into the brick building, his skull and the bones in his neck and back cracking under the impact. His limp body crashes into the dumpster below, the noise reverberating up and down the alley.

For a moment, all is quiet save the crumbling pieces of brick falling into the dumpster after Sunny. The thing advances purposely towards the silent dumpster. I snarl as I rush it, attempting to distract the creature while Sunny recovers. I swoop in, slashing at the back of its neck with my claws, but if Sunny can't penetrate the thing's thick skin with his claws, there's no way I'll be able to. If I can get the creature to turn around for only a few seconds, then Sunny can get back into the battle.

I'm only partially successful. But even as the thing backhands me easily into the alley wall, Sunny erupts out of the dumpster with a 2X4. He swings the piece of wood like a baseball bat and hits the creature square in the face, the cracking noise echoing off the brick walls. He cautiously circles the debilitated monster, not falling for the same trick twice. By now a small crowd has formed on Fairfax, likely attracted by the noises of the fight. Fortunately, we're shrouded in darkness. I can barely see what's going on myself, and my slitted eyes can see in the dark. No way a human's vision will be able to make this out. It's just too fast and too dark in here.

Meanwhile, the creature recovers from the last blow, and black, congealed blood covers its ears and nose. Fresh red blood is matting the hair at Sunny's right temple. He's also healing a deep, jagged cut stretching from his hairline down to the bridge of his nose.

Sunny and the creature continue to circle each other warily, neither willing to make the first move. I stand defensively over Alex, who remains prone on the ground.

I'm thinking that, if Sunny could knock the thing out for a few seconds, we could drop one of the dumpsters on its head and sever it. But suddenly the thing spins around and for the first time advances on me. Until now, I couldn't have said the creature was aware I was there.

Sunny roars, his attempt to get the thing to turn back. When that doesn't work, he charges. Exactly what the creature wants. It easily sidesteps Sunny's charge, helping the rushing vampire's momentum with the added force of its own strength. Sunny's skull cracks as he's driven into the wall. The creature wastes no time jumping up and landing heavily on the fallen vampire's chest, grabbing him by his hair to better expose his neck. I watch in horror as the thing strikes with its fangs into Sunny's vulnerable flesh, feeding with loud sucking sounds. Sunny struggles, but his arms are pinned to his sides by the creature's legs.

I look around helplessly for a weapon. I'm not strong enough to do damage on my own, I need my Bowie knife. I see Sunny's discarded 2X4, and rush to pick it up. I don't need to incapacitate the thing, but I need to knock it off of Sunny long enough for him to get up. Swinging as hard as I can, I drive the wood into the creature's head.

Nothing.

It doesn't budge an inch, draining Sunny's body with those horrible sucking sounds. Sunny's struggles become fainter and fainter.

Desperate now, I dart in closer and jump on the thing's back to grab it in a choke-hold to get it to stop feeding. Sunny needs time to get back on his feet. But Sunny isn't moving now, his struggles have stopped.

The creature doesn't budge. Maybe it doesn't even know I'm there. I grab a handful of its hair, but it comes off easily in clumps. I fall over backwards from the lack of resistance to my effort.

Then Alex makes a noise.

Alex!

Alex is up and on his feet. He points towards Fairfax. Following his gaze, I see the figure of a police officer shining a thin beam of light from his flashlight into the darkness of the alley.

Thank God for the LAPD.

Rushing over to the cop as fast as my vampire speed allows, I grab his gun from its holster and hit him on the head with the butt, knocking him unconscious so he can't venture farther down the alley. Adrenaline has me moving at an impossible speed. If anyone saw anything, it was likely just a ghost, a brief imprint picked up by the brain, but gone in a flash. And in any case, the crowd is now preoc-cupied with the cop—good.

I'm now back at the creature and Sunny. I place the muzzle of the gun against the back of the creature's head and pull the trigger. The gun kicks back in my hands, and I see the fire erupt from its barrel. The creature is blasted forward, off of Sunny. Brain matter splatters over the alley wall. The creature crumples to the ground, shrieking an unholy noise. I snap my eyes to the side to make sure no humans are tracking the noise, then lean forward for a second shot at the monster. I pull the trigger, I see the bullet blasted forward out of the fire, but it only travels through empty space before lodging itself into the brick wall.

The creature flees, flying up the fire escape with preter-natural speed I don't think even Sunny could match. Once it reaches the top of the building, it vanishes.

I do not follow it. My fight is over. Dammit, it was hardly any fight at all. I will be carrying my Bowie knife from now on. Fuck what people say.

Kneeling next to Sunny, I slap his face and call his name. The extensive injuries he's sustained have not yet healed, his heartbeat faint from the loss of blood. Blood loss can't kill a vampire, but it complicates things. I keep slapping his face. Finally, Sunny moans faintly.

Alex is leaning over my shoulder to see Sunny. "Will he be okay?" he asks. "Has he lost too much blood?"

"He'll be okay," I answer, almost to myself, "but he *has* lost too much blood. I need to get him to a doctor."

"Doesn't he just need to feed?" Alex asks.

Sitting back on my heels, I look at him. "No, it doesn't work that way. Our digestive systems are not linked to our vascular systems."

When he continues to regard me with a puzzled look on his face, I elaborate. "When you drink wine, it goes through your digestive system. It doesn't automatically go into your vascular system—you don't suddenly have wine for blood." This is no time for a lesson in vampire physiology, but he nods thoughtfully so I assume my answer makes sense.

"What Sunny needs," I say, again almost to myself, "is a transfusion. And there is only one place in L.A. where he can get one." I hook my hands under Sunny's armpits and start to haul him up. Alex moves to Sunny's feet to help.

"It's not a good idea for you to be that close to him." I keep my voice calm. "He's badly hurt. Instinct will kick in, and he won't know what he's doing. Drinking human blood won't cure what's wrong, but it will help. It's best if you just go home right now. When I'm done with Sunny, I'll come and answer whatever questions you have."

Alex steps back and watches me for a moment as I easily lift Sunny and get him on his feet. No sense in playing the fragile human woman after all this. Sunny hangs on me, looking for all the world like a drunken rock star—all he needs is a bottle of Jack Daniels dangling in his hand. Alex takes a deep breath, and steps back a little further.

"You promise?" he asks. "This isn't going to be it, is it?"

Understanding what he means, I say no. Then I turn Sunny away from Fairfax. Mercifully, no crowd of spectators wait at that end. The humans on Fairfax scattered at the sound of gunfire, one of them dragging the cop's unconscious body out of harm's way. But I can hear them coming back. The distant sound of sirens is becoming louder now.

"I promise. Either later tonight or tomorrow. I can't say. My *Koinon* will have business to discuss. But I'll come by."

"All right then." His voice is shaky. "I'll wait for you. I live at the Fleur de Lis Apartments. 1825 North Whitley. Number 45."

Alex jogs down the alley towards his car. After I hear him start up his motor and pull away, I bring Sunny out the same way. I spot his McLaren and fish his keys out of his pocket. Belting him into the passenger side, I close the vertical door then speed-dial a number on my iPhone.

The police are about to arrive on Fairfax; I can hear two cars and two SUV's, one with a canine unit. Yes, I really can smell the dog. Nocturnal predator, remember? And that dog could be a problem.

I have to go.

Voice mail picks up my call. "Neichia. It's Sonia. I'm coming to you now. Sunny's hurt badly. I'll explain when I get there. Call in the *Stoicheía*, we need a blood transfusion."

After sending a little prayer up to the Powers That Be, I slide into the driver's side, take a deep breath and turn the key in the ignition. Neichia's house isn't far.

CHAPTER 14

STUPID, FUCKING L.A. TRAFFIC. 10 p.m. on a Friday night, and there's still rush hour gridlock. By the time I pull up in front of Neichia's house, two figures await us at the curb. Sonny's breathing is shallow, his neck wound still bleeding. This is not good: it should have stopped bleeding almost immediately in the alley. He looks ghastly; like the puncture wounds, the bruises and cuts on his face and shoulder are not healing the way they should. The skin around his lips and nose is faintly blue, giving him the look of a fresh corpse left overnight in a freezer. Logic tells me that his wounds alone cannot kill him, but I'm scared. Really scared.

Neichia lifts Sonny's vertical door open, and I am blown back into my seat by a rush of power. Incredible power. It surges around me, through me, exploring and testing, casting the crazy forms of an aurora borealis, but in reds, greens, blues, and white.

The *Stoicheía* are here. There must be a lot of them, and they are showing off. Judging from the throbbing undercurrents pulsing from Neichia's house, the assholes are not dampening their power.

I yawn to pop my ears, and fight my way forward to release Sunny's seatbelt. Then Neichia and Bianca begin to shift him out of his seat. I crawl out after him as Neichia pulls one of Sunny's arms around her shoulders and Bianca takes his other side, and the three make rapid progress through Neichia's side gate. I am just behind them, jogging to catch up. My breathing is a little shallow, the *Stoicheía* power demonstrations are stretching the air thin as though we are at a very high elevation. God damn *Stoicheía* are not supposed to gather like this. When I requested some *Stoicheía* for a blood transfusion, I didn't mean *all* of them. Even humans would be able to detect this. For Christ's sake, Neichia's house is glowing.

Our destination is Neichia's laboratory in the backyard. She quickly punches her code into the keypad, and then we're in.

Here Bianca parts ways from us, and I feel the cool night air on my arms.

But as she starts walking down the pathway to the house, I call after her. "Bianca!"

She turns, her brow arched. "Yes, Sonia?"

"What are all the *Stoicheía* doing here?"

Bianca frowns at me. "Why, we are here to find out what happened to Sunny. He needs a blood transfusion? But he is one of the most powerful in our *Koinon*. What could have caused this? I called them in to hear from you what happened."

Shit. I am going to have to go into that house.

Well, the *Stoicheía* will have to wait. Sunny needs me right now.

I return to the laboratory to see Neichia hoisting Sunny

over her shoulder like a bag of oats, then down onto the hospital bed as easily as if he was a five-year-old child.

Under the bright fluorescent lights, he looks even more ghastly than before. His skin tone is gray. Deep red and black bruising, crisscrossed with broken capillaries, cover most of his visible body. Neichia cuts the remnants of his shirt off him, then takes his blood pressure and listens to his heart. After a few moments, she turns to me and nods.

"You are right," she tells me as the air hisses out of the deflating arm cuff. "He needs a transfusion. His blood pressure is so low, his heart is barely pumping. I've never seen this before; this kind of blood loss should only trigger a hibernation state. But he's not going into hibernation. I honestly don't know what will happen if his heart stops."

"Do you mean he could die?" I whisper.

Neichia looks down, not meeting my eyes. "It's good that you got him here as fast as you did."

I take a seat at the work table next to Sunny's bed. I watch him struggling to stay alive as Neichia fits my upper arm with a tourniquet. When she places a small rubber ball in my hand for me to pump, I tell myself over and over again that Sunny cannot die. Vampires do not die like this. But then I think of Fiona. The fresh, bleeding wounds on his body indicate that his body is not responding the way it should.

Neichia slips the large gauge needle into my vein. Vampires all have the same blood type, so we have none of the complications associated with human blood donors and recipients. I can hear outside the laboratory the sound of cars arriving at Neichia's. I can tell from the new surges in the shapes and swirls of energy that more *Stoicheia* are converging for this emergency meeting.

During the twenty minutes it takes for my bag to fill up, I sit in silence and watch Neichia work. She shines a pen light back and forth into Sunny's eyes, then examines the wounds on his face and neck with careful hands in latex gloves. The wounds are now just beginning to form scabs, certainly an improvement, though still not healing the way vampire bodies are supposed to. There must be something about this monster that interferes with our normal healing abilities. Some sort of venom, perhaps? I determine to raise this matter with Neichia once Sunny is out of the woods.

Once the bag is full, Neichia carefully extracts the needle from my arm, and I leave the laboratory, making my way back to the main house. As I get closer, it gets harder and harder to breathe. By the sound of the din of voices from within, I am correct in my surmise: there is a large number of *Stoicheia* in that house. *Stoicheia* are not known for their cooperative efforts. Plowing my way through the kitchen's open sliding door and into the living room, I step into what feels like the eye of an energy storm.

Suddenly it is easier to breathe. I relax a little, feeling the tension in my shoulders ease. Fifteen vampires sit in various positions of repose on Neichia's furniture and floor, and it looks like all the heavy-hitters are here. Except for Vladimir, of course. If Vladimir were here, Neichia's house might go up in a tornado.

I steady my legs, and motion for Anastasios, the Greek Earth *Stoicheia*, to go back to the laboratory. It's his turn to give blood. Then I find a seat next to Adrienne on the floor. She is also an Earth *Stoicheia* and has the mildest aura in the room, smelling like freshly cut grass in the summertime. Adrienne acknowledges me with a small nod, then returns her attention to the Persian vampire couple, Khort-dad and Kasra, two fire *Stoicheía* who are glowing red in the corner. They both sit in their usual postures of disciplined refinement. The two of them, Kasra sitting on a cushioned footstool and Khortdad on the floor at her feet, regard the room with cool, expressionless eyes. When they catch me looking at them, Kasra arches a brow and Khortdad glares at me as if insulted by my regard. His arrogance reminds me of the Persians described by the ancient Greek historian Herodotus, and I wonder just how old Khortdad is. He definitely stands as a perfect example of someone not able to adjust to the changing times.

I shift my position so that I'm sitting on my hip. Word-less power struggles are making the floor vibrate, and I'll be damned if sitting in certain positions isn't turning me on.

"They're arguing."

"What?" I turn to look at Adrienne's unusual, angular face. I taste lemongrass in my mouth. She has turned her gaze on me, and I think for a moment that I catch a glint of humor in her deep set, forest green eyes. She is glowing, ever so slightly, the color of an evergreen in Spring. Very soothing.

"If you watch them long enough," she says, "you can see it in their body language. They are carrying on a heated argument without saying a single word."

I look back at the Persian ancients, looking for signs of this argument. True, they are radiating red. But otherwise they look like two people just sitting in a room. Turning back to Adrienne, who has not taken her eyes off my face, I shrug.

"They just look bored to me," I admit. "Like they really don't want to be here."

"No, no," she answers. "They are furious with each other. Khortdad has done something that Kasra does not like. He is trying his best not to be intimidated by her wrath, but he is failing. I wonder what it is that he has done."

I looked back at the vampire couple, and I notice a slight distinction in their auras. Kasra's is slightly redder, and is pulsing faster than a heartbeat. Khortdad's is a more orange color, and is not pulsing at all. I am rewarded with another surly look from Khortdad. Kasra, if anything, looks serene. Adrienne leans closer to say something else, but just then Anastasios reappears and she instead shoots to her feet in a fluid motion.

"I will go do for Sunny what I can," she says to me. "I have always liked him; laughter comes so easily to him, and I admire his zest for life. So American, but in all the good ways."

She leaves me and glides through the doorway to the kitchen. I wonder how Sunny fares. I hope the infusion of fresh *Stoicheía* blood will aid his body in the healing process.

I feel the pull of someone's gaze, and turn to find Siroun's ocean blue-green eyes upon me. She glows softly with the gentle, playful energy of water.

Carradhy.

Witch.

Siroun, rumor has it, lived her human life in the time of the Vardanank, during the War of St. Vardan in 451 AD. That would make her more than fifteen hundred years old. Returning her watery gaze with a little smile, I wonder if this rumor could be true. She certainly seems otherworldly, her movements flowing from one position to the next. And those depthless eyes, like the sea itself, watching everything and nothing, moving first this way and then that way to silently absorb all we have to offer her. The longer I look, comparing her to others, the stranger she becomes. The only humanizing trait visible on her face are the fine, delicate lines at the corners of her eyes and around the corners of her mouth. Were they already present during her human life, or has she lived to that mythical point when vampire bodies supposedly begin to show age?

I realize with a start that her aura is the smallest of everyone here, just the barest hint of blue shimmering across her skin. Siroun *is* dampening her power. Jesus. What would this place be like if she weren't? Probably a cyclone.

I cannot help but wonder about Vladimir, the reclusive Russian *Stoicheía* acknowledged to be the oldest vampire living in Los Angeles. If Siroun has walked this earth for over fifteen hundred years, how old is the Air *Stoicheía* Vladimir?

As for the rest, the majority of the *Stoicheía* seem to be here. Conqueror and Conquered, Colonizer and Indigenous sit side by side. So many wars have these creatures seen, so much blood shed, so much life lived and great ages passed before their eyes. They are history itself, seated here in Neichia's living room. The history of the human world.

"Sonia," Bianca says quietly, her voice cutting through my reverie. "Please tell us now what happened to you this evening."

CHAPTER 15

I REMAIN SEATED. EVEN IN the eye of the storm, I don't
trust myself to stand. I'm having a hard enough time
just breathing. And, no. I'm not brave or stupid
enough to tell them all to knock it off. If they want to
behave like secondary school children, then they can listen
to me while I sit on my ass.

As for my story, I have it ready. I start at the point
when Alex and I entered the alleyway. I finish with our
arrival at Neichia's. Alleyway, Monster, Neichia's. Then,
as an afterthought, I mention Fiona's house. I definitely
smelled that thing at Fiona's. My whole narrative takes less
than three minutes.

The *Stoicheia* initially meet my account with silence.
I look around the room at all of the faces turned towards
me, and try to decipher their thoughts. First and foremost,
do they believe me? Strange monster vampire creatures
are every bit as hard to accept in the mainstream vampire
world as in the human one. But Sunny was
nearly killed, something not supposed to
happen to our kind. That little detail
needs to be accounted for somehow.

The Bulgarian Water *Stoicheía* Vasil speaks first. A bright blue energy radiates from him. "Please, Sonia," he begins with uncharacteristic politeness. "Could you explain to us what you meant about the vampire Fiona's house? I am not sure I understand in which context you are speaking—are you telling us that you first detected this, ah, thing, at her house? If so, then why is she not here with you? We should probably like to hear her account, as well."

I just stare at him for a moment, stunned. Judging by all of the blank faces staring back at me, the *Stoicheía* know nothing of Fiona's death and the circumstances surrounding it. But how can that be? Especially since Neichia assured me she would take care of things?

Then Bianca clears her throat, bringing the room's attention to her. I taste ashes in my mouth.

"That matter," she explains, "was brought to my attention about two weeks ago. From what I understand, the evidence suggests that Fiona was attacked in her home and murdered. I did not think this to be a noteworthy event, other than its tragic nature. It appears to have been an isolated incident and there are no leads as to who might have committed this murder.

"Now." She turns her penetrating gaze upon me. "What you are saying, Sonia, is that you detected evidence of this creature at Fiona's house?"

At first, I do not know how to answer. How could Bianca, who keeps her finger pressed a little too closely to the pulse of the L.A. vampire *Koinon*, not know about the series of disappearances that have been occurring over the last several weeks? With her network of informants, she should have been among the first to know.

"Well?" She prompts. "We are waiting."

"Yes." I finally find my voice. "Yes. I detected the presence of this creature at Fiona's house. I smelled it. But I did not know what it was at the time and could therefore not have known its significance. But when I picked up the scent again in the alley tonight, I realized that the two incidents—and at least seventeen others—are linked. This monster has been preying upon us for some time."

"That is conjecture," she says flatly. "You have no conclusive evidence of that."

I stare at her in disbelief. How could she not see the gravity of this situation? Sunny and I were attacked by some sort of zombie vampire tonight. I mean, Jesus Christ. How could something like that even exist? What the hell was it, and are there more of its kind? There are just so many questions! And tonight's attack, and its clear link to Fiona's death, should be enough to demonstrate that something serious is going on here. All of these disappearances, which I *know* Bianca knows about, are connected.

Looking around the room, I search the *Stoicheia*' faces for some hint of support or understanding. I find nothing. The Swedish Air *Stoicheia* Ragnar and the Earth *Stoicheia* Zádor appear to be dozing off. Fiery Baltasar is staring out the window, Air *Stoicheia* Anastasios is picking at a spot on the fabric of the chair he was sitting on. Khortdad and Kasra are no doubt continuing their silent argument. Nowhere in the room do I detect any sense of alarm or urgency. None of them seem to care about anything else other than blasting each other with the strength of their power.

And why would they? Apparently, this vampire creature

has left the *Stoicheía* alone. It is only targeting the younger ones—the *Neoi* vamps. But why?

Then Adrienne speaks. "What happened to the man you were with? Was he injured?"

Looking into her face, I see she is struggling to come to terms with the things I have just said. She, at least, is working the story over in her mind. She might be my only ally in the room.

"He was not injured, though I don't know how much of the attack he saw. I believe my initial shove knocked him unconscious."

This might be a lie. I don't know for sure how much Alex saw. It doesn't actually matter, in any case. He knows what we are. He's known since the beginning. I just hope, for Alex's sake, that my words taste of ambiguity instead of deceit.

Then Dragomir, the Earth *Stoicheía* from Romania, speaks up. "Were there any other witnesses? What about the police officer?"

"There was a small crowd of humans gathered on the Fairfax opening of the alley, but none of them ventured any further. We were too far back for them to see anything, though the noise attracted them. When I knocked out the police officer, they became more interested in him than the alley. They did not see me hit him—"

"—you cannot move that fast!" Vasil interjects derisively. Apparently, the Bulgarian was finished being polite.

"Well, I did. I agree that I cannot normally move quite that fast, but I figure that an enormous shot of adrenaline can help anyone do amazing things if properly motivated. And I was motivated. No one saw me." Then, after a moment, I add, "If they had seen me, then they might have come into the alley after me. And the gunshot scattered them, in any case."

Nobody could argue with that logic. Humans are curious beings, but they are not by nature suicidal. People run away from gunfire, unless trained not to.

I look around the room again at the unconcerned faces of the *Stoicheía* and then look pointedly at my watch. I have things to do. I need to go check on Sunny, and I still have a very long conversation with Alex on the table for tonight. That I want to get over sooner rather than later.

Then a small voice speaks, so small it sounds almost like a child. The accent is one I have never heard before, faint yet distinctively exotic. At first I can't place the speaker, until I taste saltwater in my mouth, and I see the crashing waves of the sea in Siroun's eyes.

Siroun is speaking to me.

I have never heard her voice, and now she is asking me a question.

"The creature," she begins, rolling her "r's" like the purring of a cat, "could you tell us again what it looks like."

I try to gauge if she is friend or foe. Is she asking me this because she feels it bears repeating, or is she about to challenge the veracity of my account? I can't tell. After she finishes speaking, her eyes dim into mysterious shadow. I wouldn't have thought she'd said anything at all, except that I saw her lips move when she spoke.

"It looks and smells like a rotting corpse," I say. "The face is so swollen, it almost does not appear human, and the skin is marbled in green and black blotches. The eyes bulge out of their sockets and the lips curl back from the gums. Its teeth are mostly missing or broken except for the two vampire fangs. The body is massive and bloated, and it wears a sort of shroud, like an Old World funeral shroud, only instead of white, this one is black."

Siroun nods, then becomes still once more. For a moment I almost think I see a glint of recognition in her eyes, but it vanishes so quickly I doubt what I saw. I look once more at all of the blank faces, cold and immovable as marble, then glance pointedly at my watch again. Bianca takes the hint.

"Thank you, Sonia," she says, "for telling us your version of this night's events. Hopefully Sunny will recover quickly so we can add his account as well. Now if you will excuse us, we have much to discuss amongst ourselves."

Fine by me. I go back out through the slider and make my way down to the laboratory. I find Sunny on his third pint of blood. He looks improved, though the wounds on his head and neck still haven't healed. His color is slightly better, and he is breathing deeply and regularly. Neichia assures me that it will be a while before he regains consciousness, so I decide to see Alex. Hopefully, by the time we finish our little tête-à-tête, Sunny will be conscious again. It's going to be a long, long night.

I head out front, down Neichia's lawn to Sunny's car parked on the street. A lone figure silently glides out of the shadows towards me. I smell the earthy fragrance of freshly tilled soil, and wordlessly the vampire Adrienne falls into step beside me until I cross the front of the car towards the driver's side. I fold my arms on the roof of the McLaren and wait for her to speak.

Standing across from me, on the passenger side, she looks

at me for a moment. I get the impression she is carefully choosing her words. As the seconds tick by, I watch her face, illuminated in the light of the street lamp overhead. Her face is not beautiful in the classical sense, each of her features too strong for a Helen of Troy or a Grace Kelly. Framed by thick waves of long, dark auburn hair, Adrienne's pale face is long and narrow with high cheekbones, deeply-set green eyes, and a proud, aristocratic nose. But these features taken all together are quite striking. Her name is modern and French, but names mean nothing at all in the vampire world. It is the voice that betrays you, and in Adrienne's voice I detect the very faint accents shaping her words into a light singsong cadence. In fact, I've never met anyone—*Stoicheía* or *Neoi*— who speaks quite the same way she does.

"They will not do anything, you know," she says.

"I know," I reply. "I knew that as soon as I finished giving my account. What I'm trying to figure out is where to go from here."

"So long as this thing is not killing *Stoicheía*, they will ignore it. Even if it kills every last *Neoi*. They may even welcome it; there has been some talk lately about the size of the younger population—many are alarmed by it, feeling it must be reduced somehow."

Figures. But it doesn't change anything. The *Stoicheía* are not going to help. And that thing came after Sunny, and will probably do so again.

"I wonder how it can tell us apart," I muse. "How it can tell who is young and who is old?"

"I do not know."

"So, you do believe me then," I say, not bothering to keep the cynicism out of my voice.

"Yes, Sonia, I believe you. And so do most of the others in the house—they just don't want to admit that they believe you, because they don't want to be forced to act."

She looks at me for a moment, frowning. She looks like she's debating whether or not to say something more.

I wait, tapping my foot impatiently on the black top. Finally, she speaks again.

"Please let me know if there is anything that I can assist you with. I can tell you what is going on in the *Stoicheía* population. If they have any changes of heart, I can inform you of that. There might be other things I can help you with." She stops then, cryptically leaving the possibilities of her last statement open. I don't say anything. We stand there for a few moments, regarding each other silently over the roof of the car.

"I must go back inside, they might be missing me," she says at last. "Good luck, Sonia, I think you might need it." And then she's gone. I stand for several moments, staring at the empty space where she stood, thinking over what she'd said. If I understand her correctly, not only will the *Stoicheía* fail to help, but they may even prove an obstacle in my investigation.

Investigate, I must: Sunny and I seem to be the only two survivors of an attack from this monster. The way it came after Sunny, with such single-minded determination, gives me the feeling that he'd somehow been targeted. I can't explain. It's just an itch I feel. Sunny is a target, which means he's probably still in danger.

For Sunny's sake, I need to find out what the hell is going on. And I need to kill that creature.

CHAPTER 16

ALEX LIVES ONLY TWO minutes from my house, about half a block south of Franklin Avenue. But I'm not at my house. I'm in Brentwood, on the West Side. I don't mind. I'm headed that way, anyway, and I need time to think.

I pull Sunny's McLaren north onto the 405 freeway, and the supercharged V8 comes alive as I accelerate to 90 mph. Powering through the six miles from Sunset to the 101 freeway, I struggle to wrap my head around the events of this evening. I have a lot of questions and no answers.

From what I can tell, the *Stoicheía* are far more concerned over possible witnesses to the attack than the attack itself. Of course, exposure to the human population is an ongoing concern of ours, but still…the *Stoicheía* don't seem shocked about the creature itself. Definitely not as shocked as I am. I mean, we're talking about a creature that feeds off vampires. In all my years, I've never heard of such a thing. Could the *Stoicheía* have encountered something like this before? Do they already know what it is? The more I think about it, the more convinced

I become that *someone* in Neichia's living room *must* know what this creature is. They know, and for some reason they aren't telling.

I flick on my turn signal and ease the McLaren into the right lane so I can take the exit onto the 101 freeway. Heading south towards Hollywood, I turn my attention back to the creature. There seems to be something Old World about it. It reminds me of the vampire Count Orlok in the 1922 film *Nosferatu*, with its hideous face, massive body, and terrible claws. *Nosferatu* is a German film, and the Count, based roughly on Bram Stoker's *Dracula*, sleeps in plague-infested soil.

This creature smelled like rotten soil, too.

I think of Adrienne's words: the *Stoicheía* will not help in this matter. So, I'm on my own. It's up to me to stop this thing, which means killing it. And to kill it, I must first find out what the hell it is, and that means research.

Taking the Cahuenga exit, I consider my options. The most straightforward approach is to interview the *Stoicheía* individually and hope one of them comes forward with the information I need. This, however, will be extremely time consuming. Protocol requires I get a letter of introduction for each interview, with no guarantee of success. If one or more of the *Stoicheía* knows what this creature is and what its presence in Los Angeles likely means *and* they're willing to share this information, they would have done so during the meeting, right? Maybe.

In any case, individual interviews are out of the question. That would just take too much time, and time is something I don't have. That leaves the more traditional research method: books. If this creature is indeed something

Old World, somebody somewhere has probably written about it. Humans are observant. And they like to write things down.

I can also look at traditional late-nineteenth-century vampire literature, like *Varney the Vampyre*, *Carmilla*, and good old *Dracula*. Much of that is based on folklore but I suspect folklore might be my best bet.

All right. I have a plan. Now for Alex.

Alex knows my true nature. Has known all along. I've promised to answer all of his questions. Do I mean it?

I think of Owen; I think of my Maker.

No, no. There are still some things I am not ready to reveal. To anyone.

CHAPTER 17

I T IS 3:37 A.M. when I finally find myself at the Fleur de Lis Apartments where Alex lives. I park the McLaren right in front of the sign with the three-pronged insignia, under the scroll number 1825. As I hesitate on his doorstep, I can smell him, as well as the strong odor of a dog recently washed in oatmeal shampoo.

I take a deep, fortifying breath and rap sharply on the door three times.

Hoping he's gone to bed, I check my watch. He opens the door and catches me in the act. We look at each other for an awkward moment. A pair of black knit pajama pants hang alluringly from his hip bones. He wears no shirt. Despite the thick tension of the moment, my eyes record the details of his body that his slim fitting t-shirts and henleys only hint at: broad, strong shoulders, muscular arms, and a washboard stomach.

But dammit, no, Sonia. *No.* He belongs to someone else. Wherever she may be, he belongs to her. That is the way of our world. We do not share humans.

"You came," he says.

I nod. "Yes. I said I would."

He opens the door wide and takes a step back. "Do I need to formally invite you in?"

I snort. "No, Alex. I'm not Dracula."

He looks sheepish, and runs a hand through his hair. "Sorry. I'm not an expert."

"And no," I say, stepping deliberately over his threshold, "we don't sparkle either."

Moving into Alex's living space, his scent slams into me like a brick wall, and all my snark evaporates. Dammit, but I do like how he smells. The uniquely musky scent of his body saturates everything around me. As Alex turns around and leads me deeper into his apartment, I catch a glimpse of the masculine, earthy tones of a bedroom through an open door on the right. Alex takes me to a large living room with dark hardwood floors. Three small windows, framed in white gossamer, provide a stark view of the roof of the building to the north. The drapes add a refined, breezy touch to the otherwise masculine nature of the room.

Alex turns, gesturing to one of the leather couches. "Feel free to make yourself comfortable. Can I get you a drink?"

Then he freezes, staring at me like a deer caught in headlights.

I smile and take the offered seat. "No."

He relaxes, laughing a little at himself, and then disappears through a pair of French doors lined with the same gossamer material.

"Why don't you make friends with Fluffy?" he calls over his shoulder.

My gaze settles on the very large, fat pit-bull lounging on an enormous doggie bed near my feet.

Fluffy gazes at me steadily with his one brown eye, wearing an expression somewhere between truculence and boredom.

"You've had a bath tonight, haven't you?" I ask. "I can smell your shampoo."

He gives me a single thump of his tail.

"Yes, yes," I say, leaning forward. "It was my fault, wasn't it? I'm sorry. I'm sure you couldn't have smelled that bad." I hold out my hand for him to sniff. "I'm Sonia. And I agree, it's a very strange thing that humans do: expecting company, wash the dog. I'll tell your dad you don't need a bath every time I come over." Then I stop myself. What the hell am I saying? Why would I ever come over here again?

Alex pads back into the living room just as I'm giving Fluffy a good scratch behind the ear. He's holding a tall glass of water in one hand and a Coke in the other. I arch a brow. Hmm, so he knows I can drink water? All right then, Alex. Let's find out what else you know.

I'm disappointed to see that he's put on a shirt. Without the distraction of his body, I notice he looks tired. Good. Maybe this little interview won't take long.

Setting the water and Coke on the coffee table in front of the couch, he settles down onto the matching loveseat and looks at me expectantly. I disengage myself somewhat reluctantly from Fluffy.

"So—" Alex begins.

"So—"

The silence stretches out between us, heavy and uncomfortable.

I break first. "You know what I am."

"You're a vampire," he says. "Undead."

I shake my head firmly. "I am not undead."

"Oh. Okay." He frowns. "Then, what? You're human?"

Ah. Alex doesn't know everything. "No. I'm not considered human anymore, but I'm very much alive. My heart beats, and I breathe, just like you. I drink blood, but it's food. I don't drink it to replenish what is in my veins. My vascular system produces its own blood, just like yours does." Much as I'd like to drink him up, it's not quite the same thing.

Alex leans back and crosses his legs, one arm draping over the back of the loveseat. "Does that make you some sort of sanguinarian then?" He looks very comfortable having an apex predator in his living room. When I don't respond, he says, "Alright, tell me. Lay it all out for me."

I can't help but snort a little laugh. "I'm a vampire. I have fangs that grow when I need to feed or am in danger. I don't age like normal humans. My body regenerates and heals almost all kinds of wounds much more rapidly than humans. I'm nocturnal and have the sensory abilities of a nocturnal predator—acute night vision and enhanced auditory and olfactory abilities. I'm far stronger than an ordinary human woman, and I also have enhanced cognitive abilities."

"Oh." He stares at the Coke can, now resting on his knee. "How long have you been a vampire? I mean, you were born human, right? This is something that happened to you later in life. Am I right? That's how I understood it with the tribe in Africa."

"Yup." I look down at Fluffy's peacefully sleeping form. "I was born human, but I've been a vampire since 1840. I was turned when I was 30." I take a breath, and smile at Alex. "I look pretty good for being 213 years old, don't I?"

He doesn't say anything right away, no doubt wrapping his head around the numbers I've just thrown at him. I reach down to pat Fluffy's head with my fingertips. I see why Alex loves his solid, comforting presence.

"And it happened...uh, you became a vampire in Australia?" he finally asks.

I consider that question for a moment, deciding how much I'm willing to tell him.

"Yes," I finally say. "In Australia. I was born in England and sent to Australia when I was sixteen."

Alex frowns, setting the coke back down on the table. "What do you mean you were *sent* to Australia?"

Oh boy. Here we go.

I take another deep, fortifying breath. "I was exiled from England on a charge of prostitution. I was convicted and sent to exile in the Australian penal colony in New South Wales, where I served for seven years."

He nods thoughtfully. But still, I detect no judgment.

"Jesus. Sixteen. So young to be put on a ship alone to a foreign country."

"Just barely, too. I arrived on my birthday, January 10, as a matter of fact."

He laughs then, but he quickly apologizes. "I'm sorry—it's just hard for me to think in terms of birthdays when talking to a 213 year-old vampire."

I don't like this. He may not be judging me, but he is objectifying me. I tell him as much. "I am not just a vampire, Alex. I am Sonia. Please try to remember that."

He dips his head like a chastised puppy. "Is Sonia your real name?"

"No," I admit. Then I fall silent. Am I ready to tell him my birth name?

Alex leans forward, feet planted, knees wide, elbows anchored on them, hands laced loosely between. It's a quintessentially masculine pose, and it looks beautiful on him. "I'd like to know your real name," he presses softly.

"It's Moira." Damn. That was too easy.

"That's beautiful. It's nice to meet you, Moira."

This makes me smile, which turns quickly into a yawn. I check my watch, and see it's past four o'clock—almost my bedtime.

Alex gets down to business. "What exactly happened tonight? What was that thing? Is Sunny going to be okay?"

"Well, I'm not entirely sure," I admit, stifling another yawn. "I've never seen nor heard of anything like it before. It's some sort of vampire creature—it drained Sunny of about six pints of blood. But I have no idea what the hell it is or where it came from. And I don't know why it attacked us."

Alex leans back, shock telegraphed on his face. "Six pints of blood? Will he survive?"

"God, I hope so," I say vehemently, sending up the two-thousandth-prayer of that night to the Powers That Be. "He received a transfusion tonight, but he's still unconscious. I'm supposed to get a call when he wakes up. No one has called yet."

Alex sits still, eyes unfocused as though deep in thought. "You know," he says finally, "I'm not so sure that the thing attacked *us*. It only seemed interested in Sunny."

I look at him in surprise. I'd come to the same conclusion myself, but I hadn't realized Alex had been that aware during the attack. It was pitch black in that alley, and I'd shoved him headfirst into a wall.

I nod slowly. "I agree. I think it was after Sunny. But I don't know why—that's part of what I need to find out."

"What are we going to do now? Are there vampire police that can go after this thing?"

I cock an eyebrow at the "we" in his question. "No, we're not organized like that. At least, not in L.A. And *we* are not doing anything. It's looking like I'm on my own."

"But why you? Isn't that dangerous?"

I don't hesitate to answer. "It's very dangerous. But so am I, Alex. And I have a feeling that thing isn't done with Sunny—I'm pretty sure it's going to come back to finish the job. And I also think it might come after me. It knows me now. And…" I shrug. "I've never been good at waiting for a fight to come to me." I stop short of telling him about all of the other missing vampires and how neatly I fit within this creature's general victim profile.

"I'd like to help."

I snort. "No. Absolutely not."

Alex leans forward, intent. "Look. I can tell you're not the sort of woman who thinks she needs help. And maybe you don't. But I am a journalist. I know how to find answers, and better yet, I know how to find people. Even if I don't have your super vampire cognitive abilities."

Hmmm.

But I need to be straight with him. "Alex. I'm not going to lie and say that having a journalist wouldn't be helpful on the investigative side of this little monster hunt, but if it's dangerous for me, and it is, then it's ten times more danger-ous for you. There's something going on in my *Koinon,* and

I don't know what it is. And should we come across that thing, well," I take a deep breath. "If it attacks you, I'm not sure I'd be able to save you."

He laughs. "No worries there. I have no desire to be on the front lines. And," he adds, a little smile playing around his lips. "I like strong, smart women. Taking orders from you won't be a problem."

I laugh, too. I can't help it. I'm that tired. And what he says makes sense. He's a journalist, good at finding answers. And strangely, I trust him.

I reach down and give Fluffy another pat. "Very well, so long as you stay off the front lines. Two pairs of eyes are better than one."

"Good," he says with a little nod. "It'll be easier this way. Otherwise, I would just have to tail you secretly, and with your super-Spidey-senses I'm not sure how successful I'd be."

I laugh again, not having any idea what he is talking about. He picks up on my confusion. "Spider Man," he says, as if that explains everything. "Comic books? Don't tell me you've never read a comic book!"

Ignoring this, I continue. "Tomorrow I'm going to check out some books at the UCLA research library. I figure someone, somewhere, has written about this thing, and I intend to find it."

"What time do you get up?" he asks.

"What? Why?"

"So I know when to pick you up!"

"Oh. Why don't you pick me up at 4:30." That's terribly early for me, but I'm not sure when the library closes. "That will put us in Westwood about 4:45."

"Sounds like a plan. I'll see you this afternoon at 4:30."

He walks me to the door and gives me a hurried kiss on the cheek as I turn to say goodbye. As he closes the door behind me, I realize I'm happy.

I'm about to take on a monstrous adversary much stronger than myself in a fight to the death, and I feel happy.

Dammit. That's not good.

CHAPTER 18

I T IS LATER THE same day that Alex and I find ourselves at the Young Research Library on UCLA's main
campus in Westwood. Things are not going as well as
I'd hoped. Once in the stacks, we discover some interesting clues in the fictional literature predating Bram Stoker's
aristocratic and sensually enigmatic Count. Before *Dracula*,
vampires more often appeared in print as disgusting and
terrifying monsters. Varney the Vampyre, predating Stoker's
work by fifty-two years, is far more revolting in appearance
and habit than the Transylvanian, and most literary vampires that followed. Nevertheless, we find nothing in the
literature suggesting first-hand knowledge of the creature as
we'd seen it. Re-animated corpse, certainly; rotting zombie
vampire creature from hell, not even close.

Our efforts are not a total loss, though. Alex unearths
an interesting study in the anthropology call numbers about
the vampire in eastern European folklore. Here we find
first-hand accounts about vampires harassing
villages shortly after plague epidemics.
The descriptions are close to what we
saw in the alleyway. In particular,

these re-animated corpses came back from the dead to go after family members and friends because, or so the informants explained, the dead were jealous of the living.

Perhaps.

And this lead becomes all the more promising when we discover that the author, at least at the time of publication, was a professor in UCLA's anthropology department. It's at the point of this discovery that I receive a phone call from Neichia. She needs me to come over as soon as possible. Sunny is awake.

For Neichia, this is as close to an S.O.S. as anyone is likely to get.

Half an hour later, I pull up in front of Neichia's house. Alex stayed at the library to do more research. Good. I'm not sure what I'm walking into, but I hear the argument before I even open the car door.

"*SIT STILL!*"

"*OOOOOOOUUUUUUCCCCCHHHHH! GOD DAMMIT, LEAVE ME ALONE, WOMAN!*"

"*I SAID SIT STILL!*"

"*NOOOOOOO! Leave. Me. ALONE!*"

"*IF YOU DON'T SIT STILL FOR THIS, I AM GOING TO SEND YOU BACK TO THE HOSPITAL BED! IS THAT WHAT YOU WANT?*"

The threat of a hospital bed looms as I ring the doorbell and wait, trying to keep the smile off my face. The sounds of scrambling around in the living room and hushed expletives come from the other side of the door as the two combatants continue the argument in muffled tones. Finally, Neichia opens the door. She's not her usual immaculate self. The strain of dealing with an under-the-weather Sunny has aged her about ten human years. Wisps of hair from her normally perfect coif stick in stringy clumps to the side of her face. She's wearing a skirt, and half of her blouse is hanging untucked. She holds a syringe about a quarter full of blood in her right hand. Shaking her head, she backs up and holds the door open for me to come in.

The living room resembles a battlefield.

Wearing nothing but his black boxer briefs, Sunny sits on the one section of the sofa that still has cushions, and he holds another half-torn cushion defensively in front of him. He wears a murderous scowl.

"It sucks here!" he announces when he sees me. "I want to go home. Now."

Ignoring her patient, Neichia turns to me. "I was just trying to take a blood sample."

"You scared of needles?" I ask Sunny. "Big scary vampire doesn't like having his blood taken?"

"I am *not* scared of needles!" he snarls. "She's taken so damn much blood. Why did I need the stupid transfusion in the first place? She's taken everything she gave me last night."

Not knowing what else to do, I shrug at Neichia.

"Sonia, did you drive here in the McLaren?" he demands.

"Yessss," I say, "I did. It's out front."

"Good," he announces. "I'm going home. I hate it here." He stands, wobbles a little, unsteady on his feet. Then he throws his cushion defiantly onto the ground, and stomps out of the room towards the guest bedrooms.

"He's going to crash," Neichia says, watching him go.

"I don't know where he's getting this energy, but it won't last long."

"Is it okay if he leaves today?" I don't know what I'll do if she insists he has to stay.

"Probably not." Weariness comes through in her tone. "But if he stays here, I'll kill him. Sonia, he's not healing like he should—I think something in that creature's saliva is causing it, but I can't pinpoint it. That's why I've been taking so much blood."

Sunny reappears in his jeans, boots in hand. I give him a once over. He looks like death, truth be told. He's already sweating from the exertion.

"That's why I came by to talk to you," I say. "To see if you can tell me anything forensic about this thing. If you find anything, could you call me?"

Without a word, Sunny stalks past us. He marches through the open door and down the front lawn to his car. He stands at the driver's side, glaring back at us. I still have his keys.

"I haven't found anything yet," Neichia says. "It's still too early. But Sonia, he really shouldn't be alone right now."

"I know." My voice is grim. I'm thinking about the creature. As long as that creature is still at large, Sunny can't be alone. Not when he's like this. "I'll stay with him. I'll let you know about any new developments."

Forty-five minutes later, Sunny and I are headed north on the twenty mile stretch of the Pacific Coast Highway between Santa Monica and northern Malibu. The drive would be beautiful during daylight hours when you could see the clean, white beaches and sparkling ocean between the clusters of beach houses and swanky restaurants. But now the deep waters are an inky blackness, occasionally relieved by the distant lights of a lonely fishing boat or yacht.

Next to me, my passenger sleeps soundly, his energy spent during his argument with Neichia. He didn't have the energy to argue with me when I announced that he couldn't drive. We've already made a stop in Hollywood, so I could pick up provisions from my house. Sunny waited in the car while I packed a small bag. In some ways, it would be easier to have him stay with me instead of schlepping all the way to Malibu, but his security system is state-of-the-art, and he has a panic room, which we're going to need if the creature makes an appearance.

A little after 2:00 a.m., I finally pull off PCH onto Sunny's street. We travel along the dark road for about a mile while he sleeps. When we finally pass the golf course on the right, I know we're close. I slow down so I don't miss his turnoff. When I make the turn, I'm on a dark driveway blocked by a privacy gate. We've arrived.

Sunny's house is a white giant, one of those steel and glass monstrosities that southern California realtors like to label "contemporary." They are fairly common in beach areas, presumably because they are expensive to build and their prolific windows maximize the ocean views

I get out of the McLaren, and cross to Sunny's door to help him out of the car. I fold his arm around my shoulder, so I can pull him, rock-star style, to the front door.

Once through the glass doors, I drag him up the staircase to the bedrooms on the second floor.

The master suite is spectacular, with the entire western wall composed of floor to ceiling windows. Black and white zebra print carpet—thick enough to sink down to your ankles—stretches from wall to wall. The extra wide four poster bed, about the size of two queens pushed together, is dressed in custom electric purple with turquoise pillows. The heavy drapes hanging down from the ceiling to puddle on the floor are blood red crushed velvet.

Axl Rose, eat your heart out.

As I ease him onto the bed, Sunny opens his eyes and looks around in confusion. "This isn't where I sleep," he mumbles, shaking his head.

Oh?

He waves his hand back towards the door, gesturing where he wants to go. I haul him back up and help him back through the doorway, where he gestures towards a door just to the left of the master suite.

By this time, he's so weak I'm almost carrying him. Neichia wasn't kidding. He's crashed hard, but I manage to get him through the door and onto the bed of this much smaller bedroom. Looking around, the room's relative austerity impresses me far more than the Rock-n-Roll love nest next door. This room faces east, away from the ocean, and it lacks the extravagant floor to ceiling windows that the western side of the house has. Those, come to think of it, would have been impractical for a day-slumbering vampire. A California king bed sits in the center. It's covered with a thick, fluffy white down comforter and soft pillows. Other than the bed, there's room for little else, but a plasma screen TV is mounted on the wall. His bedside table has only a lamp and a framed photograph on it. I pick up the photo to take a closer look, curious whose photo the magnificent Sunny Michaels has in his bedroom.

Me.

It's of me. A candid shot taken at his Halloween party last year, where I'd dressed as Morticia. I'm facing the camera, but not looking at it, my head thrown back in laughter, rather at odds with the Morticia Addams costume.

I feel a curious pang in my heart as I return the photo to its place, but then I notice Sunny struggling to arrange himself comfortably in the bed. No, no, that won't do. He isn't sleeping in jeans, certainly not in these downy bed-clothes. I yank the comforter off and grab him by the legs to pull him to the center of the bed. Then I undo the buttons on his jeans and haul them off, tossing them over my shoulder to throw away later. He'd been wearing them when the creature attacked. Bad juju. I then tuck my fingers under the waistband of his boxer briefs, and those too join the jeans on the floor. More bad juju. He's not wearing a shirt, so this job is done.

I fluff up the comforter and spread it back on top of him like a fluffy cloud. He already seems a little better, with the hint of a smile playing at the corners of his mouth. I know what he's thinking. Apparently even a near death experience isn't enough to kill the Scorpio libido. His color is still a sickly gray, however, so there will be no hanky-panky for him, even if I were so inclined. I go to the room's one small window and pull the heavy drapes closed so the morning's sunrise will not bother him. Finally, I go back to the bed and kiss him lightly on the mouth. He mumbles something incoherent and starts to snore. I leave the room, closing the door quietly behind me.

CHAPTER 19

WITH SUNNY SAFELY TUCKED in bed, I have a few things to do. Trotting back downstairs, I head for the office, where Sunny keeps his computer. He's decorated it in the same outrageous style as the bedroom, with eighteenth-century Rococo furniture painted in vibrant purple and red lacquers.

Taking a seat at the desk, I pull out my iPhone and dial a number on my favorites list. I order a two week supply of human blood, preferably O negative, delivered to Sunny's address, billable to Sunny Michael's account. It takes them a while to find Sunny in their system, and for a moment I worry that he might not be there. Sunny, after all, hunts every night. But he can't hunt in his present condition, and calling in his familiars is out of the question. They equate sex, and there's no way Sunny Michaels is having sex in his current condition. So bagged blood it is. And it can't be bovine blood, although that's much easier to come by, because it won't aid his healing process the same way human blood will. He probably wouldn't drink the bovine blood, anyway. Getting him to drink bagged O negative is going to be challenging enough.

When the vamp on the other side of the phone eventually finds Sunny's account, I change my order for three-weeks' worth. I have to eat, too, don't I? And in these dangerous times, human blood might just give me the edge I need to stay alive.

After taking care of that, I lean back in the purple Louis XV chair, staring through the giant windows towards the black ocean as I wonder what to do next. I'm at a bit of a loss, stuck in this large and very strange house. And I'm spooked. Extremely spooked, truth be told.

Then something outside, a flicker of movement, catches my eye.

I bolt upright and peer out through the tendrils of steam rising off the heated pool. I see nothing. Nothing at all.

Probably just a bird.

But it didn't look like a bird.

Nor did it move like a bird.

And it was big.

In one slow movement, I reach over to kill the light and get to my feet, leaving the office. I head to the kitchen, where I can turn the lights on outside. Even with my vampire vision, there is only so much I can see under the pitch black conditions of remote, ocean front property. All of the rooms I pass through have the same floor to ceiling windows. Feeling exposed, I step up my pace.

In the kitchen I stand at the sink, looking into the backyard.

Still nothing.

I reach over and flip the switch, turning the outside

lights on. Suddenly the patio and the infinity pool are flooded with light. But I see nothing out of the ordinary. The steam from Sunny's swimming pool is thick and heavy in the predawn chill, mingling with the marine layer rolling in and shrouding the patio in a fog heavy enough to sink your teeth into. In a few hours it will have penetrated inland several miles, enough to make itself a nuisance for early morning commuters. But for now, it just looks chilly and spooky.

I still can't see anything out of the ordinary, but *something* is pricking my vampire Spidey-senses, as Alex calls them. My canines start to throb.

Then, I remember something. I head to the garage, where the control center for Sunny's state-of-the-art security system is housed. Twelve small screens show live video feed from strategic points throughout the property. The control panel under the monitors shows many buttons, switches, and lights. But one of the monitors shows only white snow. I see no label, so I can't tell what part of the property it's meant to record.

It's probably a simple malfunction.

Nothing out of the ordinary appears on the other monitors, but an increase in the light wind brings the marine layer deeper inland.

All in all, everything looks exactly as it should.

Then why am I still feeling spooked?

Once back in the main house, I face another problem. I left my suitcase and book bag in the McLaren when I brought Sonny inside. I move to the glass front door.

Still no monsters outside.

But I hadn't seen the front door area on any of the

security monitors in the garage. I bet the malfunctioning camera is for the front door and probably includes the port cochere where the car is parked.

I have one more realization: Sunny's equipment never malfunctions. Ever. If something breaks, he fixes it the same day. Old human habits, like the need for an efficient security system, die hard. That camera must have somehow stopped working between the time Sunny left yesterday and now. Otherwise, he would have immediately repaired it.

But I need to get to that car. I'll go crazy in here, all alone, without anything to do. I use the Smart House remote control to unlock the front door and disarm that portion of the alarm system.

The car is unlocked. But as the vertical door slowly rises, I smell it.

Rotten, putrefied, flesh.

I whirl around, my back to the car. The marine layer has reached the front of the house, obscuring my vision, and the damp chill of the hour just before dawn brings goosebumps to my arms.

I need to get back to the safety of the house. I'm not strong enough to face this thing alone. But my fangs have not descended. If I trust this reflex, I shouldn't be in immediate danger. Am I willing to stake my life on it? I also notice the reek of the creature isn't as strong as it was in the alley.

But the thing has been here. That's undeniable.

As I suspected, it's stalking Sunny.

Wait. I inhale again. The smell is stronger near the car. Then I stick my head in the car. The smell is even stronger *in* the car.

I sniff around the interior like a bloodhound until I reach my suitcase, where the smell is the strongest yet.

The thing had opened the car and handled my luggage. It had probably sniffed around exactly like I am now.

And my luggage was its point of interest.

Jesus. What the fuck does that mean?

I gather my suitcase and my Louis Vuitton bag full of books, then bring the car door back down. Once inside, I lock the front door and re-arm the security system. It won't keep the creature out, but it will give us enough warning to get to the safe room.

This thing is no dumb, zombie-like creature. We can't stay at Sunny's house, I realize.

We must leave.

CHAPTER 20

A T 1:00 P.M. EXACTLY, the bellhop slides the plastic hotel key card into the lock and swings the heavy door open wide enough for me to pass through. We are at the Sunset Tower Hotel on Sunset Boulevard in Hollywood. It's Vamp friendly, owned by one of the *Stoicheía,* and both the hotel's central location and its shape attracts me. I need to remain in the thick of things. The Sunset Tower Hotel is a tall, narrow building, so if any monsters follow us there, they'll have to pass through the lobby and ride up the elevator to get us. That's too damn much exposure for a creature that lives in the shadows. I've booked a suite on the floor below the penthouse.

Vamp friendly means VIP treatment, with early check-in. I hold the door so the extremely large bellhop holding Sunny up on his feet can follow me, while a third hotel employee wheels in our luggage on the hotel's large brass cart. Checking to see which of the bedrooms holds the California king-size bed, I motion for the bellhop to deposit his charge in that room. I tip each man generously, for privacy as much as for their assistance, then send them on their way to find me a refrigerator large enough to store three weeks' worth of vampire provisions.

The trip from Malibu has exhausted Sunny, who now lays back on the bed with his eyes closed and his arms flung out on either side of him, like Christ on the cross. He's spent what little energy he had complaining for most of the 45-minute drive. He was unhappy about being woken up in the middle of the day, he was unhappy he had to leave his home, and he was unhappy about my choice of hotel.

All in all, he is very unhappy.

And now as he slides back into unconsciousness, I go around the suite, pulling the drapes closed over the Art Deco hotel's distinctive large convex windows. He doesn't comment when I strip off his clothes and pull him far enough back onto the bed so he can rest his head on the pillows. I unpack his clothes while I wait for the refrigerator. By 2:30, I'm ready to meet Dr. Miriam Ferguson, the professor of anthropology who piqued Alex's interest. I heard back from her while on the way from Malibu. I must not have sounded too crazy in my email, because she's agreed to meet with me.

Before I leave I have another look at Sunny, fast asleep now, his head turned to one side with his mouth slightly open. As I come closer to him, I pick up the unmistakable scent of blood. Looking closer, I see he's bleeding out of his nose and ears.

Shit. That can't be good.

I have Neichia's number under my favorites. She doesn't answer. I assume she's asleep. Voicemail picks up and I leave a message saying that Sunny is worse and tell her to come to the Sunset Towers. Come immediately.

Other than the bleeding, Sunny seems stable, so I decide to meet the professor anyway. I need some answers. By the time I leave, it's a quarter to 3:00. I'm cutting it close. I quietly shut the door behind me, careful not to disturb the cool, dark hush of our rooms. Then, with equal care, I fix the "Do Not Disturb" tag on the door. I don't think Sunny is so far gone he'd actually do it, but just in case I want to make sure he has no opportunities to attack any hotel employees. Needless to say, the hotel guests are also strictly off limits. Sunny's not an animal, but it's always better to be safe than sorry. I send a little prayer to the Powers That Be that he doesn't get any worse while I am gone. I hope Neichia gets my message soon.

UCLA's North Campus looks a lot different during daylight hours. At night the warm peach and red colors of the Renaissance-styled buildings are washed out in the floodlights designed to enhance the drama of the campus's architecture. But during the day, the heat from the sun radiates off the buildings and the Mediterranean colors come alive under the bright blue of the spring sky.

The sheer number of people is staggering. At 3:30 in the afternoon, the pathways between the buildings are choked with warm bodies pressed too close together. They remind me of cars on a narrow two-lane highway. Off these congested arteries of human traffic, more relaxed bodies sprawl across the lush lawns of the Sculpture Garden. Some nap in the California sunshine while others study in the shady spots. Using the map, I quickly find the building that houses the Anthropology Department.

The combination of sleep deprivation coupled with the press of humanity and the lethargy brought on by the sun leaves me dizzy and slightly nauseous from the sensory overload. My canines throb, though from a totally different reason than earlier at Sunny's compound. I need to feed, an instinct made all the sharper by the bounty of flesh around me.

Muriel Ferguson's office is on the third floor of Haines Hall. I'm not in great shape by the time I find it. I'm sweating and panting in an effort to calm my overburdened olfactory system.

Once I find the correct door, I hear Professor Ferguson inside talking on the phone. It is a few minutes past 3:30, so I knock sharply on the door. In a friendly voice she bids me to enter, then motions for me to take a seat.

To my immense satisfaction, the office is everything I'd expected it to be. I've never been in a professor's office before, but I've seen enough of them on TV and in movies to have formed some preconceptions about what it should look like. It is a long, narrow room, the full length of each wall on either side of Dr. Ferguson's desk lined with bookshelves from floor to ceiling. Every shelf is packed with books, framed photographs, and the occasional old, dirty knick-knacky-looking thing, probably some sort of priceless anthropological artifact.

I'm only slightly disappointed that no random bones or skulls are lying around, but I suppose I shouldn't have expected them since she is a folklore expert and not an archeologist.

Dr. Ferguson's bookshelves hold everything from ancient leather-bound tomes in German and French to small, paperback novels with spines broken down from multiple readings. I look at these paperbacks with interest, expecting to find some evidence of personality. She has a lot of Anne Rice, Laurell K. Hamilton, and, of course, some Stephanie Meyer. But then, these might be more indicative of research interests than personality. The woman is a vampire folklore expert, after all, so I suppose Anne Rice's novels could be considered a type of modern folklore.

Muriel Ferguson finally hangs up the phone, stands behind her massive, ancient desktop computer and turns her full attention to me. The photograph on her faculty website is a few years old. She looks slimmer, sleeker now, with her black hair cropped close to a beautifully-shaped skull, the rich, dark brown tone of her skin at odds with her Celtic last name.

Dr. Ferguson comes round her desk and extends her hand. "I'm so sorry. If I had known, I would have scheduled our meeting for this evening."

"What?" I look at her sharply, allowing her extended hand to hang awkwardly in the air. All of the sunshine fogginess evaporates. "What do you mean?"

She chuckles, her brown eyes twinkling, "Come now, Ms. Rivers, you don't suppose that I would devote my professional life to the study of vampires and then not be able to recognize one who happens to walk through my door?"

I'm stunned, and don't know what to say. First Alex, and now Dr. Ferguson. Jesus. What is going on with me? Finally, I come up with the words, "How could you tell?"

"It's a quality you and your kind have," she answers matter-of-factly. "It's almost as if you glow, only you're not actually glowing. I'd describe it as an aura, I guess." Then she laughs. "I'm sorry," she says. "I've never had anyone ask me that before. As it happens, I don't come across too many of your kind."

I give her a calculated look. Here I've been trying for the last hour to figure out a way to get information out of her without giving away too much about myself. But the damn woman calls me out before I even shake her hand.

Shit.

As if reading my mind, or perhaps it's just the look on my "glowing" face, she takes a seat in the chair next to me and tries to make peace.

"I'm sorry." She looks down, smoothing out the front of her stylishly cut jacket. "Really, I don't see many of your kind. Besides, because of the amount of time I devote to research into cultures where belief in vampirism is as pervasive as belief in Christ or the Devil, I tend to forget that, here in America, most people still don't know you exist."

I sit back in my chair and give her an appraising look. "Well, all right then. I suppose I should simply come out and tell you why I'm here."

Dr. Ferguson looks me straight in the eye and leans forward. She knows this is going to be good.

"There is a creature," I begin, "that has been—"

Here, I pause. It's one thing for her to know about me, quite another for me to expose the existence of the vampire *Koinon*. Most likely she knows something, but how much? I try to think up a way to leave the *Koinon* out of it, but I come up blank.

"Yes," she prompts me after a few seconds, "there is a creature that has—"

"That has been attacking members of my *Koinon*." To hell with it. Might as well jump all the way in.

Leaning back in her chair, she narrows her eyes in thought. If this is the first she's ever heard of the vampire *Koinon*, she's careful not to show it.

"Can you describe this creature for me?"

That part is easy. I give her the same description I gave the *Stoicheía* at Neichia's house: fangs, green and black skin, gross smell—the works. She listens attentively, then sits quietly in deep thought after I finish.

"This creature," she says a minute or two, "sounds like a vrykolakas."

"A vrykolakas? Uh, what's a vrykolakas?" I ask, slowly wrapping my tongue around all the consonants.

"A type of revenant," she replies. "It's a type of undead that returns from the grave to harass the living."

"Undead?" I scoff. "Are you kidding me?"

There's no such thing as "undead." Everybody, including vampires, knows that. Sure, I'd been calling the thing a zombie vampire monster from hell, but that didn't mean that I actually believed it. There has to be some sort of logical explanation, right?

"You don't believe." A statement, not a question. "You don't believe, even when you've just told me that you witnessed this thing first hand; you saw and smelled its decomposition. What alive thing deteriorates in that way? What else can account for the smell?"

"Plague," I answer. "Plague victims smell like that and physically deteriorate before they die."

There had been several outbreaks of plague when I had lived in New South Wales. It often came over the seas on the convict ships and decimated those living in the towns. I know plague. I know plague intimately. It's not something you're likely to forget.

"You think this is a plague victim?" she asks incredulously. "But how can it be a plague victim if it's also a vampire? Vampires are immune to disease."

"I'm not sure it is a vampire," I say defensively. "I never said it was a vampire."

"And yet you have come out in the daylight to meet with a vampire expert in order to find out what this thing is."

There was no arguing with that. My very presence in her office was implication enough. Whether I realized it or not, I'd come to the conclusion that it was, indeed, a vampire.

"You've got me there," I say. "So what exactly do you mean by 'undead?' Have these things been encountered before?"

"Oh, yes," she says. "Never in America, at least not to my knowledge, but they have been encountered in Europe."

"Where? When?"

"Well." She shifts a tall stack of books off to the side so she can prop her elbow up on her desk. "There are a few recorded individual cases, like Peter Plogojowitz from the Hungarian village Kisilova, and the Serbian ex-soldier Arnod Paole. The oldest recorded case that I know of is the shoemaker of Breslau, who returned from the grave in 1591 to terrorize his relatives and neighbors. Then," she continues, shifting her weight forward as she warms to her subject. "there are more general references: the German Nachzehrers and the Greek vrykolakas. There is a saying that the vrykolakas in Santorini are as numerous as owls in Athens." At this last part, she splays her hands wide like jazz hands and moves them through the air in a dramatic rendition of an exploding firework. "Sorry," she adds, when she sees the look on my face. "I love this subject."

"How does one become an undead vampire?" It's almost too horrible to consider.

"There are some theories," she says. "Babies born with teeth are said to be more likely to become revenants, as are those who die from murder or plague. The illegitimate child of illegitimate parents is also supposed to be more prone to come back from the dead, though that belief seems to stem more from Christian moralist values than anything else." Dr. Ferguson spins in her chair towards the far bookcase and begins scanning the titles. "Suicides are also supposed to come back from the dead. That is why in traditional European cultures, the head is commonly removed from the body before the burial of suicides. Ahhh, yes," she says, pulling a thin, ratty volume from the shelf. She then spins in her chair back around and hands it to me. "It is only in the case of Arnod Paole that a vampire is implicated in the cause of revenantism. Arnod, apparently a generally unpleasant individual who got himself murdered in a field one day, complained during his lifetime of being plagued by vampires."

I look down at the book Dr. Ferguson has handed me. It's in German. I don't know German. "But we have all those things in America," I say. "Why aren't there any American revenants? And if there are no American revenants, where the hell did this one come from? And," I add, holding up the book, "I can't read this."

She chuckles, and in a very un-professor-like gesture, thunks her forehead with the heel of her hand. "Sorry.

Occupational hazard. We all know German around here. But," she continues, back to business, "I don't know why revenants have not been a problem for North America. Vampires such as yourself are not native to the Americas, either. Your kind originates in Europe, as do revenants. But as to how it got here, that is an interesting question. I'm afraid someone must have brought it here."

I don't bother to tell Dr. Ferguson that my Maker originated in Aboriginal Australia. Somehow I feel that will take our present conversation off course. That is a conversation for another time.

Instead, I ask, "Someone brought it here on purpose?"

Dr. Ferguson nods. "I'm afraid so."

Okay, one problem at a time. "How can I kill it?"

"Kill it? I'm sorry to say that this will be extremely difficult. It is zombie-like. A true undead. It is true that different cultures have come up with creative ways of dealing with revenants. Russians were rather fond of abandoning them in deserted wastelands, which I suppose would be effective enough if you have deserted wastelands to spare. It sort of adds a whole new flavor to being sent to Siberia for punishment. Not only will you have to survive in one of the bitterest climates known to man, but you'll also have to fend off the starving hordes of revenants left there to wither away."

She chuckles at her joke.

I rub my temples. I'm so tired. "Okay, so I can't kill it? What the hell am I supposed to do?"

She waggles her index finger at me. "This revenant is not your main cause for concern."

I frown, not understanding.

"Let's say you do manage to kill it in a way that keeps it down. Decapitation sometimes works, *sometimes*. Burning won't work at all. Neither will staking. Your best bet is to find its daytime resting place when, according to the stories, they are helpless. They are not like your kind. They cannot come out during the day. Problem with that is, in a place like Los Angeles, its resting place could be virtually anywhere. Yes, they prefer graveyards. We have a *lot* of graveyards, have you ever noticed that? Anyway, what you need to worry about is finding its master and killing *that* vampire. And that vampire won't be a revenant, but a vampire like you. If you just kill the revenant without the master, it's likely that the master will just summon another revenant."

"It has a master? A vampire like me? But that's impossible. This thing is killing vampires like me. How can its master be one of us?"

"A revenant is a blood-sucking zombie. Its actions are the result of compulsions—we are told that he *must* do, not that he *likes* to do. It's a miserable, accursed condition. He essentially has no free will, which separates him permanently from his humanity. Normally, revenants will just go after humans. In all of the written accounts, it goes after humans. But this one doesn't. It goes after its own kind. This is a different behavior than what we've seen in the texts. *Someone* is compelling it to behave in this way, and that someone is a vampire. It has to be. A human is not powerful enough."

"But," I cut in, "it's not going after its own kind. We are nothing like these revenants. We are not the undead."

Dr. Fergusson nods. "You are more like this revenant than you know. It's kind of like the difference between

Homo sapiens and Homo neanderthalensis, two different species who were nevertheless similar enough to each other to not use the other for food. The fact that this revenant is feeding on vampires of your kind indicates he is being directed to do so by the master who is controlling him. It has essentially become a cannibal, and it wouldn't do this on its own. Find the master, and you'll find the revenant."

Dr. Ferguson checks her watch. "That is all I can tell you for now. I have to give a lecture in fifteen minutes, and I need to get my notes in order. What I think you should do now is go see the vampire Vladimir. I think he might be able to help you track down this revenant's master. In any case, it'll be good for him to know that there is a revenant running amok in Los Angeles. Something tells me the rest of the *Stoicheía* have probably failed to mention it to him."

For the second time since coming into her office, I sit there in complete shock. I don't know what surprises me more, that she knows Vladimir or that she knows the *Stoicheía*.

"I cannot see Vladimir," I tell her. "He doesn't see visitors. Maybe I can find someone else to talk this over with."

"No!" she says sharply. "Do not go to one of the other *Stoicheía* with this. The fact of the matter is that one of them is most likely the master. You don't want to accidentally go to the wrong one. Vladimir and I are old friends, and I feel confident in sending you to him for advice. He lives at the Chateau Marmont in one of the bungalows behind the hotel. I'll call ahead so he'll be expecting you. But I really must send you on your way."

Old Friends? With Vladimir? This woman is full of surprises.

CHAPTER 21

As I take Sunset back into Hollywood, I realize I
don't know what Vladimir looks like. I've always
imagined him to be a Russian prince of the tall,
dark, and handsome variety, with a penchant for tight
breeches, heavy boots, and long, hooded capes. The only
thing I actually know about him is that he is the oldest
vampire living in Los Angeles. Technically, he is one of the
Stoicheia, but as far as I know he's never participated in any
of their politics.

Once I hit the Strip, I slow the McLaren down as I
approach Harper Avenue on the right. The Marmont's dis-
creet, ivy-covered entrance comes up fast. I've not been
to the Chateau before, but the hotel piques my interest
almost as much as the vampire. Except I'm not afraid of the
hotel, and Vladimir does scare me a little. He has a reputation for antisocial behavior, and even with Dr. Ferguson
calling ahead to tell him I'm coming, I'm not sure how
much weight a human's introduction will carry
with someone so old and powerful. I'm
banking on not much.

A long line of black limos

parked along the North side of the Strip signals that I have arrived. I see the small neon sign, a medieval shield with an arrow going through it, indicating the entrance to the subterranean garage.

Once I've ditched the car, I head up a short stairway and immediately find myself in a predicament. The sign in front of me indicates that the bungalows, where Vladimir lives, are off to the right, and the hotel lobby in the main building is to the left. I have no idea where I'm supposed to meet him. I don't even know if he's awake. Muriel's phone-call introduction may have found its way only into his voicemail.

One problem at a time, Sonia. I go to the front desk, the most logical first step.

The lobby is located on the ground floor of the large French chateau. My first impression is of heavy draperies, stained glass windows, and heavy beamed ceilings. The atmosphere is relaxed and quiet—full of people, though their movements are slow and deliberate and they all speak to each other in their library voices.

No one stands out immediately.

Despite the room's dark interior, most of them still wear their large sunglasses, the kind that hide the top half of the face. Most of the sofas are full, taken by "the talent," while "the management" sit in the carved chairs, leaning forward to pay homage and make money. They are all completely self-involved in their little shows, and there isn't a vampire among them. There are some undeniably good looking young men, but nowhere do I see my Russian prince.

There is one person, however, who marks my arrival, though he stands out among the beautiful people in the lobby like one of Santa's elves in the middle of a Paris fashion show. He is chubby, with a round belly spilling out over his stained jeans with matching holes in each of the knees. Looking to be a few inches shorter than me, which would put him just over five feet tall, he has a large balding spot on his very round head and most of his face is hidden behind a full, unkempt white beard. His eyes twinkle good-naturedly, and as I return his gaze he waves at me cheerfully like a guileless five-year-old.

The name 'Timothy Leary' comes to mind.

Returning the friendly little hobbit's wave with the briefest of smiles, my stomach sinks when he makes his way across the room to me. I redouble my efforts at finding Vladimir, hoping that he might miraculously appear and save me from an awkward conversation with the odd little man.

Then I feel it.

The unmistakable thrum of power.

Great electric power.

And it's growing, becoming more and more intense. All the hairs on my arms raise, as does the hair on my head, so that I resemble a damn dandelion. I feel like I'm about to be struck by lightning. The person bearing this power is coming physically closer to me.

But the only person approaching is the little hobbit.

No!

Can't be.

Can it?

It is.

By the time the little man stands before me, I'm caught in a static storm of power. The great weight of his long life presses down on me, crushing my lungs, while at the same time his electric vibrancy shoots my heart rate up and hits my blood stream like a speedball.

Fuck. I bend over, holding my head. How on earth did I miss it when I first walked into the room? Surely I should have picked up on his presence down in the parking garage, not to mention the very room in which he now stands.

"Hello, my dear," he greets me, as a zap of electricity shoots up my spine. "I believe you must be Sonia. My name is Vladimir."

CHAPTER 22

Ten minutes later I sit in a mahogany-framed armchair in the living room of Vladimir's cozy little hillside bungalow, his tabby cat Tchaikovsky purring rhythmically in my lap.

Vladimir is fussing about in the drawers of the antique-looking commode beneath the not-so antique-looking plasma screen TV, an empty pipe in one hand and the other presumably engaged in a search for his tobacco.

I feel better now from my vantage point of observing the large bald spot on the crown of his head, as well as a little too much of his plumber's décolletage where his tattered jeans ride a bit too low and his t-shirt a bit too high. I still feel the power of his age radiating off of him and cutting through the stillness of the room, but it is nowhere as intense as it had been in the lobby.

He is shielding, thank God.

But even diminished, I still detect a quality to that power, the static electricity of an air *Stoicheia*. The hairs on my arms and the back of my neck still stand at attention, and I keep having to smooth my hair down to keep from looking like Drew Barrymore in the movie *Firestarter*.

Siroun, as the second oldest vampire in Los Angeles, must also be shielding her power to some degree.

Who else among the *Stoicheía* is doing the same?

After my conversation with Dr. Ferguson, I understand my primary goal: I need to discover the identity of the vampire controlling the creature. I also need help dealing with that vampire in such a way that will render the revenant powerless.

Best-case scenario, Vladimir will assist me. Worst-case scenario, he won't, which will leave me dead in the water.

I don't want to think about the worst-case scenario.

Vladimir finally gives a cry of triumph and slams the drawer shut with a flourish. I watch as he carefully fills his pipe with tobacco leaf taken from a well-worn leather pouch, and I wonder offhand if he knew Tolkien.

When he finishes with this little ritual, he takes a seat on the carved mahogany-framed sofa to my left. There he sits in his worn out "I'm with stupid" t-shirt, puffing away at his pipe while regarding me steadily with his golden brown eyes. Now that his master has settled, Tchaikovsky abandons me and leaps back into his lap.

Protocol demands that he speak first. I remain silent, waiting.

At just about the time the silence becomes uncomfortable, Vladimir speaks. "So you are Sonia, the vampire from Australia. I have heard it told that you spent 100 years alone in the Outback. And that you knew Pemulwuy. He was your Maker."

Holy fuck. *How the hell does he know who I am?*

The look on my face makes him chuckle, a jolly sound, and strange to be coming out of a vampire predating Jesus Christ. But, then again, for all I know it's typical.

"I am Sonia from Australia," I affirm. "I did spend some time in the Outback, yes. And Pemulwuy was my Maker."

"When I traveled that part of the world, I heard rumors of the Witch in the Outback." Vladimir strokes Tchaikovsky's smooth head. "I also heard rumors that you are very good with a knife."

I snort. "I am not a witch. Pemulwuy believed such arts were only for men. And yes," I say, "I'm good with a knife."

"A curious skill for a vampire, I would say."

I shrug, but I don't answer. He's not entirely wrong.

"Why did you move to Los Angeles?" he asks abruptly. "I remember that you came here in 1977. Why?"

I blanch, then quickly look away, focusing on one of the brass lock plates on the massive armoire positioned against the wall across from me. I feel the stirrings of anger deep inside of me, and grip the scroll-carved ends of my chair. Vladimir has asked me the one question you do not ask. Not here. Not in L.A. We all have our reasons for coming to Los Angeles, and I certainly had mine. But I am not prepared to talk about it, not to anyone and especially not to another vampire. I feel tenderness in my teeth, and realized that my anger is causing my canines to elongate. Tchaikovsky hisses at me from Vladmir's lap.

I need to calm down. It is a tribute to Vladimir that he doesn't do it for me, doesn't use his power to soothe me and mollify the anger I know he can detect. The very old ones can do that. By allowing me to work through these feelings myself, he is graciously showing me the respect normally conferred to equals. This, more than anything, calms me and brings me back from the flashpoint. Slowly, deliberately, I release the chair's arms and smooth my hands up and down my thighs as I take one or two deep, cleansing breaths.

"I had my reasons," I say lightly, though we both know I'm not fooling anyone. "As we all do," I add, hoping that he would take the hint. Then, in an effort to change the subject, I comment on the fine quality of the room's reproductions. "I'm surprised to find furniture like this in a hotel, even if that hotel happens to be the Marmont."

Vladimir doesn't answer at first. I feel the pressure of his gaze on my face, but I'm determined to avoid looking him in the eye until I have reassurance that we are letting his question drop. He waits a few more moments, as if deliberating, then finally takes my lead.

"They are not reproductions," he replies. "They are all originals, and they all belong to me."

He takes a few more puffs on his pipe. I realize that I can no longer detect the shimmer of power on his skin. He is definitely shielding now, and I notice that the longer he smokes his pipe, the more human he seems to appear. Interesting.

"The other question was a trick," he informs me after a minute or two, still puffing away. "I already know why you came to Los Angeles. Your instincts to protect *Them* from the *Koinon* are good. Just be sure to remember that you must also protect *Them* from yourself. Do not allow yourself to get too close, no matter how tempted you are. For your protection, as well as ours."

Suddenly this jolly little elf doesn't seem so jolly.

Leaning back in my chair, I shake my head. How this rat bastard knows my secret, I don't know. I'm not even sure I care. I have never spoken about my family to anyone, not even Sunny, and I'd *thought* I *was* being careful. I never go anywhere near *Them*, except occasionally to the little boy's soccer games. But even then, I always sit far off to the side, and I wear a different disguise each time.

I feel his eyes on me, and I look up to meet his gaze. I now see kindness in his expression, and gentle understanding. I return it with hatred. I feel violated. That little part of me that has remained human all these years has been torn open and exposed by another vampire.

He allows me a few moments to seethe before clearing his throat to call my attention.

Good. Back to business. No more talk of *Them*.

"What exactly did Dr. Ferguson say to you on the phone?" Best to start out slowly, see what he already knows. With any luck, Muriel has taken care of most of the back-story for me.

"Well," he begins, "she told me about your revenant problem, though not in much detail. Just that there is a revenant running loose in Los Angeles, targeting vampires, and that you wanted to ask me some questions about it."

Hmmm. A safe enough answer. I decide to be bold.

"According to her, this revenant must have a master. Do you know who the master is?"

"Do you know the motivation behind these vampire killings?" Vladimir asks. "I do not know who the master is, but if you know the motive, that could shorten your list of possible suspects."

"How in the hell am I supposed to know the motive if

I don't know who the master is?" I demand in exasperation. Then I catch myself: Jesus, did I just curse at Vladimir? *The* Vladimir?

Vladimir's eyes grow round and he blinks at me a few times, but he does not tear me apart with his mind, thank God. "In good detective fiction," he says, "knowledge of the motive often precedes knowledge of the perpetrator."

He has me there. I take a deep breath and try to refocus my thoughts. A lead *has* to come out of this interview. It just has to. I sit up straight, the words just on the tip of my tongue, then slouch back into my chair.

"What?" he asks eagerly. "What is it? What are you thinking?"

I sigh. "It doesn't make any sense. It doesn't work out."

He smiles. "Humor me."

"Well," I begin, "I've never heard of any other revenants wandering around in North America, and neither has Muriel. There's only this one here in L.A. So, what is it about L.A. that stands out from other American cities? The first thing that comes to mind is that we don't have a formal government—we have no *politeia*, we aren't a *hetaireia*. We've got more of an *oligarchia* thing going on."

"And why does that not work out?" he asks, twirling his beard.

"If it has something to do with a power struggle, like a rival *hetaireia* coming in from the outside to impose themselves on us, then the victims would be the *Stoicheía*. They would have to be the ones taken out. But this creature isn't touching any *Stoicheía*. It's going after the *Neoi* vampires. The relatively powerless ones."

"I see," he says, now picking at the beginnings of another

hole in his jeans. "But what if the *politeia* isn't being imposed from the outside? What if it is coming from within?"

"Wouldn't it just be the same thing?" I ask. "Wouldn't it be *Stoicheía*, who are targeted, not the *Neoi*? What power do any of the *Neoi* have?"

"That is a very good question." His tone matches an elementary school teacher talking with a particularly dunce student. "What power *do* the *Neoi* vampires have?"

"I don't know." The exasperation is back in my voice. "That's what I'm asking you."

"Okay." He stops picking at his jeans and focuses all of his attention on me. "I think you're onto something, as they say here in America, with the *politeia* approach. But you're looking at the problem from the wrong angle. Ask yourself, why doesn't Los Angeles have a *politeia*? What makes the vampire population in the City of Angels stand out from vampire populations in other cities in North America, *other* than its lack of *politeia*?"

Vladimir waits patiently while I think. The Russian vampire is no longer sharing his power with me. I didn't even realize he was until it was gone. Now I'm beginning to feel tired, my eyes gritty from lack of sleep. I want this interview to hurry up and end so I can get back to the hotel.

"Its size," I say, rubbing my eyes. "We have a larger population than anywhere else I know of."

"Yes." He jabs at the air in my direction. "And who makes up the majority of the vampires in Los Angeles?"

I give him a blank look.

"*Stoicheía* or *Neoi* vampires?"

"*Neoi*," I answer, "by leaps and bounds."

"And what do you think would happen if some *Stoicheía*

such as myself decided to try to impose a *politeia* on a very large population of *Neoi* vampires living free and clear of any coercive system of Law?"

"We would rebel." Suddenly this is starting to make some sense. I push back my sleepiness and stop rubbing my eyes. "So, kill off a big chunk of the *Neoi* vampire population so that they no longer pose a threat in numbers to the *Stoicheía*. Any rebellion could then be put down."

"Oh," he replies, "it goes even further than that. After a while, when a sizable enough chunk of *Neoi* vampires have been killed off, what do you think will be in the hearts of the survivors? The survivors who know nothing about this revenant and its connection to one of the city's *Stoicheía*?"

Suddenly I see it all clearly. It's diabolical. And it's genius. "We will be calling for some sort of authority to come in and take care of the problem. Like a police force. And you only get that kind of institutional response from a *politeia*."

He sits back triumphantly. "The *Neoi* vampires, the would-be rebels against *politeia*, will be the very same vampires demanding its creation."

"And that would be the motive." I am a little dazed. "The whole thing is an inside job."

CHAPTER 23

I FINALLY HEAD BACK TO the Sunset Towers just a little after 7 p.m. Though the sky still bears the rich orange and red hues of the sun's final rays before it sinks down into the Pacific, I judge it late enough to finally give Neichia a call. Much to my surprise, she answers on the first ring.

"Oh, thank God," she says. "I've been waiting for hours to call you. I'm glad you're an early riser."

"I'm not an early riser. I never made it to bed this morning. I've been waiting for hours to call you!"

"Why? What's happened?" she demands. "How is Sunny?"

Her rush of anxiety fuels my own. My foot presses down on the accelerator, and I begin weaving dangerously back and forth between Sunset's two lanes, passing slower cars to my left and right.

"He's not doing well, Neichia. He's not getting any better. In fact—"

I pause as I cut off a large SUV in the left lane, narrowly missing the Jaguar that had been in front of me in the right.

"In fact, what?" Her voice sounds stressed.

"He seems to be getting worse." I weave into the right lane, then again cut back into the left.

"What are his symptoms? Is he bleeding?"

"Yes." The irate driver of a BMW blasts me with his horn and flips me off. "When I left him, he was bleeding from his nose."

"Any other symptoms?"

"Just bleeding and exhaustion. He's lost his strength."

"Good," she says as I hit the gas and make a diagonal move from the right lane into the left, nearly hitting cars in each lane. I cut off the Porsche in the left lane so closely, the driver slams on his brakes, black smoke rising from his tires.

"Did you just say 'good'?" I ask, incredulous. I ease off the gas and my speed drops a notch. In my rush to get back to Sunny, I don't want to cause collateral accidents. "Do you know what this is? Can you treat him?"

"Yes," she says.

I feel an enormous wave of relief.

"I've been working the last twelve hours on an anti-venom treatment that should do the trick. If I leave now, I should be in Malibu a little after eight."

"We're not in Malibu." I ease the McLaren up to a red light at Sweetzer. "We had to move to a hotel for now. Didn't you get my voicemail? We're at the Sunset Towers in Hollywood. I'll explain the situation when you get here and you can tell me about this anti-venom treatment. For the sake of life and limb, I'd better get off the phone for now."

"I'll be at the Towers in twenty minutes."

Thirty minutes later Neichia steps into the quiet elegance of our suite, her old fashioned black leather medical bag in hand. Upon my own arrival a half an hour earlier, I immediately checked Sunny's condition and found him in much the same state he'd been when I left. Blood still trickled in thin, but steady streams from his nose and ears, although he'd now managed to smear a good deal of it all over himself, the hotel's chocolate-colored bed linens, as well as the ivory buttoned fabric headboard. Housekeeping won't be happy with us when we check out.

Once I close and latch the door behind her, I don't waste time on social pleasantries. I lead Neichia straight to the master bedroom where her patient lays unconscious. While she hurries to Sunny's side to check his vitals, I grab the writing desk's small chair and position it so she has somewhere to sit while she tends to Sunny. I then sit at the foot of the bed and watch her work.

"Tell me about this anti-venom," I say in a hushed voice. "How do you know it will work?"

She takes the stethoscope out of her ears. "Once I'd completed the transfusion two nights ago, I'd expected him to have made a full recovery by the time he woke. The first indication of trouble came when it took him so long to regain consciousness." She pauses a moment, drawing the sheet down and feeling along his abdomen.

"Then," she continues, "when he did regain consciousness, I could tell he hadn't regained his full strength. This suggested to me that he still had something in his system, something deleterious to his health. That was when I began taking blood samples and trying to isolate the poison." She smiles ruefully at the memory.

I return a grim smile. It shocks me to think it had been only yesterday.

She opens her bag and removes glass vials of fluids. "His reaction to the bite wound reminded me of rattlesnake bites. So I checked for rattlesnake venom, or at least something like rattlesnake venom. It was similar, but not exactly the same." Selecting one of the larger vials, she places it on the bed and returns the rest to her bag.

"Then when Sunny left, I did a bit of detective work since I no longer had a patient to work with. Anyway, next, I tried Cobra venom without any success, and, to make a long story short, I finally tried Fer-de-lance, or "lancehead" venom and found an almost exact match with what was in Sunny's system. And, looking up the effects and symptoms of this particular venom, it was indeed a match: bleeding from the bite, nose, gums, and mouth. Blood cannot coagulate and hemorrhages into muscles and nervous system. That would account for the weakness. If this venom were left for this amount of time in humans, they'd die within a matter of hours. But Sunny's not a human, he's a vampire."

"But he's not just a vampire," I chime in, "he's a bloody ripper!"

"Indeed," she replies. "Anyway, I acquired some anti-venom from USC's county hospital. Lance heads are indigenous to central Mexico, which is close enough for them to keep some anti-venom on hand. Then I had to adapt it for vampire blood, which is what I've been doing for the past twelve or so hours. But I think I've got it. This should work."

She presses the syringe into Sunny's arm.

"Aren't you supposed to inject that into an I.V. or something?"

She looks up at me, a sardonic smile on her face. "You've been watching those doctor shows again, haven't you?"

"Maybe. Yes."

"Are you a vampire doctor?"

"No."

"That's what I thought. He's going to need four injections over the next twelve hours. Once every three hours. Is that something you think you can handle, or do you want me to stay?"

I want her to stay. Having her here makes me feel better, like Sunny really is going to be okay. With her here, I no longer feel responsible for his welfare, and if anything goes wrong, she would be on hand to deal with it. I have to admit, I'm not as convinced as she seems about this lancehead anti-venom. But, looking down into her tired, blood-shot eyes, I can tell she is exhausted.

"Go home and get some sleep," I tell her. "I can handle the injections. Once every three hours."

"Are you sure? Because I can stay. I can just go grab a quick nap in the other bedroom. It really wouldn't be a bother."

"Go home and get some sleep," I repeat. "I can handle the injections, and in case they don't work, I'm going to need you at your best."

Once I send Neichia on her merry way, I feel unsure about what to do. I use my phone to set a timer for Sunny's injections, and then sit down in the living room and stare blankly at a space of wall, tracing the gold and tan geometric patterns on the cream-colored wallpaper with my eyes. I am exhausted, bone-deep, gritty-eyed exhausted. My body aches and wants to lie down and rest. But my mind is too wired to sleep. At times like these, I wish I still drank coffee. Then, I realize it's been nearly twelve hours since I last fed. No wonder I feel so awful! Dragging myself off the sofa, I make my way over to the half-size refrigerator special-ordered for our suite, grabbing a clear pint glass off of the mini bar on the way.

After seeing to my repast and popping it into the microwave, I pull out my phone and dial Alex's number.

"Sonia?" he answers on the first ring. "Thank God."

I should have called him hours ago to tell him that everything was okay—the last thing he'd had heard from me was a text telling him that Sunny and I were relocating to an undisclosed hotel because we were being stalked by the creature. I feel terrible. I start to apologize, but he cuts me off.

"Please," he says. "It's okay. We're at war. No need for apologies or explanations. Just tell me where you are. I'll leave now."

I give him the hotel's address, and we hang up. I'm left with an odd, warm feeling, that has nothing to do with the human blood I've just drunk.

Alex Chevalier really is an extraordinary human.

Too bad he belongs to someone else.

Alex is true to his word. I have just enough time to change into fresh clothes and fix myself another pint of blood when I hear the knock on the door. I chug the last of my drink, then check in the mirror to make sure there's no residual left on my teeth. My fangs are still out. Making a mental note to keep my mouth as closed as possible until they recede, I open the door to let him in.

"Hey," he says, giving me a quick peck on the cheek. "How's Sunny? Is he doing any better?"

I touch my face lightly where he's just kissed me. "My friend Neichia came by almost an hour ago and gave him some sort of anti-venom. We're hoping it'll work."

"Anti-venom?" Alex frowns, taking a seat on the sofa. "You guys have an anti-venom for that monster? You know what it is?"

I sit next to him, but not too close. "I've been busy." I tell him about my trip to Muriel Ferguson's office at UCLA and my subsequent meeting with Vladimir afterwards, though of course I don't name him. I trust Alex, but I'm not yet sure how much. I conclude with Neichia's findings and her theories regarding the lancehead venom.

Alex listens quietly, every once in a while nodding his head to something I say. Once I've finished, he sits silently as he absorbs all the details.

"So this thing is a revenant," he says at last, "a type of undead vampire."

"According to Dr. Ferguson, yes."

"Do you believe her?"

I think this over for a moment. "Yes," I finally say, "I do. Her description fits all of this creature's characteristics."

"And it has a master, something you called a '*Stoichei*'?"

This gives me pause. How much can I tell him about the vampire *Koinon* without betraying them? If he goes public with this information, would anyone believe him? Would he go public? He never published anything about the African vampires. I know. I checked.

Alex seems to sense my hesitation.

"Look," he says, "I understand there are things you're not ready to tell me. Maybe never will be. I get that."

He pauses, searching my face for some sort of acknowledgement. It's now fully dark outside and his dark gray eyes look almost black in the dimly lighted room. I reach across and switch on the torch lamp on the table next to him. I keep forgetting he can't see in the dark.

"Alright," he says after I don't respond. "I'm assuming that this *Stoichei* is another vampire."

"A *Stoichei* is a type of vampire. I'm not sure I can tell you any more than that. At least, not yet."

"Fair enough. So Ferguson ID'ed the thing for you, but tells you that you have to go after the *Stoichei* first."

"Yes."

"Then she sends you to another vampire to see if he can help you identify the master."

I nod.

"Did he?"

"No," I say slowly, "he didn't know who the master was. But he did come up with a possible motive, which theoretically should narrow the field a bit."

"Oh."

There is a sharp knock on the door, followed by a voice announcing room service.

I instantly launch into stealth mode, and I'm at the door in a flash. I've moved too quickly for Alex, who suddenly jumps and does a double-take at my new position.

Pressing my face to the door, I close my eyes and inhale deeply. Cheeseburger, sweet potato fries, soft drink, and more importantly, human, male, late teens to early twenties.

His pulse is regular and nothing in his body chemistry suggests he's anything but perfectly relaxed. Perhaps a little too relaxed. He smells faintly of marijuana. When I look through the peephole, I see a top-heavy fish-eyed view of a blond kid with ocean-bleached surfer hair and a light smattering of acne. No Uzis, rocket launchers, or machetes. Still, when I open the door I am careful to block the opening with my body—any concealed weaponry will have to go through me. And unless he manages to cut off my head, I'll almost certainly survive the attack. He will not.

"Um, Sonia?" Alex's voice is a little hesitant behind me. "I'm sorry I didn't mention it. I ordered myself dinner at the front desk."

Sure enough, all the kid wants to do is deliver Alex's food. I tip him twenty bucks, then wheel the cart in myself. Alex falls upon the food like a Savannah lion on a wounded zebra, and doesn't speak another word until he's scarfed down every last sweet potato fry. I feel terrible. I'd detected the remnants of prolonged anxiety off Alex when he came through the door, but I'd been so distracted by the kiss I hadn't given it any thought. He must have been really worried, and I wonder when he ate last. I make a mental note to keep better track of his body chemistry. I need to take better care of my human.

No, Sonia. He's not your human, remember?

"Can you tell me the motive?" he asks after sucking down the last dregs of his Pepsi through the straw.

This is a heavy question, and enough to snap me back to the present. My mind switches gears to the problem at hand, and I stare at him for a moment, deliberating.

The *Koinon*. It's always about the security of the *Koinon*. He's a journalist.

But dammit. All this secrecy isn't working. I'm going to have to trust him.

I take a deep breath, and I do it. I tell him everything I know about the string of vampire disappearances/murders, from the blood bath we found in Fiona's bathroom to the attack on us in the Fairfax alleyway.

Is it reckless? Yes. But I'm exhausted and need a second brain on this. Sunny is still unconscious. So Alex is going to have to be that second brain.

He listens quietly. By the time I get to Vladimir's proposed motive, I have thrown caution to the wind and told him about vampire government, Los Angeles's unique lack of one, and the possible reasons why. I finish by telling him all about the *Stoicheia*, or at least as much as I know about them.

Fuck it. Fuck it all.

When I'm out of words, he says, "What you're essentially telling me is you suspect that all of this is going down over a change in government."

"Yes."

"But even with this motive, the list of suspects is still too long. Too many individual vamps, or a small group of vamps working together, could be involved in this."

"Yes."

"Then we have to approach the problem from another angle." He leans back, lacing his fingers behind his head as he rests it on the back of the sofa. I try not to notice the way his t-shirt inches up to reveal a tanned strip of skin above the hips of his low rise jeans and the tantalizing line of dark hair trailing down from his belly button.

"If there have been so many killings, why hasn't the media caught on?" he asks.

"I think because most of the attacks are happening in the home, like Fiona's."

"Then what happened with you and Sunny?"

"Well, I thought about that. All I could come up with is his security system. It's too hard to get him at home."

"But even harder at a hotel?"

"Yes. No one knows we are here, except you and Neichia."

He nods, "Fair enough. So what about this? If specific vampires are being targeted, and targeted in their homes, where is the master getting their addresses?"

"What do you mean?"

"Do you guys have a vampire registry?"

I frown at him, uncomprehending.

"You're all constantly moving around to keep from freaking out your neighbors, right?"

"Yes. Every fifty years."

"A regular citizen can't just go to the DMV and get people's addresses. We have stalking laws and all that, right?"

"Uh-huh."

"So your master vamp either has someone on the inside leaking information, or vampire changes of address are being tracked another way."

"The *Riassegnessa*!" I sit bolt upright. "The Relocator! She's in charge of our changes in address and identity! And she keeps files on all of us!"

CHAPTER 24

I DREAM OF AUSTRALIA.

I stand before the looking glass in my room, gazing nervously at the stranger looking back at me. She is beautiful, every part the fine lady in her wedding dress and veil.

Can this really be happening?

Am I about to marry Owen?

"Yes," the little voice in my heart says. "Yes, you are."

And then what will my life be like? Wifehood... Motherhood?

I suck in a little breath, as much as my lacings will allow. I could be a mother. A little smile plays around my lips. What will our children be like? Will they be gingers like Owen? Or will they look more like me? Will they be boys, or girls? Or will Owen and I be blessed with both?

A sharp rap sounds at the door. It is Marta, our neighbor who helped me dress this morning.

"It's time," comes her rough voice.

"It's time," I murmur to myself. Time

to begin my new life. Time to leave the fifteen-year-old prosti-tute back in England once and for all.

Time to be happy.

When I wake, a blurry figure looms over me. Before my eyes can focus, I recognize Sunny's scent. He isn't happy. Rubbing my eyes, I sit up in bed and try to focus. He's naked, and he has something in his hand.

"What the hell is this?" he demands, shoving a cold bag of O negative under my nose. "And where the hell are we?"

Seems he is feeling better. Neichia's anti-venom worked.

I reach over and grab the alarm clock off the bedside table. It is 5pm. Time to get up anyway. Alex is coming at 7:00. With a sigh, I lean back against the padded headboard.

I remind myself to be gentle. Sunny has been through a lot.

"What's the last thing you remember?"

"I don't know," he says, plopping himself down in a chair in the corner of the room. "I guess I remember being at Neichia's and for some reason I was tearing apart her couch. But I was in my underwear, so that must have been a dream."

"No," I inform him, "that really happened. Do you remember the fight?"

He narrows his eyes and thinks for a moment. "Yes," he says finally. "I remember a fight. In an alley. But I figured that must have also been a dream because..." His voice trails off and he looks down at the floor.

"Because why?" I prompt.

"It's stupid. You're going to laugh."

"I promise I won't laugh."

"I thought it must have been a dream, because I was fighting a monster."

He looks at me defiantly, his eyes challenging me to laugh. On some level I register the irony of the situation. Here sits Sunny the Vampire, twenty-first century monster extraordinaire, afraid to trust the veracity of his memory because he was fighting another kind of monster. Monsters not believing in monsters. That is kind of funny.

"I'm afraid it wasn't a dream." I bring him up to speed with the events of the last couple of days. As I progress through my story, I can sense his mood growing darker and darker. By the time I finish, his handsome features have twisted into a thunderous scowl.

"And what is this for then?" he demands, tossing the bag of O negative onto the floor.

"It's for you," I tell him firmly. "You aren't strong enough to hunt yet and you can't hunt in the hotel."

"Why the hell not?" he challenges. But the challenge is in his voice alone. He knows perfectly well why not, and his body chemistry reflects that. I tell him as much and his shoulders slump and he sticks his lower lip out like a petulant child. Then I notice he still has blood smeared all over him.

"Why don't you go take a shower," I suggest in sympathetic tones. "Then put on some clean clothes, and I'll warm up a glass of O negative for you."

"Fine!" He stands up and stomps out of the room with as much dignity as his nakedness allows. I sigh again, this time truly heartfelt. He won't be happy when I tell him he can't come to Pasadena with Alex and me.

Two hours later, we rumble slowly through Alpine Street in the Madison Heights neighborhood in Pasadena. I would have preferred to make the trip in the quieter McLaren, but after about half an hour of heated arguing, I had to concede. The McLaren doesn't have a back seat and the Cougar does.

That's right, we have Sunny with us after all.

He will put up with hiding out in a hotel indefinitely, he will put up with the temporary restrictions on his hunting activities, and he will put up with the store-bought bagged blood. But he will *not,* under any circumstances, put up with being left behind. Alex, to his credit, stayed out of the argument completely and pretended to watch *Extra* while Sunny and I battled it out in the next room. Eventually, I had to give up. There is simply no winning with Sunny, and he's often willing to take arguments to heights that the rest of the civilized world would shy away from.

Now he sits quietly in the back seat, looking out his side window in perfect contentment. He will apologize later for the things he said, and I will forgive him because the fight was really my fault anyway. I knew, deep down inside, that he wouldn't allow us to leave him behind, a sentiment I could have been more sensitive to since he'd been unconscious for almost two days. He'd been literally left in the dark while the rest of the world carried on perfectly well without him.

And, in the end, it probably doesn't matter whether we are in the McLaren or the Cougar. Madison Heights is very old by Californian standards, the streets laid out in the nineteenth century, and most of the homes dating during the first two decades of the twentieth century. Consequently, all of the oak trees lining the street are about a hundred years old, their thick, mature branches knitting together overhead to form a sort of dark, leafy tunnel that mutes the rhythmic rumbling of the muscle car's hemi.

In between the oak trees the old fashioned street lamps have begun to glow, and a few of the houses have already turned on their porch lights. Most of the houses are variations of the craftsmen bungalow, each with their characteristic covered front porches supported by massive columns, and low-pitched roofs with deep, shadowy eaves and exposed rafters. These craftsmen are duplicated up and down both sides of the street with the odd Spanish or New England colonial revival interspersed here and there for variety. It's a neighborhood of lush green lawns, well-tended hedges, and white picket fences. It is not the sort of neighborhood in which to have bad habits.

"Is that it?" Alex asks, pointing to a rustic brown house with side shingles and stone detailing on the porch columns.

"Yup," I affirm after checking the house numbers on the curb. "That's Elfie's house."

"Should we park in front, or would it be better to drive up a little ways and park there?" Alex asks.

"In front," Sunny says. "As of now, this is just a social visit. If we park up the street, our intentions will look suspicious."

Alex wordlessly pulls the car up in front of Elfi's house and cuts the engine. We all sit and share a moment in silence.

Alex is the first to speak. "Do you guys normally show up at each other's houses unannounced like this?"

Sunny snorts. "Nope. Never."

"Aren't you worried that this is going to look kind of weird? The two of you arriving like this together?" We'd already decided that Alex should wait in the car. He didn't argue.

"Yes," I say, looking pointedly towards the back seat, "this is going to look very weird. It would be better if just one of us goes in."

"Do you want to wait in the car?" Sunny asks me with exaggerated patience.

"No."

"Then I guess we're both going."

"Why aren't there any lights on?" Alex asks.

He's right. The house is completely dark. No porch light, no interior lights. It appears dark and empty.

"That doesn't mean anything," Sunny says finally. "She probably just forgot to turn on the lights. Happens to us all."

"Yes," I agree, though I'm not so sure. Something seems off.

Opening the door, I scramble out of the low-slung car with my customary grace, happy that I am wearing jeans and boots rather than a skirt and heels. I then tilt my seat forward so Sunny can emerge. To my chagrin, he does so in a single, fluid movement, his bones seeming to bend like a cat's as he squeezes through the tiny space. Graceful bugger doesn't even get caught in the seatbelt.

"That's not bloody fair! You're younger than me."

"What's not fair?" he asks, smoothing the front of his vintage cowboy shirt down over his jeans. "It's not fair that I move like a gazelle and you move like a hippopotamus?"

"Oh, shut up," I retort, spinning on my heel and marching up the driveway to the front door.

"It's because I'm athletic," he says, jogging up next to me. "I played a lot of sports when I was a kid. You probably weren't athletic when you were a human, so you're not as graceful as I am."

"Kiss my —"

"Now, now, Sonia," he interrupts in a patronizing tone as we start up the stairs to the porch. "It's time to focus. Do you want to knock, or should I?" Then he winks at me and knocks on the door before I can answer. Apparently after two days of relative peace and quiet, he is looking to make up for lost time.

Turning towards the front door, I wait while running our cover story over in my head: Sunny is stopping by because he wants to make a change to his blood account. And I've tagged along because I'm considering a move to Pasadena. We're conveniently ignoring the fact that Sunny's little errand could have been accomplished easily by phone, and I'm not due for a move for another fourteen years.

"Something's wrong," Sunny observes when our knock gets no response. "I don't think she's home. It doesn't seem like she's been home in a while. And I smell something."

I sniff at the air on the porch. I smell it, too. Ammonia, lots of it.

I try the front door. "It's open," I say unnecessarily as the door swings wide.

Sunny steps inside and I follow on his heels, quietly shutting the door behind me.

CHAPTER 25

ONCE INSIDE ELFI'S HOUSE, I sniff the air again.
Then I sneeze. Damn. Someone really got
enthusiastic with the cleaning supplies in here. It
smells like the interior of an old Kmart from the seventies.

But no trace of the creature's scent.

None at all.

This seems odd. Whether Elfi is the master or a victim,
I would expect to detect the presence of the creature. But
there is nothing, not even the barest hint of graveyard decay.

To the left is the dining room, which opens directly
onto the kitchen. Straight ahead is a large living room, and
to the right are two small doors. The first opens onto a coat
closet and the second into a narrow hallway with several
more doors, presumably bedrooms and hopefully an office.
Wordlessly, Sunny and I split up.

We know what we're looking for: we need to find where
Elfie keeps her computer.

I head into the dining room, and he makes
a move for the bedrooms. We'll meet up
again in the living room in the middle.

The old mahogany wood

flooring creaks under my footsteps as I cross through the dining room to the kitchen. I take a moment to look around. Vampires often neglect kitchens. The refrigerator is the only useful appliance, and even those tend to stand empty, as we prefer a locked device in a more secure area of the house. Mine, as I've said, is in the basement with my bedroom. But it can be a useful place for hiding things, especially from other vampires.

Elfie's refrigerator stands as empty as the day it arrived on the delivery truck. Not a big surprise.

Closing the door, I take two steps backwards in the tiny 1920's kitchen, and lean back against the counter with my eyes closed, waiting for my night vision to return. Then, while my olfactory senses are temporarily freed from visual distractions, I smell it: vampire blood.

A vampire has bled somewhere in this kitchen.

With eyes firmly shut, I push off from the counter and follow my nose. When my hipbones bump against the counter, I open my eyes and find myself standing at the kitchen sink. Looking around the polished granite countertops and the pristine sinks, I can't immediately find the source of the blood. I check the tile floor in front of the sink, but it, too, is perfectly clean.

Too clean.

Like the rest of the house, the kitchen has been scrubbed down.

But I smell blood, so whoever has done the scrubbing, missed a spot. Then my eyes travel upwards from the floor, over the sink, over the window looking out over the front yard, and then I see it. On a hook hanging from the side of the cabinets next to the sink, a dish towel. A well-used dishtowel, by the looks of it. Snatching it down, I put my nose to the dirty fabric and inhale.

Blood.

Vampire blood.

But that's not all.

I also smell sulfur, and something else…perfume, a distinctive scent favored by only one vampire I know.

The rest of the rooms on the western side of the house yield nothing. When I make my way back to the barrel-vaulted living room, I find Sunny already there, lounging on Elfi's couch in front of the red brick fireplace.

"Find anything?" I ask, taking a seat in the rocking chair.

"Her office has been cleared out," Sunny informs me as he scratches an itch on his flat belly. "Computer's gone and all of her file cabinets are empty."

"I found blood in the kitchen," I say. "On a dishtowel. It's vampire blood."

"I'm guessing that it's probably Elfi's." He pauses before adding, "Judging by the way someone scrubbed this room down, it probably happened in here. Looks like she's not the master after all."

"Dammit. I liked Elfie."

"So we're back at square one. Shit."

"Not exactly. There was something else on that dishrag—"

"What?" he asks, sitting up a little.

"Sulfur."

"I smelled that, too. On the porch. So that does narrow the field a little."

"I also smelled Black Opium perfume."

Sunny is still, a blank look on his handsome face.

Then, it clicks.

"Oh, fuuuuuck," he groans, leaning back in his seat. "Not *her*."

"Yup. Her," I reply. "Are you really surprised?"

"If she's the master, we're in deep shit."

"Yes. We are."

Just then, we both hear the sound of a car door closing out front, followed in rapid succession by two more car doors closing. Somebody is here.

"Fuck!" I borrow Sunny's F-bomb as we both hurry to the dining room windows. "Alex is out there."

"No, I'm not," says a disembodied voice from the foyer. "It got hot in my car. I came in about fifteen minutes ago." Alex materializes in the doorway to the dining room. Dammit. All these cleaning chemicals are messing with my nose. I didn't even pick up his scent.

"Who's here?" he asks.

Good question. Sunny and I stand at the window, straining to see around the craftsman's massive stone pillars down to the street below. I barely make out the figures of four men, all dressed in black, clustered around Alex's car, one of them looking carefully at the license plate.

"It's Constanzo," Sunny announces, "and three noobs. What the hell are they doing here?"

"Well," I point out, "if Bianca's the master, it makes sense that she'd have her favorite pet watching this place. Do you recognize any of the others?"

"No." Sunny moves to another window. "I've got a pretty good view of them now. They're just a trio of your typical noob vamp clones, all dressed in the Armani uniform with slicked back hair. If they had Ray Bans on, they'd look like the dudes in *Men in Black*."

"Yup," I say as the quartet moves away from the car. "I can see them now. It's Constanzo all right. What should we do?"

"I dunno. Looks like a kill squad, if I ever saw one."

"Agreed." I move away from the window, letting the drapes fall back into place. "We need to get Alex the hell out of here. He can go out the back and wait for us a few blocks up the street."

I turn to Alex and he nods his assent as he tosses Sunny his car keys.

"You going to be alright?" he asks me in a low voice, his eyes betraying his uncertainty.

"Don't worry about Sonia," Sunny cuts in as he moves to the door. "She could break Constanzo in half if she wanted to. And I can definitely take the other three."

Alex leans his forehead against mine in a disarmingly intimate gesture. "Be careful, promise?" Then he hurries out the French doors in the back just as a sharp knock resonates through the foyer.

Discussion is over, they're here.

Sunny waits for me to reach the foyer before he opens the door. I look back just in time to see Alex close the French doors quietly behind him. I meet Sunny's eyes. We nod briskly to each other as he jerks open the front door.

Constanzo stands on the porch, his three goons taking up position behind him.

"Sunshine, Sonia." Constanzo smiles, showing us his canines. Fucker. He's gone through the change.

"Constanzo." Sunny steps back, inviting him in. It's still human hours. We need to move this inside.

"What a coincidence that I should find you here," Constanzo says as he saunters into the room, the goons following single file. "We've been looking everywhere for you two. My *Archoatess* has some urgent business she needs to discuss with you." He flashes me a smile over his shoulder, carefully revealing the full length of his deadly fangs. He means business.

I bring up the rear, following the last goon. "Your *Archoatess*?"

Damn. This is a dangerous word in the vampire world, one that's caused entire communities to be wiped from existence. It's the language of the Old World, of blood feud and war. Think Romeo and Juliet, Montagues and Capulets, only vampire style. This language should have no place modern Los Angles, but if Bianca is indeed now an *Archoatess*, and has cultivated a following of lesser vampires, as the word suggests, then it seems Vladimir's theory is correct.

"Why, the Lady Bianca, of course." Constanzo's smile widens, flashing more fang.

I smile back, shifting through the change in front of the Italian prat. If he wants to play, we'll play. Meanwhile, Sunny remains silent in the corner, lounging casually in his seat, his face fixed in a bored expression. But no one has forgotten his presence. Constanzo has fixed his attention solely on me for the time being, but each of his three goons throw a wary glance towards Sunny's corner at regular intervals.

I wonder how much they know about him. Do they think they can take him? They outnumber him, and Sunny is still recovering from the creature's venom. I have a feeling the goons' confidence, or lack-there-of, is the only thing keeping this charming little *tête-à-tête* from disintegrating into an all-out brawl. Unfortunately, *I'm* not even sure how up to the fight Sunny is.

As if reading my thoughts, Constanzo turns his attention to Sunny's silent form. "And you, my brave warrior," he purrs seductively. "My *Archoatess* heard you had become terribly ill after some sort of attack. I must confess that, when we could not locate you at your home, we feared the worst."

Sunny responds by focusing his eyes on Constanzo for the first time. I can see from where I sit they are entirely black, as if the pupil has spread to devour not only the blue irises but also the whites of his eyes. I know right then there will be no peaceful conclusion to these threatening little demonstrations. Somebody is going to die. I hope it's Constanzo. I unhinge my jaw and nonchalantly lace my clawed fingers to grip my knee.

Meanwhile, Constanzo, idiot that he is, shows no hint of awareness that anything is amiss with Sunny. He has turned his attention back to me. Big mistake.

"I am afraid you'll have to cancel the rest of your plans for tonight," he says. "My associates and I are under orders to bring you to *Archoatess* Bianca immediately."

As if on cue, the three goons behind him unclasp their hands and flex them at their sides, bodies rigid with the promise of violence.

"I don't think so." I speak slowly, uncrossing my legs and planting my feet firmly on the ground as I rest my hands loosely on the arms of the rocking chair. I give a little push with the balls of my feet and begin to rock back and forth in the chair, quietly radiating menace. Sunny continues to stare at Constanzo with his deadly black eyes.

Suddenly, the blond goon closest to Sunny turns towards him and rushes. Not daring to take my eyes off of Constanzo, I have only the blurred impression of movement before I hear the distinct cracking sound of breaking bones. I see from the corners of my eyes that Sunny is holding up the limp body of the blond goon in one hand.

In the other he holds a machete. Where the hell did he find a machete?

The blond vampire struggles against Sunny. There is another blur of motion, and then the wet squelching sounds of a head being severed from its body. Sunny is efficient, the sharp blade cuts expertly through meat, tendons, and bone, and then the sound of a body hitting the floor, the thump of a head following.

Nobody dares to move. Constanzo keeps his eyes fixed on me, a sick smile still plastered on his face.

Sunny crouches, throws his arms wide, and tilts his head back. The most terrifying scream comes from him. He sounds for all the world like a pissed off Pterodactyl from one of the Jurassic World movies. And holy fuck, I've heard that sound before: something similar came from the *vrykolakas* the night we were attacked.

The two remaining goons face Sunny, their promised violence somewhat diminished. Drenched in blood and gore, Sunny straightens back up and turns his black stare onto Constanzo. I know Constanzo can feel the weight of Sunny's deadened eyes. Almost imperceptibly, his neck seems to shrink as if he's trying to pull his head down between his shoulders like a turtle.

"I think you had better leave now," I say softly. "Or else he's going to kill you."

Constanzo's smile slowly slides down into a grimace.

The two remaining goons each take a step back.

We won. For now.

CHAPTER 26

"SO WHERE DID YOU get the machete?" I ask from Elfi's master bedroom as Sunny steps out of the shower, toweling the damp curls of his hair.

From the moment Constanzo and company left forty-five minutes ago, hurling promises of future death and destruction over their shoulders, I've been in a frenetic state. First, I had to sit in the living room for about ten tense minutes with a murderous Sunny and a decapitated goon until Sunny's eyes went somewhat back to normal. I'd never seen eyes like that before, and I wasn't taking any chances. Only when I could see the whites of his eyes again did I deem it safe to get close enough to strip him of his bloody clothes and throw him naked out into the backyard until his bloodlust passed completely. While he prowled around outside, stalking the small nocturnal animals of Elfi's neighborhood, I searched the contact list on his cell phone until I came across a number listed under the heading, "The Cleaners." I placed a call, requesting a clean-up service for one dead vampire body.

I also contacted Alex, suggesting that he walk to Lake Avenue and find a comfortable coffee shop where he could wait for us. Way ahead of me, he gave me the address of the Starbucks where he'd been cooling his heels for the last 30 minutes.

As I finished my call with Alex, Sunny reappeared at the French doors, his fangs still out and a freshly-drained cat hanging forgotten at his side, indicating he was ready to come back inside. He obviously still wasn't himself, so I chased him off the exposed deck and out into the more secluded darkness of the back yard with some strong words about staying away from the neighborhood pets.

I'd scarcely a minute or two to think of what to do next when the doorbell rang, signaling the arrival of Sunny's three-vampire clean-up crew. Once I brought them back into the living room, two of them changed into their coveralls while the third handed me a small duffel bag containing a fresh set of men's clothing, a pair of boots, size 13, underwear and socks, and several small bottles of various men's grooming products. They opened the two larger duffel bags they'd brought with them. Soon, the floor was littered with their various tools of the trade, ranging from devices that looked like medieval instruments of torture to industrial-size bottles of cleaning agents.

Sunny reappeared at the French doors, sans dead cat, asking for the second time to be let back into the house. His fangs had fully receded, and I smelled no aggression coming from him, so I let him back inside. His face, neck, and arms were still covered in the dead vampire's blood, so I shoved him into Elfi's shower in the master suite with the bottles of shampoo, conditioner, and body wash from the duffel bag. Then, not wishing to watch the cleaners chop up and dissolve the vampire body, I sat on the bed and waited while

Sunny washed off all of the gore. That's when I thought to ask about the machete.

"I found it under the bed in one of the bedrooms," he answers as he continues to towel himself dry. "Once I saw that all of Elfi's files were gone, I figured she must be dead, so I took the machete."

"You really think she's dead?"

"Don't you?" He strides into the bedroom, naked as the day he was born, naturally bronzed skin still radiating warmth from the shower. Boy probably never suffered a self-conscious moment in his life.

"Yeah." I studiously refuse to admire his body as he dresses. "I suppose I do. I don't see there being any other way. She would never willingly allow anyone to take her files, and she would be too dangerous to hold captive. And there would be no reason for that, anyway, once her files were taken. She's too damn efficient for her own good, I guess."

"Uh-huh." The bed sags under his weight as he sits down to put on his boots. "I thought the same thing. Now what do we do?"

"Since it looks like Bianca has killed a *Stoichei*, that might change things. Let's wait until we pick up Alex before we talk any more about this," I suggest. "It'll be better if we all discuss this together."

Once back in Hollywood, the three of us decide to hold a council of war in the hotel suite's living room. Sunny sprawls across the sofa, and Alex and I each take a seat in the matching armchairs positioned on either side of the sofa. For Alex's benefit, Sunny has switched on the two *torchères*, each of them now flooding their respective corners with light.

"So *now* will you tell me what the hell happened?" Alex demands impatiently. "You guys were in there forever. I drank two *venti* caramel lattes while you were gone, and that was *after* I stood freezing my ass off on the corner of Alpine and Los Robles for thirty minutes, waiting for you guys to drive up."

Sunny and I look at each other, silently deciding who should fill Alex in.

A sharp double knock on the door intrudes, and a courteous male voice calls out, "Room service."

My hackles rise. Judging by the look on Sunny's face, he's responding the same way. Alex seems the only one not bothered.

"That was quick," Alex says, bouncing up. "I only called them ten minutes ago."

In a flash, Sunny is at the hotel room door, peering through the peephole. I'm right behind him.

"You know this guy?" he demands, stepping aside so I can take a look. It's the same surfer kid who'd delivered Alex's food the last time.

"Yes," I say cautiously. "Same guy who came before." I turn to Alex. "When did you order room service?"

"From the lobby," he replies. "You guys were bickering about something."

We'd been bickering about whether or not we should change hotels. I was all for moving to somewhere a little less conspicuous than Sunset Boulevard, but Sunny argued that changing hotels would make no difference if we were already being watched. We might actually be safer staying somewhere more conspicuous. More witnesses.

"*ROOM* service." The voice on the other side of the door is more emphatic now, followed by a louder double knock.

Alex opens the door, and once he takes charge of the food, Sunny slips the kid a $100 and closes and latches the weighted door behind him.

"Well, if he's going to eat, I want to eat," Sunny declares, fixing me with a pointed stare.

"You know how the microwave works," I say.

"But you do it so well," he whines.

"Fix your own damn blood. You're a big boy, you can do it all by yourself—"

"Do you guys always fight like this?" Alex blurts as he spreads mayo on his cheeseburger.

Chastised, I get up to fix two pints of warmed O Negative.

Once we are all seated with our nourishment of choice, I bring Alex up to speed about Constanzo and the death squad. I leave nothing out about the scene at Elfie's house, not even the decapitation of one of Constanzo's clients.

"Well," Alex says thoughtfully after chewing for a few moments, "I can see why it took you guys so long."

Sunny and I nod in agreement.

"Is that normal?" Alex asks, turning to Sunny. "Having to come down from a blood lust like that?"

"You didn't encounter anything like that in Africa?" I ask Alex as Sunny shakes his head.

"Ha. I didn't encounter *any* of this in Africa," Alex says, devouring a french fry.

"There are a few things I need to talk to Neichia about," I say evasively.

"What?" Sunny zeros in on me like a hawk. "Why? And why do you smell worried? You don't think I'd attack you, do you?"

"No. I just need to talk to Neichia." I pray she gets back to me soon. I'd fired off a text from the car on the way home. Truth is, I am worried. Very worried. His eyes had turned black and he'd sounded like the *vrykolakas*. And no one knows how a *vrykolakas* is made. If vampires can make vampires, can revenants make vampires into revenants?

Sunny narrows his eyes at me. "I was just pissed. I liked Elfie."

"That's what happens when vampires get pissed?" Alex asks him. He pops a few french fries into his mouth, his gray eyes bright with interest.

Sunny flashes me an unreadable look. "I guess. I mean, I almost died because of Bianca. And Constanzo was just sitting there with that superior little smile on his face, and he was being so condescending, I just wanted to remind him who he was dealing with." Sunny folds his arms across his chest and turns to gaze out the window. He's done speaking on the matter.

"Oh," Alex responds, reading Sunny's closed body language. I can almost hear him making a mental note to ask me more about it later. Without missing a beat, Alex turns to face me. "I guess that means Bianca must be the master then, right?"

"Right," Sunny and I say in unison.

"And Constanzo is one of her henchmen?"

"Yes," I answer.

"He'd like to think so," Sunny says at the same time.

"And the creature? Did the creature kill the vamp living in that house?"

"No. The creature has never been to that house," I say, "but I have a theory about that."

Sunny and Alex look at me with interest.

"I think Elfie must have been the first vampire killed, and by Bianca herself."

Both nod their agreement.

"Either she was killed before the creature arrived in America, or maybe Pasadena was too far away from the Hollywood/Beverly Hills area for the thing to travel by itself and nobody was particularly keen on sitting in a car with it."

I pause for them to laugh at my little joke. Neither do.

"But it did make it all the way up to my place in Malibu," Sunny points out. "Which is farther away than Pasadena is from Hollywood and Beverly Hills."

"True." I consider that fact. "So maybe Bianca killed Elfie before it arrived."

"Makes sense," Alex interjects. "That way Bianca could have her hit list ready to go by the time the creature got here. How do you think it got here?"

"Probably through San Pedro," Sunny muses. "Beyond that, who knows?"

We all sit quietly for a moment, each contemplating the logistics of shipping a reanimated vampire corpse half-way across the world. For the first time I find myself considering the fact that this conspiracy must have spread beyond the geographical limits of the metropolis. Somebody found this thing, reanimated it, or, if it was already reanimated, captured it, and shipped it right under the noses of the port authorities. That would require money and organization, and probably political connections in the human world.

"So now what?" Alex finally asks. "We go after Bianca?"

I answer with a firm no. Alex knows damn well that he is here to help with the investigation, nothing more. "Now that we know who is behind this, *we* are done. From here on out, Sunny and I have to handle this alone. But," I continue, directing my attention to Sunny, who sits with a look of grim satisfaction on his face, "we are *not* going after Bianca. It's too dangerous. She's too powerful, and we don't know yet how big this conspiracy is. For all we know, she's got half the *Stoichei* population on her side."

"Then what are you going to do?" Alex's question beats Sunny, who opens his mouth to protest.

I ignore the mutinous look on Sunny's face. "Since Bianca has killed another *Stoichei*, this changes things. Some *Stoicheia* might be more inclined to involve themselves in the situation now that one of their own has fallen victim."

"That's assuming the *Stoicheia* are not already involved in the conspiracy," Alex points out.

"I'm pretty sure they're not, at least not all of them." I pause, wondering how much I should tell him. "The *Stoicheia* have a pretty sweet deal. We function as an *oligarchia*. That affords each of them a heavy vote in any business that should arise in our community. To make Bianca queen will end all of that. They'd have to organize themselves into a court and a formal government, and they're not going to like that. Besides," I add, "I'm pretty certain the *Stoichei* I have in mind is not involved."

"Fine, fine…we don't go after Bianca," Sunny agrees. "At least, not *for now*. But I think Alex needs to come stay with us in the suite. After what happened tonight, it's not safe out there for a human."

I agree, even as Alex shakes his head.

He offers a quick shrug. "I can't. I've got Fluffy. I can't leave him."

Sunny's face lights up at the mention of Fluffy. "Bring him. I'll talk to the concierge. It'll be fine."

Alex frowns. "Are you sure? Fluffy's not a small dog. We can't exactly sneak him in here—"

"Trust me, the concierge won't say "no" to Sunny Michaels," I say, interrupting Alex's caution. "No one will stop you."

"But what about my work?" he asks. "I'm still on contract with a couple of magazines. If they decide to send me somewhere, I have to go."

"Coming and going during daylight hours should be fine," Sunny tells him. "And either Sonia or I can tag along with you on any calls you get after the sun goes down."

Alex still looks doubtful, but in the end he agrees.

"If Alex is going home to pack and get Fluffy," Sunny says, "what are we going to do?"

"We," I say with a hint of mystery, "are taking a trip down to the beach."

CHAPTER 27

ADRIENNE THE VAMPIRE'S PENTHOUSE condo is housed in one of the many steel and glass full-service buildings built into the side of the cliffs overlooking Santa Monica's beaches. Her elevator is private, her ceilings cathedral, and her western and northern walls unrelieved floor to ceiling glass. From where Sunny and I sit in her living room, we can see the white foam of the rolling waves cresting against the lonely blackness of the ocean. The thundering surf crashes through the silence of the early morning hours.

Adrienne, perched on the edge of the sofa in front of us, is flawless, from her French twist and the timeless air-brushed quality of her natural toned make-up, to her purple silk pantsuit and camel toned Manolo Blahnik heels.

I suppose superior grooming talents are natural enough when you've had six hundred years or so to master them.

Inching back on the couch cushion, Adrienne fixes us both with a mesmerizing stare of her huge ever-green eyes. She looks first to me, then to Sunny, before she speaks.

"It's good to see you've made

a full recovery, Sunny," she begins. "Your condition had Neichia very worried."

"Thank you," he mumbles, shifting his gaze to the floor. "Uh. Neichia told me you were one of those who donated blood to me. Thank you for that." Then, to my utter astonishment, I see the pink flush of a gentle blush creep up his neck under his golden brown skin.

"Of course," she says lightly. "It was nothing at all. You see, I have always enjoyed your company in so many ways. So in a way it was selfish of me to want to preserve it. I am glad to see it worked."

Sunny's flush becomes a little more pronounced, and I have to fight the urge to point out it was the anti-venom that saved Sunny, *not* the transfusions.

Adrienne then shifts her attention to me. The shade of purple she's wearing brings out matching flecks in the deep green irises of her eyes. I see golden flecks begin to glow softly, her irises seeming to move slowly like dazzling kaleidoscopes.

I recall her watching Kasra's and Khortdad's argument at Neichia's house the night of the attack. Adrienne sees things that others don't, and her intense scrutiny now makes me uncomfortable. I close my eyes, feeling sun drunk, and shake my head to physically wrench myself away from the power of her gaze.

Pemulwuy's voice whispers in my ear…. *Carradhy. Witch.*

Adrienne's friendliness does not make her my friend.

Adrienne is dangerous.

Adrienne's eyes have cleared by the time I regain control over myself. It helps to remember what has brought us to her in the first place. Only four nights ago, she told me the *Stoicheía* would not get involved because no *Stoicheía* had been attacked by this thing. Many of the *Stoicheía* would probably view the thinning of the *Neoi* ranks as a positive move towards balancing the ratio of *Stoicheía* to *Neoi* vamps. Vladimir, too, indicated unease amongst the Elders, regarding the large population of younger vampires in Los Angeles.

But now a *Stoicheí* has been killed, as well.

And not just any *Stoicheí*, but Elfie, the Relocator.

Would her death be enough to galvanize the *Stoicheía* into action?

Was Adrienne the correct person to turn to for this? She sits across from us, doing a very good job of looking harmless.

I begin conservatively. "Four nights ago, the night Sunny and I were attacked by the revenant, you indicated that I might come to you for help should I need it."

Adrienne nods. "I did. But I also indicated that my help has certain qualifications." She uncrosses her legs and leans forward. "I'm neither among the oldest nor the most powerful in the *Koinon*. I believe I told you I'd be most useful in my ability to keep you apprised of any changes in *Stoicheí* opinion about this creature, or their willingness to help. I regret to say that no such changes of heart have taken place. This matter remains a problem for the *Neoi* only. I'm sorry."

I glance at Sunny. This is more or less what I expected to hear. Sunny remains silent, sipping his bloody tea while watching the waves break down below on the beach. His face is unreadable.

I look back to Adrienne. "I have some new information that might change this attitude of non-involvement among the *Stoicheía*."

Adrienne's elegant features register mild surprise. "Only the death of a *Stoichei* would bring that about."

"There has been such a death."

Adrienne's deep-set eyes widen ever so slightly. "By the creature?"

"No," I admit. "Not by the creature. By the creature's master."

"Tell me," she orders calmly. "Tell me everything you know. Please begin the night of the attack and leave nothing out. This is very important."

So I tell her everything. Adrienne listens silently without interruption. Sunny also remains uncharacteristically silent, but, then again, he'd been unconscious for most of that time.

"So Elfreida is gone then," Adrienne says once I complete my account. "That is most unfortunate. She will be very difficult to replace."

"I hadn't really thought of it that way," I concede, "but you're correct. Our *Koinon* cannot function for long without a *Riassegnore*."

Adrienne sits silently for a few moments, deep in thought. When she finally speaks, her words make my heart sink.

"Elfie's murder alone," she says, "might not be enough to rouse the rest of the *Stoicheía* into action. If what you say is true, that Bianca is this creature's master and is, therefore, the mastermind behind these murders, there are many amongst us who would think twice before tangling with her."

I open my mouth to interrupt, but Adrienne holds up her hand. "Furthermore," she continues, "these murders are evidence in and of themselves that the time has come for a formal *politeia* to be established in Los Angeles. There's been much talk of this lately amongst the *Stoicheía*, and apparently Bianca has taken it to heart. But if we come together to bring Bianca down, who or what will stop the next ambitious tyrant from attempting to seize power? Perhaps their methods will be even more violent than Bianca's? This would be bad, and not only for the *Neoi* vampires. The security and secrecy of the entire *Koinon* could be threatened."

"So you won't help us," I say dully.

"I will help you, but only if you help me in return."

I hesitate. "What do you have in mind?"

"Have you ever heard of a *krisis*?" she asks.

Sunny and I both shake our heads.

"Tsk, tsk, Sonia. You're terribly ignorant of our ways. Sunny, I can understand—he's still a child. But you, Sonia… Being raised vampire in Australia without a *mater* or *pater* to teach you our ways has made you little more than a child yourself, though I know that you are at least two centuries old."

She gives me no chance to respond. "A *krisis* is a trial adjudicated by the most senior elders of the vampire *Koinon*, the *dikasterion*. Although we have never held a formal *krisis* in Los Angeles, the tradition itself predates *hetaireiai* and will be perfectly legal within our *Koinon*."

"Not to sound rude or anything," Sunny interjects, "but if that is the case, then why do we need your help? Why can't we just call our own *krisis*?"

Adrienne smiles at him indulgently. "Because, young one, only an elder, or in our case a *Stoichei*, can call a *krisis*, and only *Stoicheía* can hear the case as *dikastai*. And since we have no tradition of *krisis* in Los Angeles, it will most likely take several *Stoicheía* to call this *krisis*. I will have to call upon my allies in order to push this through."

"And what happens if the *dikastes* find Bianca guilty?" I ask.

"She will be put to death, along with any followers found guilty along with her."

"That'll work." A vision of Constanzo flashes through my mind. "And what do we have to do in return for this?"

"You two must take me as your *Archoatess*."

There was that dangerous terminology again. The rebellious Australian in me doesn't like the sounds of it. "What exactly would that entail?"

"As I just said, the consensus among the *Stoicheía* is that the time has come for a *politeia* to be established in Los Angeles. That *politeia* will need a king or a queen. I want to be that queen."

"You want to be *basilissa* of Los Angeles?" I ask, incredulous. "Why?"

"Why, indeed," she replies. "I suppose mainly to keep those like Bianca from seizing power. And if it wasn't Bianca, it would probably be Khortdad, which, believe me, would have been much, much worse. I believe that the time has come for us to become a proper kingdom, to join the rest of the world and take a seat on the *Synedrion*. The era of benevolent *oligarchia* has passed, my friends, and the era of Constitutional Law, *Nomos*, is dawning. I want the throne for myself, mainly because of the many whom I'd prefer not to see have it."

"But what about Vladimir? Or Siroun?" I ask. "Surely the throne should go to one of them. They're the oldest and most powerful in our *Koinon*."

"I agree with you. It would be preferable for someone of Vladimir's or Siroun's age and power to assume the throne, but unfortunately with such age and power often comes a sort of apathy regarding worldly affairs. Both Vladimir and Siroun live as recluses, no longer involving themselves in the affairs of the vampire *Koinon*. Neither of them have any desire to rule Los Angeles. Therefore, it must fall to lesser vampires."

"It's true," Sunny agrees. "We hardly ever see the old ones anymore." Focusing on me, he says, "Even you decided to come to Adrienne rather than asking Vladimir for help with Bianca. On some level you knew he wouldn't be much help, although he's far more powerful."

Out of the corner of my eye, I see Adrienne frown slightly at the "far more powerful" part of his speech. But I have to agree with Sunny's assessment regarding Vladimir. Vladimir hadn't told me outright that he would not help me any further, but I definitely got the sense that he was already as involved as he wanted to be and that I must go elsewhere for any further assistance.

"So you have seen Vladimir," Adrienne says. "Not quite what you would expect, is he?"

"No," I answer dismissively, "he's not. But let's get back to the whole queen of Los Angeles thing. I get it that you want to rule, and I get it that you believe you'll be a better ruler than most. But what I don't get is why you need our help? Surely this is a matter for *Stoicheia*. What exactly do you expect from Sunny and me in this bargain? What can we give you that others can't?"

The surf continues to thunder below as I ask my questions. Now the waves sound closer as the tide comes in.

"It's a question of numbers," Adrienne replies. "As I mentioned before, I'm neither the oldest nor the most powerful in the *Koinon*. To be perfectly candid, I'm not even the third most powerful. In order for me to become queen, I need assistance to build my client base. I have my *Stoicheía* allies, certainly, but I need *Neoi* allies, as well. I don't know if either of you are aware of this, or if you've already been approached by other *Stoicheía*, but for the last six months or so many of the *Stoicheía* have been courting followers from amongst the *Neoi* ranks. They're building their own private armies of supporters."

Suddenly I understand why my instincts told me not to trust the *Neoi* vampires at Ely's party. And why I didn't turn to them after Sunny and I had been attacked. Even when Adrienne told me the *Stoicheía* would do nothing about the revenant, and that some of them even thought culling the *Neoi* population wasn't such a bad thing, my first instinct had been to go after the revenant alone rather than turn to my fellow *Neoi* vampires for help. There's no telling how many of them already work for the *Stoicheía*, nor how many of those *Stoicheía* are in league with Bianca.

"I can't give you specifics about what I'll need you to do in the next six months," Adrienne continues, "or in the next year or two years, but I must be able to count on your support when I make my bid for power. I need guarantees that you'll work for me, not against me."

I nod slowly as she delivers this little speech, though I get the distinct impression she's leaving out something important. Nevertheless, I admire her candor, and I can tell that, strictly speaking, she's telling the truth—just not the whole truth.

But I still don't like the sound of this new *politeia*, and I don't like committing myself to such nebulous future responsibilities. Still, I can see the logic of Adrienne's arguments. If I had to make the choice right then between Bianca or Adrienne as queen, my vote would be for Adrienne all the way. In fact, the only other *Stoichei* I can think of that I might have preferred to see on the throne over Adrienne would have been Elfie, but Elfie is dead.

"So, in return for our support when you make your bid for power, you will initiate this *krisis,* which will try Bianca for her crimes against the *Koinon*?"

Adrienne nods. "That's correct."

"But if you want to be queen so badly, why don't you just initiate this *krisis,* anyway? Isn't it already in your best interests?"

At this, she simply smiles enigmatically. Once more I see the golden flecks in her eyes begin to glow, but this time I look away before I can be ensnared.

"I have my reasons," she says, "for staying out of this particular fight. At the very least, there will be a brief period of time between the moment when Bianca becomes aware that a *dikasterion* is being formed against her and the moment of her final arrest, when she will be free to either confront the vampire accusing her of murder or flee Los Angeles altogether."

"She's going to flee then," I say flatly. "She'll be safely out of the city before we can bring her to justice."

"Do you really think so?" Adrienne asks me. "Perhaps then you do not understand Bianca's position very well. Do you really think that after all this effort, she will simply pack her bags, as you say, and begin living as a fugitive?"

Before I can answer, Adrienne answers for me. "She won't flee. Through her spies, for which she is famous, even among the *Stoicheía*, she'll learn that I'm the one accusing her, and she will then come after me. I'll be in danger until she's finally arrested."

"Can you fight her?" I ask. "How much of a match are you?"

Adrienne considers this a moment, and I notice that her eyes are back to normal. "I'm older than Bianca, but it will still be a close fight. She has more followers than I do. She also practiced the dark arts during her years as a human courtesan. Many of us have wondered if she brought any of those powers over with her when she passed out of her mortal life. We don't know, so I honestly don't know who would win."

I look at Sunny, and he nods almost imperceptibly. I nod back.

"Okay, we're in, Adrienne. How long will it take for this *dikasterion* to be formed?"

"It will take about 48 hours to put the process in motion. Then once the formalities are in place, the *krisis* will probably take no longer than a night. The execution will follow immediately after the verdict is delivered."

"You seem pretty convinced that Bianca will be found guilty."

"Yes. Vampire justice usually depends upon which party has the strongest following. But in this case, Bianca may be beyond the help of her allies and clients," Adrienne says with conviction. "Bringing this thing into the New World from the Old is bad enough. It's dangerous, and it threatens the security of the whole *Koinon*. When she sent it out to attack Sunny in public, she jeopardized our secrecy. Add Elfie's murder, and we're precariously close to a state of anarchy. Bianca will almost certainly be found guilty."

"Alright then." I stand and Sunny follows. "You can count on our help in any way that you need it. How can we contact you in the meantime?"

"You can't," she tells us as we shake hands. "I will go into hiding. Until the *krisis*, you will be on your own unless I contact you first."

CHAPTER 28

SUNNY AND I BEGIN the thirty minute drive back to Hollywood in silence. I find myself so wrapped up in my own thoughts, it's not until we've traveled several miles on 10 East that I notice Sunny's lack of chatter. Glancing over at him, I see that he sits slouched low in the driver's seat, his head hunkered down between his shoulders. I catch glimpses of his face in the brief headlight flashes from the westbound cars, and I see his lingering dark scowl. But Sunny has never been one to suffer in silence. I chalk this unusual behavior up to exhaustion. It's nearly 5am and only a few hours earlier he'd been close to death. I don't know, and neither does he, how long it will take before he's back to his normal strength.

In any case, his silence suits my own brooding mood quite well. I have my first chance to think through the implications of what occurred. Sunny and I are now Adrienne's clients, whatever that means, and in return she's promised to galvanize the *Stoicheía* into action and take care of our little Bianca/revenant problem for us. And then she intends to make a bid to become Queen of Los Angeles, and she expects Sunny and me to help.

Although getting rid of Bianca and her revenant qualifies as a definite plus for us—particularly the part where we get to return to our respective homes—I can't help but wonder if we're actually getting the raw end of the deal in this bargain. The more I think about it, the more I realize I'm not entirely sold on the idea of bringing vampire *politeia* to Los Angeles. What exactly would that mean for us?

The only other city I've ever spent time in is Sydney, where I lived from 1946 to 1977, the year I made the move to America. When I first moved to Sydney, there had been a nascent *politeia* in place, but I'd always stood outside of it. There had never been very many vampires in Australia, and what few lived in Sydney at the end of World War II had better things to do with their time than bother with me. I was the crazed witch from the Outback, who had spent a century in solitude living off blood from her livestock.

In truth, I think they were afraid of me, as if I had some sort of disease they feared they might catch if they spent too much time in my company. And to be sure, I was a little crazed in those first couple of years back in civilization. Life had passed me by, and all at once I found myself catapulted into a modern world that seemed so alien to me. Even though Sydney was a Coven with a Queen and the rule of Law, they'd left me alone, so I don't know what living in such a structured *politeia* means. What I do know is that Los Angeles's Coven won't leave me alone. My new alliance with Adrienne guarantees that, one way or another, my life here in the last holdout of the Wild West is about to change in a major way.

I cannot help but wonder, however, just how inevitable the establishment of a vampire coven really is? Adrienne had made it sound inevitable, and her arguments certainly seemed sound enough. If what she said is true, that the *Stoicheía* are talking about the establishment of a coven, then Bianca's bid for power will be the first of many, should she fail. And, as Adrienne suggested, who knows how brutal these successive attempts will be?

Suddenly, Sunny pulls a hard right and cuts diagonally across four lanes of traffic at high speed in order to make the La Cienega exit. For his efforts, he wins a gasp and a smack on the arm from me, a blasting horn blow from a car who had to slam on the brakes in order to miss him, and flashing high beams from the Range Rover he cut off at the exit.

"Sorry," he mutters as I yank on my seatbelt, which has seized up and now cuts into my collarbone. "I was thinking about something. Lost track of where we were."

"You just need some sleep," I grumble as the seatbelt finally releases its death grip and gives me some slack. "Just stay awake until we get to the hotel." I know better than to ask him if he wants me to drive. Doing so would accomplish nothing more than provoking an argument.

"Who else amongst the *Stoicheía* might be considering the throne of Los Angeles for themselves?" I ask suddenly. Maybe talking will keep him awake. "If Bianca is brought down, and Adrienne fails in her bid, who will be next?"

"No one good." Sonny shakes his head. "Khortdad? If anyone is secretly plotting world domination, it's gotta be him."

I nod. "Agreed. And Los Angeles seems as good a place to start as any. But I cannot imagine Khortdad garnering support from the other *Stoicheía*." He is a small, bitter man with a streak of cruelty running through him, making him generally unpopular.

"And Kasra has too strong a hold on him. She'd be a better candidate for the throne if she wanted it," Sunny says.

I glance at him, surprised. I had no idea Sunny was watching the *Stoicheía* as closely as I was. In truth, I tended to dismiss Sunny when it came to intelligence. I might want to amend that.

"What about Anastasios? The Greek would probably be happy to take the throne, though he faces the same problem as Khortdad—he's not going to win any popularity contests any time soon. The Macedonian Jovan would be a better candidate, and he has the right combination of ruthlessness and intelligence needed to secure the throne. I'd put him on the short list."

Sunny grunts as he switches on his high beams. "If there's a short list, add Dragomir, Vasil, and Zádor right after him."

Once again, I am surprised by Sunny's familiarity with the power brokers in the *Stoicheía*. "True," I say. "A Romanian, a Bulgarian, and a Hungarian. Those three have the capacity for violence needed in a long-term power struggle. Not a good sign."

As we pass through the darkened and deserted La Cienega Park, I turn my attention to the ladies. "I think Kasra's place on the list is tentative in the first position. I don't know if ruling Los Angeles would appeal to her. We can't forget though that her people built the Persian Empire, and if that's indicative of her natural inclinations, I'd say we can expect serious trouble from her. What do you think of Siobhan?"

"The Hebrew vampire? Same as Kasra, I'd say tentative at best."

"True, she's equally difficult to read and also dangerous in her potential for power strategies." I pause a moment, in thought. "We'd better add the names Derya and Grusha after Kasra and Siobhan.

"The Turk and the Russian?"

"Yes. They lack the subtlety of Kasra and Siobhan, but I think they have the potential for violence."

"Aren't Derya and Grusha a couple?"

I nod. "They are, yes. Which makes them even more dangerous united. And what about Bianca?" I continue, "Where does she fit in all of this? Do you think she'd really be that easy to defeat? I mean, lets assume that all of these vamps have been chomping at the bit for the throne of Los Angeles, and Bianca is the one who has come out on top. Or maybe she's just the first to come up with a workable plan. I think I may have been underestimating Bianca all these years."

Sunny's voice is quiet. "Do you think Adrienne has been underestimating her as well?"

As we sail across Wilshire Boulevard on a long green light, I stare blankly out my window at the row of darkened, empty restaurants, wondering for the first time what exactly Bianca will do when she learns of the *dikasterion*. Adrienne told us she will have to go into hiding, so she clearly expects trouble. And surely Bianca won't just sit around passively waiting for this *dikastai* to prosecute her—she will fight. Once again, I wonder how extensive Bianca's plot must be. How many vampires are involved? How many other *Stoicheía*? Are any of those on my list of usual suspects already in league with her?

As Sunny turns us onto Sunset Boulevard, I feel a chill

pass through my body. "Bianca is no dummy," I say. "Of course, her plot is far more extensive than importing a monster from the Old World to kill off the *Neoi* vamps. It has to be. She's got to have some sort of following among the more powerful *Stoicheía*. But maybe not *too* powerful; she won't want the competition."

Then it hits me.

Oh, my God.

That is what Adrienne left out in our little interview.

I know exactly what will happen when Bianca catches wind of the *dikasterion*, and I know exactly why Adrienne has gone into hiding. We are on the brink of civil war.

As we pull up to the hotel's porte cochere and ditch the car, I wrack my brain over and over again as we make our way up to our room. Have we done the right thing going to Adrienne? Could we have solved this problem another way?

No.

Even if we miraculously manage to take out Bianca, her posse of known associates and unknown *Stoicheía* supporters, and kill the monster, it will take only one *Stoicheí* from my list to step up and easily take her place. And if a *Stoicheí* as relatively conservative as Adrienne entertains thoughts of grandeur, the others surely do as well. Only three weeks ago, Neichia speculated that we may all be in trouble. Now, I know exactly what she meant.

"Sunny," I say, once we close the door to our suite behind us. "It's going to be war."

I am in a daze. The full comprehension of the past three week's events hits me square in the face, along with exhaustion. And there's one more problem to worry about. A big problem.

Neichia still hasn't called me back.

I've been watching Sunny closely, and I see nothing to indicate that he's anything other than a perfectly healthy vampire specimen. Still, I'm worried. Really worried. What if there are going to be long term effects of the revenant's venom? God, I need to talk to Neichia.

The sunrise has turned the world outside into dreamy shades of periwinkle and violet, and I can't take any more. I need my bed. I tell myself everything will be okay after I've had a good twelve hours of sleep. But, even in my debilitated state, I taste my own lie.

Things are going to get a lot worse over the next twelve hours, and many of us may face the launch into oblivion. Sunny and I will need to get off the Strip and find a more remote hideout, and who knows whether we will be able to convince Alex to come or not. Since he did not return to the hotel, he's obviously not taking our warnings seriously. He's probably sitting in his apartment, drinking coffee while scrolling on his phone. Maybe he's trying to decide if he'll take a shower and switch on his scanners for breaking news stories first, or take Fluffy on a quick walk around the block. Nice simple things. I've been wrong to involve him in my world.

Then, as I head wordlessly towards my bedroom, Sunny calls after me. "Sonia! Sonia, please. Come back. I have to ask you something before you go to sleep."

Perplexed, I shuffle over to the armchair he holds out for me. Flinging myself down with all the panache of a sack of potatoes, I'm even more surprised when he doesn't take a seat across from me, but instead kneels on the floor at my feet, taking my hands into his own.

"Sonia," he presses, his voice fraught with urgency, "I need to ask you to please, *please*, promise me you will do what I'm going to ask you now."

At the second "please," he kisses my hands and bends over them, touching them to his forehead in a gesture of supplication. I stare at the top of his bent head, alarmed until he gradually straightens up and looks again into my face. His troubled eyes hold so much pain, I fight the urge to say yes to whatever he asks of me, just to bring my happy-go-lucky Sunny back to me. But these are not happy-go-lucky times, and I'm not about to agree to anything without first hearing what it is.

"If you are going to ask what I think you're going to ask," I warn, "the answer is 'no.' No way."

"I need you to leave town," he tells me. "Leave town now. Pack your bag, get in the McLaren, and drive until you are out of the state—"

"Absolutely not," I insist, not letting him finish. "No way."

"I own a house in Tucson. You can stay there for the night, but you'll have to leave the next morning—"

I wave him off. "No. I'm not leaving."

"You can't stay anywhere attached to me. After Arizona, you must ditch the car and then you can go anywhere. Just not back to California—"

"Blast it, Sunny!" I yell to stop him. "I bloody damn well said *no*."

He continues. "Just don't contact me. I can't know where you're going. It's the only way you'll be safe."

"You're not listening." I'm shouting now to shock him into shutting up. "Stop telling me what to do, because *I'm not going anywhere.*"

I wrench my hands angrily out of his grasp and brace them on the chair's arms so I can hoist myself up. But even as I do this, he bends his head down to rest on my knees, and he takes a deep, shuddering breath. His body chemistry has altered, shifting his scent ever so slightly. With a shock I realize that I am picking up the unique salty signature scent of tears.

I relax back into the seat and after a moment's hesitation, bring my hand up to stroke the soft curls on his bent head.

"You must leave," he says quietly, choking back a sob. "If it weren't for me, you wouldn't be in this mess." His bowed head pushes into my hand as I continue to run my fingers through his hair.

"How can you say that?" I ask, my voice low and soothing. "Of course, I would be here. You have nothing to do with that."

"Yes, I do!" he cries fiercely. "The creature came after me. Not you! If you had just left that alley when I told you to, you wouldn't be here in this mess."

"And neither would you," I point out, though still carefully keeping my voice soft and soothing. "And you don't know whether that thing would have come after me. For all we know, I was next on Bianca's list."

"No, that's not true," he says heavily. "Bianca and I have a history I never told you about. That's why she hates me. And it's why I hate her. She sent the creature after me for revenge. You would have been safe."

"If that's the case, then she'd probably have sent the revenant after me in a jealous rage." I let out a quick, light laugh, hoping the joke in my voice will distract him and maybe get him to laugh, too.

"Gechina turned me as a gift for Bianca," he says heavily. "I was to be her slave, her toy. But things did not go according to her plan—I was too strong for her. I did not need her. I never needed her. And then I met you."

"She knew I loved you," he continues, shocking the laughter right out of me. "She knew I've always loved you, from the very first night we met. But she hated *me* for it, not you."

He raises his head from where it rests on my knees and looks up into my face. His tears still cling damply to his dark eyelashes and the midnight blue of his eyes burn with the inner fire of cabochon sapphires.

"I love you," he whispers. "You have to know that. I love you. I'm *in* love with you."

I feel the sting of tears as I nod slowly in acknowledgement.

"Good," he says. "Then you know why you have to leave. I can't live in this world without you. You can take Alex and go find a quiet place to hole up and be happy for a while."

"You tell me you love me," I say, smiling as fat droplets slide down my cheeks, "but then you tell me to go hole up with another man?"

He flashes the shadow of one of his boyish grins. "I like Alex. I think he's good for you. And," he continues, his smile growing a little wider, "Alex has a shelf life. I don't. I've got eternity, baby, and you're worth the wait."

I can't help but laugh.

"Besides," he goes on, "I'm not ready to settle down just yet. I've got a few more groupie orgies left in me."

I agree and say so. "Don't worry, I'm not about to slap a wedding band on you just yet."

"But someday you will," he tells me solemnly. "Someday you will."

"You're probably right. And until then I have Alex to keep me occupied, huh?"

"Yes." He pauses and takes a breath. "Somewhere far from here. I'll give you guys sixty years or so, since I know you'll stick around till the end, and then I'll come looking for you."

"And if I turn him?"

"If he survives the transition, then I will kill him." This he says with a faint smile, but I know he's serious.

"We can talk more about that later," I say dismissively. "In the meantime, we've got a civil war to worry about." I raise my hand to stop the argument before he starts it again. "I'm *not* going anywhere. And you damn well know it."

"I get it," he says with a heavy sigh, laying his head back down on my knees. "But I had to try. I don't know what I would ever do without you—I don't think I could go on,"

"And that," I tell him, running my fingers gently through his hair, "is exactly why I can't leave."

One more deep sigh, and his body shudders as the last of his pent-up sobs finally escape.

But there are no more tears.

CHAPTER 28

AUSTRALIA, NEW SOUTH WALES.

IT IS DARK IN *Owen's sparsely furnished bedroom. The only light comes from the small candle on his bedside table, whose valiant efforts still leave most of the room in shadow. On the other side of the bed stands the new bedside table that Owen built for me, and on it sits a brand new candle standing tall with a long, white wick that has never been touched by fire. Briefly, I think of lighting the new candle to give Owen's some help in its battle against the shadows, but then, looking down at my pale bare feet, I realize I am more comfortable in the darkness.*

All too soon, a quiet, almost hesitant knock sounds on the door.

"Come in," I call softly, pleased my voice doesn't falter. I look down at the shiny yellow wedding band on my left hand, wiggling my fingers against its strange feel as I hear the door slowly open. After a few moments, the door closes and I force myself to look up into the eyes of the man who is now my husband.

Owen stands in the corner of the

room farthest away from me, taking in the sight of me standing next to his bed in nothing but the fine linen chemise I had
bought to wear beneath my beautiful wedding gown. The gown
itself now hangs on the door of his wardrobe, and my stockings,
corset, and petticoats lay folded neatly on a chair. My satin slippers, now tinged slightly pink from the red dust of Australia,
are arranged neatly on the floor next to the chair.

"You've left your hair up," he says quietly. I bring my hand
up to touch the elaborate curls and braids fixed into place with
about a thousand pins earlier that day by my friend, Anne, a
lady's maid back in England.

"May I," he begins, then hesitates as he casts his eyes down
to the floor, reconsidering whatever he planned to say. Suddenly
I know he is as nervous and unsure as I am.

"Yes. Owen?" I ask, amazed at the strength in my voice. "Is
there something you would ask of me?"

"I was wondering..." He brings his eyes back up to meet
my own. "I was wondering if you would permit me to take
your hair down."

"Of course, husband," I answer, perplexed, "but you do
not need to ask. You may do whatever you like. You are now
my husband."

"No!" Welsh fire flashes in his eyes. "That is not the sort
of marriage that we will have!" More gently, he says, "I will
always ask. And you will only say yes if it suits you."

Silence falls between us as I consider the ramifications of
his words. The husband giving up the rights of master over his
wife? I have never heard such a thing before. More commonly
men try to extend and enforce these rights, never to give them
up. How could such a marriage even function?

"Well," I say finally when I realize he is still waiting for an answer, "my answer is yes. You may take my hair down."

He comes towards me then and puts a hand on each shoulder, peering intently into my face.

Vaguely, I register confusion.

Something is off. This is not what is supposed to happen. Owen is supposed to go into my old bedroom and retrieve my brush. He will carefully and gently take all the pins out, unravel the braids, and then brush out the kinks in my hair. He will then kiss my shoulder, then the back of my neck. I will turn to him and kiss him on the mouth, then we will lay down and make love. That is what is supposed to happen.

"Moira," he says to me, his eyes fixed closely onto my face, "Moira, can you hear me?"

I am confused. This is not what is supposed to happen. But how can I know what is supposed to happen? What is going on?

"Moira," he says again, "Moira, you are dreaming. This is a dream. But you need to wake up! Something is wrong!"

I close my eyes and shake my head. No. This can't be a dream. I am here with Owen. We have just been married, and this is our wedding night. We are going to make love. It is going to be wonderful, and then he will hold me as I rest my head on his shoulder, and we will sleep until morning. And then—

"No, Moira," he says, almost as if he can hear my thoughts, "This is just a dream. But you need to wake up! You need to wake up now, because something is wrong! Something is wrong, Moira! Wake up!"

"But I don't want to wake up." I sob as realization dawns on me. "I don't want you to go!"

"I won't go," he promises. "I will come back. But you have to wake up now! Something is wrong."

With a gasp, I sit bolt upright in bed and mouth a single word: Alex. Alex isn't here, he is in trouble. Something has happened to him. I know it as certainly as I know my own name.

Throwing the bed covers aside, I leap out of bed and rush out into the living room where Sunny lounges on the sofa like a panther, clad only in his cashmere pajama bottoms and sipping a pint glass of O-negative through a straw.

"Good evening, gorgeous," he says, keeping his eyes glued to the TV screen. "I've bought *Twilight* on Amazon. Care to join?"

"No!" My voice is high pitched and loud in my agitation. "We've got to go. *Now*. Something's happened to Alex."

"Don't worry about Alex," he says in exaggerated reassurance. "He's *fiiine*. I'm sure he'll be here any minute. Come watch this with me, the guy playing Edward looks like the valet at the Roosevelt who scratched my car—"

"You've seen him? You've spoken to him?"

"The valet? Of course, I did. I spoke to his manager, too, and got his ass—"

"*No!*" I roar. "*Alex.* Have you spoken to Alex?"

"Why," he says patiently, tearing his eyes away from the TV screen for the first time, "would I speak to Alex? He's probably been working all day. That's what humans do."

"So you haven't spoken to him?"

"*NO.* I haven't spoken with Alex." Sunny's eyes flash, a warning that I'm pissing him off.

"Then we need to get over there now and check on him." I modulate my voice. I need Sunny to be helpful and cooperative, and when he's angry he is neither of those things.

Sunny stares at me for a long moment. "What makes you think he's in trouble?" he asks finally, slurping the last dregs of his drink through the straw.

After a moment's hesitation, I tell him the truth. "Owen told me."

His eyebrows climb towards his hairline, "And when did *Owen* tell you Alex was in trouble?"

"Just now." I ignore the clear disbelief in Sunny's voice. "While I was sleeping."

"*Owen* comes to you in dreams?" You could cut his incredulity with a knife.

"Yes, he does," I say defensively. "I'd thought they were just memories, but now it seems it's really him."

"Like a ghost?"

"Sort of. Yes. Like a ghost."

"There's no such thing as ghosts, Sonia."

Now I'm surprised. "*You* don't believe in ghosts? How can a vampire not believe in ghosts?"

"There's. No. Such. Thing." He pretends to be patient. "Ghosts, ha."

We glare at each other across the living room. Without looking, Sunny turns off his movie so he can devote his full attention to staring me down. It works.

"Fine," I say, "but I know what I know. I don't care whether you believe me or not. I am going over to Alex's now. I would appreciate it if you came with me in case I run into trouble."

"Okay," he grumbles. "But I'm coming only so I can see the look on your face when Alex opens the door all safe and sound. Besides," he adds, "I want to meet Fluffy."

Well, what can I say? When I'm right, I'm right. Or, to be fair, I should say that when Owen's right, he's right. Not that I'd doubted my paranormal experience for one second. The place on my shoulders where Owen touched me still tingles. I've been dreaming of Owen for years. The realization that it is really him left me overjoyed at first. But now that I've had some time to think about it, I find myself conflicted. My love life is complicated enough without adding my long-dead, love-of-my life husband into the mix.

Sunny and I trudge human-style up the stairs in Alex's apartment building to the fourth floor, while Sunny explains the payment he plans to exact for strong-arming him into this wild goose-chase. Once we make it back to the hotel, with Alex safely in tow, I will have to watch the entire *Twilight* series with him, start to finish, with no complaints or sarcastic commentary. Alex will have to watch, too, since this whole thing is his fault in the first place.

"You know you're lucky," he tells me, "it could be a lot worse. You're getting off easy with these sparkly vampires. But when we get back to the hotel…" His voice trails off into silence. I've just opened the door from the stairwell to the fourth floor, and we are hit full in the face by the pungent, coppery, unmistakable smell of blood. Canine blood.

As we stand there a moment, trying to detect the presence of any other vampires, we glean additional information from the blood scent. Strongly present are the pheromones released for aggression and fear. This blood was shed while the animal protected something or someone. And it still lived. It still bled somewhere on this floor.

Sunny suddenly is all business.

Conscious of the presence of humans about—at 7pm, the floor buzzes with human activity in their apartments—we walk slowly to Alex's door. We adjust our speed to match that of two humans casually making their way down the hall to a friend's door.

Just because we aren't using our vampire speed, that doesn't mean that our vampire senses are not busy. Our slow rate of progress down the hall enables us to pick up a great deal of information along the way. By the time we reach Alex's door, we both know that Constanzo, along with two or three other vampires not known to us, had passed through this way. Alex also recently passed this way, although we couldn't say for sure if he numbered in their company or not.

The fact that I can detect faint excretions of the human pheromones for anger and fear suggests that he might have been in their company on the way out. But they didn't take the stairwell down; they must have used the elevator, probably to ensure that they didn't run into us. Vamps always take the stairs. We move faster than elevators.

Or sometimes, if no one is around, we jump.

Once we make it to Alex's apartment, Sunny tries the door and finds it unlocked. As we swing the door wide, now confident there are no more vampires left on this floor, the smell of blood once again smacks us full in the face. And now we can also hear the rapid heartbeat of a wounded and frightened animal.

Fluffy.

There isn't much left for us to do in the apartment other than tend to the dog. We know who has taken Alex and, by the rate of scent decay, we can tell that he's been gone less than two hours—probably snatched at about the same time Owen came to warn me.

"See what you can learn," Sunny growls. "I'm going to find Fluffy and see if anything can be done."

He then heads to the kitchen, where the sound of the heartbeat is coming from, leaving me alone in Alex's entryway. I hear the low rumbles of a growl followed shortly by a whimper and two weak thumps of a tail. Sunny has found his quarry.

Alex's apartment is a disaster—or some of it is. I reconstruct what happened with little difficulty. They entered through the window, and he made his stand with only a baseball bat to protect himself in the opposite corner. He went down with a fight. The baseball bat is shattered, a sign that they cornered him there.

The rest of the living room is pristine. This was no battle. And there aren't any traces of human blood anywhere in the room, suggesting that he'd been sitting in the living room and immediately backed into the corner with his bat while they entered the apartment. They had cornered him and then torn Fluffy apart. Why? A bat and a dog are no match for any vampire, and Alex faced three or four of them. It would only take one to stroll right up to him and relieve him of his weapon. Even if he'd hit them square in the face with it, they wouldn't have been seriously hurt.

And the dog? Why the dog?

Dammit.

They wanted Alex scared so that I'd pick up the residual scent of his fear. It worked. He was scared. But also angry. Very angry. Judging by the way the bat had been pulverized, he'd given one or two of them a pretty good couple of whacks before they took it away from him.

So they came in through the window, mutilated his dog, and toyed with him in the corner all so I would pick up his fear. For what?

So rage would get the better of me and I'd rush to his rescue without taking the time to pick up reinforcements along the way. As I stride to the French Doors, cold, hard anger thrums through my veins… and there is something else.

Carradhy… Witch.

Shut-up, I answer. I can only take one paranormal experience in a day. Pemulwuy will have to mind his business until tomorrow.

Constanzo and his goons have made a critical mistake. They've done their job too well. Oh, yes. I am angry. Angry to the point I'm almost numb to it, and I am thinking more clearly than ever before. They won't harm Alex until after Sunny and I arrive. Worth nothing to them dead, they'll keep him whole and safe in the meantime. And terrified. I know this with the same certainty that I know Owen, *my actual Owen,* came to warn me in my dreams.

Witch, my Maker whispers this time.

God Dammit, shut up!

Passing through the French Doors, I come upon Sunny crouching next to the prone and bloody body of Fluffy. Alex's dog has been torn down the side from neck to tail, and through the bloody fur I see the shiny white glint of bone across his ribcage. Looking up at me with his one brown eye, he offers me a single feeble thump of his tail in greeting.

"He's torn up pretty bad," Sunny says soothingly as he strokes Fluffy's head, "and he's lost a lot of blood. But his heartbeat is strong. He may have a chance. Did you pick up anything from the living room?"

"Just that Constanzo and his followers are going to die tonight," I say as I squat down to stroke Fluffy's head. "They left no clues to their whereabouts, so I suppose they've taken him to Bianca's. It's the most obvious place I can think of."

Sunny straightens up. "Bianca's it is. But first I need to arrange for a neighbor to take Fluffy to the emergency veterinary hospital. I figure we'll just have to say he got attacked by a mountain lion while camping."

"Mountain lion? That'll make the news. It'll send the forest rangers out hunting for P-22."

"I know. But how else could he have sustained these wounds? I'm not going to just let Fluffy lay here and die. And he will die unless he gets to the vet ASAP."

I sigh, stroking Fluffy's head. "Go work your magic on the neighbor. Try the one next door; I think she watches Fluffy when Alex goes out of town. I'll stay here with the dog."

"Alright," he says, flashing me his most devastating smile. "Wish me luck." He straightens his clothes and then swaggers casually out of the kitchen, oozing sex all the way.

The good Samaritan next door won't know what hit her.

CHAPTER 29

Turns out, Sunny's sexual charisma isn't needed. Alex's next door neighbor, a matronly Polish woman named Mrs. Zielinski, agrees to take Fluffy to the veterinary hospital right away, no questions asked. When she follows Sunny into Alex's apartment. I see the lady's kind heart breaking when she sees the state of her "handsome puppy dog."

She doesn't leave the dog's side while Sunny gingerly gathers the Fluffster in his arms and carries him downstairs to Mrs. Zielinski's Volvo station wagon. She strokes the poor dog's head and murmurs to him in Polish all the way. Apparently, this is not Fluffy's first ride in her car, as she already has a clean dog bed and several other doggie amenities ready to go. Watching them pull away from the curb in front of the Fleur de Lis Apartments, Sunny and I feel satisfied we're leaving Fluffy in capable hands.

Now we just need to rescue Fluffy's owner from a nest of evil vampires in Beverly Hills. Easier said than done. We don't even know how many vamps we'll need to fight. Apparently on our own. While Sunny wasted his charms on Mrs. Zielinski, I'd placed a few calls and found that my two most powerful contacts were unavailable: Adrienne has gone into hiding, and remains unreachable by phone. Vladimir asserts his pacifism, wanting no part of this war one way or the other. I briefly consider calling Neichia again, but dismiss that idea: Neichia—and her research— are far too valuable to our *Koinon* to risk her in a turf war over Los Angeles. No one can readily take her place should anything happen to her.

I left a message on Adrienne's voicemail, although I have little hope of her running to our rescue. A fight like this is dangerous and she's too smart to risk her neck when we know nothing about what we're up against. Bianca may have amassed a private vampire army.

Once Mrs. Zielinski and Fluffy finally pass out of sight, defeat settles on my shoulders, but I turn to Sunny, anyway. "I guess it's off to Bianca's to fight an impossible fight."

Sunny strokes his chin while deep in thought. "Are you sure you want to do this?"

I know what he's asking me. Alex is not officially my human. But now that he is in danger, my feelings for him are clear. I can't love him. He belongs to another. But I do feel *something* for him, and it is not disgust. No, those feelings passed almost immediately. He means something to me. At the very least he is my friend... perhaps a little more. And it is my fault he is in this mess. I cannot leave him to die.

"Yes," I say, resignation clear in my voice. "I want to do this. I *need* to do this."

Sunny sends me a sharp look. "But not with that attitude, we're not. I have no intention of dying tonight. But if we're going to make it through this, I need you charged and ready to go. We're both dead if you admit defeat now. As much as I love you, I'm not ready to die for you just yet."

"You have a plan?" I ask in disbelief. "How can you already have a plan when we don't know exactly who we're fighting?"

"I don't have a plan. *Yet.* I'm still working out some simple details. But for Simple Detail Number One, we need to make a short stop before we head out for Beverly Hills."

"A short stop? Where?"

"You'll see," he tells me. "It's on the way. Sort of."

Sunny's mysterious destination is a large, windowless building in Culver City with an adjacent parking lot. It looks unremarkable in every way, from its generic box shape to its putty-colored stucco. The parking lot has about ten spaces, plus a designated loading area near the door, which suggests it's a business of some sort, though no sign advertises what that business might be.

Whatever it is, Sunny is familiar with the place.

I stand at the door, eyeing the security camera fixed on us, silently blinking its little red light while Sunny expertly punches in a series of numbers on the keypad next to the door. The keypad responds by issuing a long, obnoxious beeeeep and angrily flashes its red light at Sunny.

He mutters something to himself, then punches in the numbers again, this time more deliberately. I look on silently while Sunny tries again, and then yet again before the keypad flashes a green light. We hear the locking mechanisms in the door go through a series of complicated maneuvers, each with its own sound, until finally a heavy deadbolt retracts with a loud reverberating click.

"I changed all my passwords last week," he explains as he holds the reinforced door open for me to follow him.

Once inside, Sunny rearms the security system and flicks on the lights. We stand in a long hallway lined with gold records hanging on the wall. The place reeks of stale cigarettes and marijuana smoke.

Sunny marches down the hall and uses a set of keys to unlock another door. By now, I know where we are. Sure enough, once through the door, I'm standing in the control room of a music studio, complete with a massive, complicated-looking mixing board and countless other electronic gizmos.

"I thought you'd moved your studio up to Malibu," I say as I eye all of the equipment. "This place doesn't look as though it's been stripped down."

Through the glass window over the mixing board, overlooking the actual studio, I see the room is still littered with guitar amps, coils upon coils of neatly wrapped cables, and towards the back a fully assembled drum kit. A small isolation booth for recording vocals still has its stool and microphone.

"I did." Sunny slides into the captain's chair behind the mixing board. "This is the first studio I had before I moved up to Malibu." As he speaks, he fumbles around under the mixing board, searching for something.

"Then why does this place still look so new? And why is the computer new?" I ask, still perplexed.

"Ah-ha!" he crows triumphantly. I hear a click, followed by the sound of a deadbolt sliding open in the far wall.

My eyebrows climb. "Secret door?"

"Yup." He walks to the wall and gives a section of it a little push, causing the door to disengage and swing open. "But to answer your earlier question, I moved everything up to Malibu, while I kept this place for sentimental reasons. But I've been moving everything back down here. Malibu is too isolated."

"Ah." I hear him rummaging around in the space behind the secret door.

"I'm too much of a people person," he explains as he rematerializes, holding a Dirty Harry .44 Magnum in one hand and a 12 gauge sawed-off shotgun in the other. He places these on the countertop next to the computer, then disappears back into the secret room.

"I've been looking for a new place for the last few months," he calls out over the noise of his vigorous rummaging. "There's a place in the Pacific Palisades I might buy, but the damn owners can't make up their minds whether they want to sell or not. They're a nice old couple..."

He stops talking and this time he reappears with a long, slightly curved Samurai *katana*, whose wicked blade is sheathed in a gorgeous gold-lacquered *saya* wrapped near the hilt with a golden silk *sageo* for tying the scabbard into the belt. This he places on the table, where its conspicuous elegance looks out of place next to the two guns.

"The old couple wants to move permanently to their vacation home in Newport Beach, but their grown children are having some problems letting go of the house they grew up in."

"The Pacific Palisades still isn't all that close, you know." I pick up the *katana*, and pull it from its sheath. It looks deadly. "It's still about a thirty minute drive from my place."

"True." He ducks back in the room and then emerges with a sheathed Bowie knife and a shorter, black ops military-looking blade in one hand and a 9mm Browning Hi-Power in the other, all of which he adds to the growing pile of weapons on the counter. "But it's a lot closer than Malibu."

I sheath the blade. "Why not Santa Monica?" I call after him as he disappears once more into the secret room.

"Santa Monica is okay, I guess." Now he's back, this time with a machete and a shoulder rig for a gun. "And there are plenty of people around, which is a plus. I like the sounds of their industry."

I watch him add the machete and shoulder rig to the pile. "That'll make for good hunting."

"I never hunt near my studio," he calls out from the hidden room.

Now Sunny comes out of the secret room with a weapon I've never seen before. "Jesus Christ, what the hell is *that*?"

"This," he says with a wolfish grin, holding out the massive handgun for me to see, "is The Beast. It's called a Desert Eagle."

"It looks heavy," I say, taking in the massive barrel and telescopic sight. "Where in the hell did you get it?"

He carefully places the Desert Eagle next to his cache of weapons. "I think this one came from a drug dealer."

"And why," I finally ask, "do you have an arsenal in your recording studio?"

"Security." He shrugs. "I have a lot of very expensive gear in here, and with all the soundproofing, music studios are ideal places to rob. Someone could break in here, shoot me dead, and then rob the place, and no one would know what happened until the cleaning lady eventually discovered my body."

"But you're a vampire," I remind him. "You're your own security system. And no one could shoot you dead anyway, unless they blew your head off with a shotgun or had silver bullets. And no one has silver bullets."

"True. But I was a human producer before I was a vampire producer. Back in the day, I needed to protect myself. So I bought the Desert Eagle. The rest of this stuff people gave to me."

"All those weapons? People gave them to you?" I ask in disbelief.

I'm now sitting in the captain's chair, doing my best to overcome the urge to punch all the buttons and mess with levels on the mixing board.

"Yup. It's the same with my porn collection. I've never actually bought porn, though I have a pretty formidable collection." He pauses and glances at me, then the mixing board, and finally at the weapons. "Why don't you come over here and choose something before you mess up all my settings while I'm not looking?"

Scooting my chair closer, I go first for the large Bowie knife. The blade looks to be about thirteen inches. Both the front edge and the clipped back edge are wickedly sharp. A brass strip reinforces the heel for blocking and the trapping guard is also brass. The blade has a wooden handle, lending it a good heft and nice balance in my hand. I test the point tentatively first with my finger, then drive it into the side of one of the outboard gear cabinets. It sticks and holds. All in all, it's a pretty good knife.

"I'll take this," I announce.

"Alright," he says, handing me the leather sheaf. "Then I'll take the *katana*... if you don't mind."

"That's fine." I reach for the 9mm. "This is the Anita Blake gun."

"What?" He slings the *katana* on his back. "What are you talking about?"

"Nothing." I pick up the Browning and open the action. Everything looks in order, so I reach for the shoulder rig. "You got ammo for this?"

"Of course," he says. "And wait until you see it."

He disappears into the back again, and when he emerges, he hands me an unmarked box of 9 mm bullets.

"Holy shit," I say, looking into the little box. "These are silver plated. Where the hell did you get silver plated bullets?" That is one bit of vampire lore that's true. Silver bullets, though not an automatic killer, do pack more of a wallop than regular bullets. It is yet another one of Neichia's little projects to discover why.

"Never you mind that," he says.

I smirk. His evasive answer tells me everything. They obviously came from a paramour.

"Alright," I say, changing the subject. "That leaves us with one more knife, the machete, and the rest of the guns. I think you should take the knife."

"How about *you* take the knife for back-up since you know how to use one, and I'll take the shotgun."

"But the shotgun has no killing power," I protest. "What good will it do you?"

"At point blank range, it might. Flush up against the skull, it could take the head off. But even if I can just get a clean shot to the face, it should disorient the vamp at the very least, maybe enough to let me swoop in with the sword for a kill."

"Gotcha." I pick up the second blade to inspect it. Out of its sheath it looks like a smaller, more modern version of a Bowie knife, with a 7-inch fixed blade, partially-serrated on the heel about two inches from the guard. It's much lighter than what I'm used to, but it has a good balance and is small enough to hide.

"As you wish," I agree, "but I'm good now with the two knives and the gun."

"Take the machete," he says. "It's good for hacking heads off, and it has a shoulder strap."

I nod and sling the machete onto my back. Sunny gathers up the remaining weapons and returns them to the secret room.

Just a small gesture, putting his weapons away, but at that moment it seems particularly poignant. Like our pointless discussion about real estate, Sunny returning his toys back to where they belong makes the same basic assumption: We will both make it back.

CHAPTER 30

WE TAKE RODEO DRIVE and cut through Beverly Hills, silently passing those exclusive shops on the 300 and 400 blocks—Christian Dior, Cartier, Dolce & Gabbana, FENDI, Gucci, Giorgio Armani, Valentino, Harry Winston, Tiffany & Co., De Beers, et al—now darkened and lonely, mist threading through the palms on the deserted sidewalks. A cold sense of foreboding creeps down my spine.

Sunny turns the McLaren onto Bianca's quiet street shortly after 11 o'clock. A dense night fog has rolled inland, clothing the late evening hour in a spooky chill.

Once we pull up to Bianca's massive gates, the foreboding turns to dread.

"The gates are open," Sunny observes.

I eye the massive ironwork structures. "What do you think it means? Broken gates? Hell of a time to have broken gates."

"No," he says softly, "they're not broken. She's left them open for us, because she's sent her human security team home. No witnesses."

"Oh. Shit."

"My thoughts exactly."

Navigating up her long driveway, I peer out into the cloudy darkness of her estate, wondering where she's been keeping her revenant all this time. Has it been here? Is it lurking out there even now?

Once we arrive at Bianca's circular drive, we see several other cars, though I can only identify Ragnar's HUM-V on sight.

Interesting.

So our Viking vampire has gone over to the dark side, has he? What has Bianca offered him in return? He is older than Bianca by several centuries, so his backing of her flag is a major boon since it really ought to be the other way around. What can she give Ragnar that he can't otherwise get on his own?

As Sunny pulls the McLaren into place beside a silver Porsche Carrera GT, I get my first taste of them.

Newcomers.

Bianca has guests, and judging by the fact that I can sense them from inside a car, outside of her mansion, they are old. Very old.

I turn to Sunny. "Feel that?"

"What?"

"The new vamps. What do you think it means?"

Sunny frowns at me as he puts the car in park. "What new vamps?"

Carradhy.

Witch.

Then I notice a lone figure making its way out from one of the shadowed recesses of the villa's ground floor loggia.

By his shape and the way he moves, sort of stumbling across the gravel in the mist, I identify him immediately as Simon. So she hasn't sent *all* of her humans home.

"Good evening, Simon," I call as I pull the McLaren's door down to close. "Bit chilly for you to be out here alone, isn't it?"

"Um. Yes." Simon blinks at us owlishly through his glasses. "Mistress Bianca asked me to wait out here for you. I've been waiting for a few hours." He blinks again.

I get the impression he is blinking away the residual effects of a nap. And he doesn't seem particularly bothered by the fact that Sunny and I are both armed to the teeth. Sunny holds the shotgun loosely in one hand and has slung the *katana* across his back. I have the Bowie knife and Browning in plain view, and the machete strapped to my back.

"If you'll follow me, please," he says, turning towards one of the staircases. "Mistress Bianca will want to see you right away."

"And who else is waiting with *Mistress* Bianca?" I ask, falling into step behind him.

"Um." He hesitates. "I don't think the Mistress would like for me to tell you that. They are all with her, so you can see when we get there."

"And where exactly is 'there'?" Sunny asks. He follows closely behind me as we walk through the brightly colored entrance hall. But instead of crossing to the *salon* as I had on my earlier visit, we take a right and walk through a pair of tall, ornately carved doors into a formal dining room.

"The Mistress awaits you in the grand ballroom." Simon leads us through the dining room.

"Oh," we answer in unison. Of course, she'd wait for us in the grand ballroom.

"Jesus," I whisper to Sunny behind me. "You're not picking up on this?" I can't get the taste of them out of my mouth. The weight of their age presses down on me, making it hard to breathe. I rub my arms up and down to dispel the gooseflesh.

"Picking up on what?"

Carrad—

Oh, shut up! I snap at the voice in my head.

We follow Simon through several opulently appointed rooms—Bianca's residence being modeled after villas that predate the common use of hallways—until he leads us to another pair of large, ornately carved doors. Those doors open onto an interior courtyard with a massive glass and iron skylight that occupies nearly the entire ceiling.

From where we stand, in a recessed balcony overlooking the room below, we can see that at the far wall, a large, giltwood throne has been set up on an elevated dais, flanked by several smaller giltwood chairs on either side. Bianca, of course, sits upon the throne, and seated to her right are Ragnar, Anu, and Nemesio.

Dammit. I hadn't picked up on them at all. The strangers had me completely distracted.

One or two steps behind the throne, Constanzo and his goon squad stand on either side, like bodyguards. Well, I hadn't picked up on them either, but their presence is at least predictable.

The strangers sit to Bianca's left.

Simon leads the way down a small, spiral staircase, and then across the large, parquetry floor. We walk towards the throne in silence. As we approach, none of the assembled vampires speak.

Closing my eyes, I quiet my mind as we walk, stretching my auditory and olfactory senses to their limit, pushing myself past the distraction of the newcomers.

Alex is nearby.

And he is alive.

Thank God.

But his scent signature is too faint for me to determine his physical condition or his mood. Best case scenario, I'll find him healthy and pissed off. Worst case scenario, drained and terrified.

And the revenant isn't here. I can detect its stench nowhere on the property. *That* would be easy to pick up. Interesting. Wouldn't Bianca want to keep that thing close by? Within calling distance at least, so it could be summoned to finish us off after she's finished playing with us?

Or is it a control issue? Just how obedient is the monster to its mistress?

I glance over at Sunny. He nods. Does that mean he knows Alex is close? Perhaps he's also thinking along similar lines regarding the revenant. I'd love to ask him, but our time is up. We've crossed the length of the floor and now stand before Bianca and her assembled allies. As Simon bows deeply before the self-proclaimed *Basilissa* of Los Angeles, the other vampires coldly stare at us, their expressions blank except for Constanzo, who sneers at me.

Then, to my astonishment, Simon proceeds to prostrate himself on the floor Persian Court-style, pressing his forehead down to the polished wood. As Sunny and I watch this awkward demonstration, I wonder what on earth Bianca has promised her human secretary to inspire such a syco-phantic demonstration of loyalty. But I know the answer before I have even finished forming the question: Without doubt, Bianca has promised Simon the gift of immortality.

I catch Sunny's eye. He raises an eloquent eyebrow, and I see he's come to the same conclusion. Bianca prob-ably made the promise to Simon without mentioning the extreme risk involved in the process. If she has forewarned him and he still wants to attempt the transition, then he is a fool.

The vampires continue to stare at us in a silence pulsat-ing with tension. I assess the three unknowns to Bianca's left. The vampire sitting next to Bianca is a female of Celtic origin, with blazing orange hair, brilliant green eyes, and freckles faded from centuries spent out of the sunlight. Her body could have been no older than 15 or 16 when she was turned, but no trace of childhood remains in her eyes. Those eyes watch me carefully, but I can't detect malice in them, only wary curiosity. She doesn't appear to be armed, unless she has weapons hidden behind her giltwood chair.

The man sitting to the Celtic vampire's left is very small, not much larger than the Celt. He looks to be of Gallic origin, with black eyes, black hair touched elegantly with silver at the temples, and a strong Roman nose. He wears an expression of haughty boredom, more concerned with picking at something under one of his fingernails than with anything having to do with Sunny and me. He, too, appears unarmed.

The third vampire seated on Bianca's left is a woman as large as her two companions are small. From her seated position, she looks to be somewhere around 6'5" or 6'6", with a sturdy, athletic build. She has pure white, baby fine hair that floats around her head and shoulders in cloudy wisps. Her skin is almost as white as her hair, giving her the look of an albino, but her eyes are the pure, radiant blue of a clear spring sky. Those eyes are full of questions, and I detect the barest hint of uneasiness in her.

I roll the taste of these newcomers around in my mouth. They are dampening their auras, but they cannot hide everything from me. The teenager feels around 900 years old, the Gallic vampire around 1200, and the giantess about the same. With a shock, I realize I've just pinpointed their ages.

Carradhy.

Witch.

Dammit. I'll have to worry about that later. If there is a later. I've brought a knife to the wrong sort of fight. Of course I'd realized this would be the case back at Sunny's studio, but what was I supposed to do? Bianca has Alex.

And what is Bianca waiting for?

What are these newcomers doing here? I taste a level of ambivalence in them that I find lacking in the vampires on Bianca's other side. What are they ambivalent about? And why aren't they armed?

Suddenly, Ragnar surges to his feet. "Bow down before your *basilissa.*" In a movement too rapid for me to track, he pulls an ancient double-bladed battle axe from its sheath on his back, and stands ready to fight. It is a fearsome display, and I'm immediately reminded of the Vikings in the Byzantine Varangian Guard. Could that perhaps be Ragnar's origin? In that case, his role as Bianca's supporter makes perfect sense. Originally supposed to be imperial bodyguards, the Scandinavians in the Varangian Guard soon appointed themselves emperor-makers, controlling their charges from behind the scenes. When their puppet-emperor inevitably resisted against such control, the Guards would simply kill him and raise another, more pliant puppet-emperor in his place. I wonder briefly if Bianca is aware of this. Knowing your history can come in mighty useful in the vampire world.

"Now, now, Ragnar," Bianca says as she stares down at Sunny and me from her superior vantage point, "I am not their *basilissa* just yet. First, we have some things to discuss."

"Who are your new friends, Bianca?" I ask as Ragnar reluctantly sits back down. "Have you brought in some hired guns?"

"In a sense, yes," she answers, smiling at me coldly. "These three are my constitutional consultants, Penarddun of Dublin, Thibault of Paris, and Farahilde of Vienna. They are assisting me in drawing up *Nomos* for Los Angeles."

"Bianca," Farahilde says, speaking for the first time, her tiny, girlish voice totally at odds with her colossal size. "Why are these vampires armed? What is going on here?"

"These vampires are armed," Bianca responds coolly, keeping her eyes focused on Sunny and me, "because they have come here tonight to kill me. Haven't you?"

"Is that true?" Penarddun turns to ask, her voice heavy with the sing-song cadences of Irish Gaelic. "Have you come here tonight to kill your *basilissa*?"

"She's not our *basilissa*," Sunny declares. "She's a murdering tyrant."

Apparently finding this exchange more interesting than whatever he was trying to extract from under his fingernail, Thibault leans back and whispers something in Penarddun's ear. A look of annoyance flashes across Bianca's face, though I can't tell whether she's responding to Sunny's words or to whatever Thibault is up to.

"No revolution is ever bloodless," Bianca pronounces as she focuses her attention back onto Sunny. "The casualties sustained by our *Koinon*, though very tragic, have remained within the numerical range of acceptable collateral damage. Far more would die, both human and vampire, should Los Angeles be allowed to continue in its present state."

"So the death of the few to benefit the many," I answer sarcastically. "How very Machiavellian of you, Bianca."

"Ah," Bianca responds, "you are more right than you know, my dear Sonia. Niccolò, though a tedious bore at dinner parties, had a very astute understanding of the political dynamics of power. To rule through fear is indeed more humane than to rule through love, since it's fear that promotes peace among subjects, while love promotes only anarchy."

"So it was in the name of peace then," I countered, "that you imported an Old World revenant and used it to cull the population of Los Angeles's *Neoi* vampires?"

"*Pardonez-moi, votre majesté*," Thibault suddenly cuts in, "*mais je n'arrive pas à comprendre pourquoi vous réprenez d'une accusation des personnes ploncs.*"

"I answer their charges," Bianca explains to the French vampire, "because I want them to understand why they must die tonight. I want them to understand that what I do, I do for the greater good of the whole vampire *Koinon* of Los Angeles."

She refocuses her attention back on me. "So, to answer your question, Sonia, I did indeed import the revenant to cull the population of *Neoi* vampires in the name of peace, as well as in the name of security."

"Security?" Sunny exclaims. "That thing attacked us in public! Its presence here in this city poses a *greater* risk to our security."

Bianca sighs. "You are failing to see the big picture, as the Americans say. As my consultants here will attest, the population of vampires in Los Angeles has been allowed to grow unchecked for far too long. The greater the number of vampires in any given area, the greater the risk for exposure. The size of the Los Angeles *Koinon* threatens the security of all vampires everywhere."

"It's true," Penarddun affirms as the two other Old World vampires nod in agreement. "The size of the *Neoi* vampire population in this city threatens us all. It would never have been allowed to grow to such a large size if you had a proper *politeia* in place here. *Basilissa* Bianca's actions here might seem overly harsh, but they have been undertaken for the good of us all *and* with the blessings of the *Synedrion*."

"Yes," Farahilde concurs. "What is more, your armed presence here in your *basilissa*'s throne room is evidence enough of the dangerous subversive elements in your *Koinon*."

"And what about Elfreida the *Riassegnessa*?" I demand. "She was a not a *Neoi*. Was she also a subversive element in the *Koinon*?" At the sound of Elfie's name, the Austrian vampire's eyes widen slightly, but Nemesio cuts in before she can answer me.

"Enough of this!" the Spaniard commands. "I don't know why all of you are allowing them to speak! These traitors have come here to kill *Basilissa* Bianca so they can raise that whore Adrienne, the False-*Basilissa*, to the throne! We must kill them now so we can get on with more important business."

Ragnar and Anu nod in solemn agreement, but the three Old World vampires suddenly snap to attention at the sound of Adrienne's name.

"*Comment?*" Thibault turns to Bianca as she cast a malevolent look in Nemesio's direction. "*Le Vampire Adrienne est votre rival au trône? Pourquoi n'avez-vous pas mentionné ceci avant?*"

"I didn't mention it before," Bianca answers carefully, "because I do not give credence to rumor. As far as I know, these two have come here tonight to kill me so they can prevent a *politeia* from being established, so anarchy can continue in Los Angeles uninhibited."

She is good, I have to give her that. But even with the careful modulation of her voice, she can't completely conceal the fact that she is lying. The three Old World vampires bend their heads together in a brief consultation, the level of their voices kept below the range of Sunny's and my hearing.

While the Old World vampires confer with each other, Bianca keeps her face carefully schooled in an expression of impassive composure, despite the fact that she can probably hear what they're saying. Meanwhile, Ragnar and Anu look worried and Nemesio looks downright murderous.

After a few moments, the Old World vampires come to some sort of decision. They each straighten back up in their seats, and turn as a body to focus their attention back on Sunny and me. Penarddun, apparently their spokesperson, speaks first.

"Whom do you serve?" she asks me.

Remembering the agreement Sunny and I had reached with Adrienne just the previous night, I realize for the first time the significance behind that decision.

"The Vampire Adrienne," I answer, the truth of my words ringing through the cavernous room. Behind Bianca's impenetrable facade, I detect the first glimmer of uncertainty in her eyes.

"*La même Adrienne qui a été par le passé connue comme Isolde, l'épouse du vampire Tristan? Qui a quitté L'Angleterre sur la morte de Tristan?*" Thibault demands, his black eyes burning.

I turn to Sonny. "He's asking whether Adrienne is the same vampire who used to be called Isolde, the wife of the vampire Tristan, who left England after Tristan's death.."

I turn back to the French vampire. "We've never known her by any other name than Adrienne, but she might be old enough to be the Isolde of which you speak. We don't know her reasons for leaving England."

"I thought Isolde was supposed to be Irish," Sunny whispers as the three Old World vampires discuss my answer once more amongst themselves.

I look at him and shrug. I, too, had thought Isolde was Irish. Adrienne doesn't sound like she's Irish, at least not the way Penarddun does. But, then again, who am I to say what Irish or English people sounded like over a thousand years ago?

Once more the Old World vampires straighten back up in their seats, though now they turn their collective attention back to their hostess.

"Bianca," Penarddun says, addressing the Italian

vampire with the significant omission of any royal title, "is this rival Adrienne the same Isolde, former consort of the Cornish vampire Tristan?"

All eyes turn expectantly to Bianca. In those few silent moments as Bianca chooses her words, tension thrums through the room. Bianca's allies to her right seem restless, as does Constanzo and his goons still standing behind Bianca's throne. The three Old World vampires keep their attention on Bianca's face, their vampire senses carefully tuned to perceive even the faintest taste of a lie in her words.

"Yes," Bianca says at last, "Adrienne is the same Isolde of Ériu, consort of the Vampire Tristan."

"Then your title," Penarddun says icily, "is not nearly as secure as you led us to believe."

"You brought us here under false pretenses," the giantess Farahilde declares, anger accentuating her Austrian accents. "We came here only to help you construct a constitution, *not* to fight in your war." She stands and the other two Old World vampires follow.

"Do not contact us again," Thibault says, speaking in perfect English for the first time, "until this issue has been settled."

"But you must settle it," Penarddun warns. "In the meantime, the *Synedrion* will be watching. A fully functioning *politeia* must be in place before the year is out."

And then they are gone, their movements so quick they seem to simply vanish. It's a nice effect.

Bianca, who is probably old enough to see them depart, doesn't turn to see them go. She keeps her eyes trained on Sunny and me the whole time, her fine Italian features twisted and ugly. I can feel the rage rolling off of her in waves, causing my stomach to lurch. Despite the departure of the three Old World vampires, Sunny's and my position has not improved much. If anything, Bianca now wants blood more than ever. We have now humiliated her in front of her distinguished guests, and probably tarnished her name in the process.

Now she'll make us pay.

"Simon!" she barks at the still prostrate form on the floor, "Get up, you fool, and bring in the human. Ragnar! Relieve—"

Everything suddenly goes into slow motion.

I believe Bianca is ordering Ragnar to relieve us of our weapons, but the rapid pump action and then unexpected roar of Sunny's shotgun drowns out her words. I have just enough time to register a ringing in my ears and the spray of blood as Ragnar topples over backwards, chair and all, before one of Constanzo's goons comes for me.

It's begun.

CHAPTER 31

ONSTANZO'S GOON IS MOVING fast, blade out, poised for a tomahawk-style, high-line snipe with enough force behind it to crush my skull. Planting my feet, I get the Bowie knife up for the block before impact. Steel hits steel, the goon's blade skidding along my outer edge as he leans all of his strength into me.

Dammit. Bastard is strong.

From the corner of my eye, I see Ragnar surge to his feet, roaring with deadly rage through the bloody remains of his face. He advances on Sunny with his ax.

Deflecting the goon's blade off to the right, I bring mine down in a deep, inward slash across his torso, then quickly dance back, hands up and ready. I go rapidly through the change, teeth throbbing, senses sharpening.

The goon, whom I recognize from Elfie's house, glances down at the ragged tear I've left across his upper body, then looks up at me and hisses. His canines have fully descended into razor sharp fangs, and I can see he's filed down his bottom row of teeth into equally dangerous points. But his teeth aren't what bothers me. I have eyes only for the wicked plain-edged knife in his right hand with its Japanese-style Tanto point. Though several inches shorter than mine, which would make blocking with his blade more difficult, it's still new and looks expensive, perhaps even custom. That means high quality steel, almost certainly a higher quality than my old Bowie knife, which translates into a sharper, stronger blade better able to hold its edge.

This could be a problem.

Suddenly, the goon closes with a straight stab to my midsection. Bastard is fast, no time for a disrupting attack to his hand. Instead, I wrench my body out of the way, swinging my right foot to the rear, pulling the Bowie up and back, catching his blade on its heel. Then, taking advantage of his proximity, I disengage his blade, rotating my own while firing an inward angular thrust over his left arm and into his neck, punching a nice hole, but missing the carotid artery.

The goon's pale eyes widen with shock, and perhaps fear. Having a Bowie knife plunged into your neck will do that to you. I know this from personal experience. Before he recovers, I give my knife a nasty twist, ripping it out of his neck and snapping my arm back to follow up with a vertical thrust to the groin.

Long ago, Owen taught me to always go for the groin. Although it's difficult to hit the femoral artery, the shock value is high, especially if you are fighting a man. And wouldn't you know that, for nearly two centuries, every knife fight I've ever been in was against a man. Shocking, I know.

I can tell he's still trying to make sense out of the big

hole I left in his neck, but as I come in low, his masculine instincts kick in. He swivels his hips out of the way so that I catch him on his outer hip. Tearing my blade free before he can take advantage of my proximity, I dance back a few steps, reflecting on the two things I've learned about my opponent.

His straight thrust to my midsection tells me he's a young vampire, still clinging to human strategies of engagement. Not too much damage can be done to a vampire with a knife to the midsection. My own diagonal cut was to shock and unsettle him, not to do any real harm. He has probably already healed himself of the wound, though I take a certain satisfaction in ruining his lovely designer shirt beyond repair.

And I far outclass him as a fighter. I am older and more skilled with a knife than this goon, and I've been able to take advantage of the fact that he's grossly underestimated me. But he's still fast—far faster than I'd have expected from someone so young. He is still dangerous.

And I can see by the grim look on his face that he no longer underestimates me.

We continue to circle each other in silence. Out of the corner of my eye, I see Ragnar lunge towards Sunny with impossible speed, angling his battle ax to cut into Sunny's neck. Sunny, matching Ragnar's speed, slides forward and seizes the Viking's wrist, shoving the ax out of the way. Then, moving close to Ragnar's body, he slides the point of his sword under the Viking's weapon arm, slamming Ragnar's shoulder with his own while he raises the point of his sword over Ragnar's head. Ragnar desperately struggles against him, but it's too late. Sunny angles his sword into a horizontal position under Ragnar's neck and pulls, cutting deeply into the Viking's throat.

Anu begins to scream.

The goon, smiling a little as he thinks to take advantage of my momentary distraction, closes fast with a low line straight thrust to my groin. Someone needs to have a talk with him about the birds and the bees in a knife fight. Low-line attacks to the groin don't affect women in the same way they do men. A painful nick on my pelvic bone is about the best he can hope for unless he manages to get one of my femoral arteries. So, angling my body to narrow his target and protect my inner thighs, I catch his blade easily on the heel of my own.

Not deterred, he disengages quickly and fires a highline thrust to my throat.

In his haste, he over extends himself.

Exactly what I've been waiting for.

I snap backwards, out of the way, then arch my blade in a backhand angular attack to the left, over and outside his guard, plunging my knife deeply into the soft area where the neck meets the shoulder. And I strike gold, severing his subclavian artery as I twist the blade to free it from the suction of his flesh.

Black, arterial blood gushes out of the goon's wound as he hemorrhages all over the floor. Still, it's not a killing blow. His body will repair the wound quickly enough for him to resume the fight, but he is too young to realize this and the sight of so much blood panics him. Dropping his blade to the floor, he staggers back, holding his hands up to the wound as if to catch the blood pouring out of it.

From his scent, I know this is the vamp that attacked

Alex's dog, so I show him no mercy. Lunging forward with a highline back cut across his throat, my blade's front edge cuts into him deeply, scraping against his neck bones as I partially decapitate him. He falls forward onto his knees, exposing the back of his neck. I put some muscle into it, and a few expert cuts, like a butcher through bone and sinew, is all it takes. I launch the bastard into oblivion. The head falls with a thud to the floor, its body crumpling after it, pumping out blood to the rhythm of the goon's still-beating heart.

Glancing quickly around me, I have just enough time to see Sunny backpedaling across the floor, vaulting over Ragnar's headless body as he fends off a furious assault by Anu, who alternates her attack between the wickedly sharp broadsword she holds in one hand and the honest-to-God war hammer she holds in the other. This is an unfortunate turn of events. I'm not sure Sunny has it in him to kill a woman, murderous vampire villain or no.

But those few seconds of thought are all I can spare for Sunny's plight. Like a hydra monster with one of its heads cut off, another goon has come to take the place of his dead compatriot. And this one—whose name I remember is Jeremy—has a distinct advantage. Having seen me fight and kill Goon Number One with some of my best moves, he knows I can handle a knife, and that I'm fast.

We circle each other silently, each trying to goad the other into action first. I decide to test the waters. If I can neutralize Jeremy, I can assist Sunny in his moral dilemma.

I need to know two things: Can he fight? And how fast is he?

I spring forward with a highline thrust to the throat. As

expected, he twists his body out of the way. Yes, he's fast. But I'm faster.

Suddenly, he feigns an inward angular attack to the left side of my neck.

I duck under the blow, my body moving to the right just as he snaps his arm back and fires a backhand thrust catching me squarely on the right shoulder as I come up out of the duck.

The combined force of his thrust and my own body movements causes the blade to bite deep, down into my shoulder bone.

I feel nothing at first, but as my body recovers from its initial shock, the searing pain of the wound, burning like liquid fire, explodes through my shoulder and arm as he tears his blade out of me. Blood pours from the wound. I have to raise my guard to keep it from compromising my grip.

Son of a *bitch*! God damn complacency will get you every fucking time!

I made a rookie mistake. Something Owen would have berated me for if I'd pulled it during a sparring match.

Still, now I know a few things about Jeremy. He's better with a knife than I first thought, perhaps as good as I. He's smart. He's fast. I have to dig deep into my bag of tricks to come up with something he won't expect.

At that moment, I hear a yelp somewhere to my left and glance over to see Sunny ducking under a swooping blow from Anu's war hammer, the blunt head of the weapon just missing his face. Dammit…he's not fighting back. His misplaced chivalry is going to get him dead. I need to hurry this along.

Turning back to Jeremy, I decide on another ruse, though this time I'll make it count. Dropping my wounded shoulder to appear more hurt than I really am, I invite him to come in with a thrust to the left side of my neck.

Jeremy dutifully obliges, anticipating that I'll leave the non-wounded side open and vulnerable while I'm busy favoring the wounded right shoulder. As his blade fires towards me, I abruptly slide forward, crowding into his body. I use my speed to grab his blade hand by the wrist before he can adjust his attack to close-quarter range.

As I execute the block, I drive my body even closer, squaring my shoulders with his, and I head-butt him straight in the face. Men never expect this move from a woman, and I catch the look of surprise on his face just before his nose crunches under the force of my forehead.

Jeremy staggers back, blood flowing out of his broken nose. I quickly take advantage of his disorientation with a left-hand strike to his chin, then a feigned vertical thrust to his groin.

Predictably, he scoots the family jewels backwards beyond my reach, bending at the waist like a matador so he can deliver a high-line straight thrust to my eyes.

As the attack comes in, I strike his blade hand with my left. This redirects the force of his blow away from my face while I move my blade hand to the left. I drag the blade across his extended right forearm in a horizontal chop.

My blade cuts deeply into him. As his weapon slips from his fingers, clattering to the floor, I know I've severed his radial nerve.

He is done.

"Don't do it, Jeremy," I growl as he eyes his fallen blade.

"You know you can't beat me left-handed. Don't even try it—I don't want to have to kill you tonight."

Then, out of the corner of my eye, I see Sunny go down with Anu on top of him. Taking a few steps back, I glance cautiously over at the duo. Anu has dropped the war hammer and now holds Sunny down with her left hand while using her right hand to aim the sword at his throat. Sunny has dropped his *katana* on the way down. He's using one hand to try to pull Anu off of him by the hair, while the other grips Anu's right forearm to keep her from plunging the sword into him. The sword point hovers dangerously close to Sunny's windpipe, mere inches away from a killing blow.

Glancing back at Jeremy, I know Anu will soon realize she cannot not take Sunny single handed, and will need both to plunge that sword into him. Normally this wouldn't be a worry, but given his awkward position and the fact that he has dropped his sword, Anu might be strong enough to kill him. She is at least as old as Ragnar, and with that age comes amazing strength. I need to knock Anu off of Sunny, and I need to do it quickly.

Forcing myself to wrench my attention away from Sunny to concentrate on the vamp standing in front of me, I notice that Jeremy has relaxed his stance, his useless right arm hanging at his side as it begins its healing. This is a very good sign.

"I don't want to have to kill you tonight," I repeat, looking him in the eyes as I take a firm step forward. "This is not your war. Our fight tonight is with Bianca and Bianca alone."

Taking a second step forward, I pause a moment to read for any aggression in his body language. Then I take a third step towards him and now stand within reach of his blade. If I can get the blade out of his reach, he'll be effectively neutralized. Then I can help Sunny.

"I don't know what she's promised you," I continue, still careful to look him in the eye, "but it can't be worth losing your life."

As I slowly squat down, reaching for Jeremy's knife while keeping my eyes carefully trained on his face, several unexpected things happen all at once.

Somewhere to my left, a door opens, followed immediately by the scuffling and grunting sounds of a physical altercation and the loud cracks of wooden furniture being smashed. Next, a heavy thud. Even without seeing it, I'm sure a body hit the floor, immediately followed by thundering footsteps and the unmistakable sound of a shot gun's slide action.

I have no more time to fool around with Jeremy. I grab his blade off the floor and scoot myself backwards to a safe distance, looking towards Sunny just in time to see Alex fire the shotgun at point blank range directly into Anu's body. The force of the shot at such close range blows Anu's form off of Sunny, the spreading projectiles taking her mainly in the head, neck, and upper chest.

Sunny, free of the Finnish vampire, grabs his *katana* and executes a floor kip back onto his feet and advances on Anu's crumpled, bloodied body. His face is grim.

I turn back to Jeremy. Something is wrong. His body has gone limp, sagging downwards towards the floor, though he is still standing, surprise showing in his eyes. Blood pours out of his mouth, and a crimson stain on his white shirt spreads outward from his heart and soon covers his entire chest.

"Jeremy?"

Jeremy's body convulses, and he drops to the floor like a marionette with cut strings. On his way down, I catch the flash of steel as it licks across his shoulders before his head rolls off and falls with his body to the floor.

Constanzo now stands in Jeremy's place, *en guard* with a short, bloody sword pointed at my throat. He has murder in his eyes.

CHAPTER 32

"ORA PROSSIMO, LA MIA *bella Sonia, non potete combatterli con quella lama barbara. Be sia civilizzato e prenda la spada di Anu.*"

The Italian vampire, having killed his own goon, apparently for no good reason, now stands before me in the classic fencing stance: weapon arm forward, left arm tucked neatly behind his back. He uses a Roman *gladius*, or short sword, for his weapon of choice. If authentic, the *gladius* would be centuries older than Constanzo, who was just a few decades younger than me. It would also be a very well-made weapon and one I couldn't fight effectively with a Bowie knife.

Unfortunately, this seems to be exactly what Constanzo is trying to tell me. He gestures towards my weapon arm when he says the words *con quella lama barbara*: barbarous weapon…barbarous knife? Then he points off to the left, towards Anu's lifeless body, when he says *e prenda la spada di Anu*: take Anu's sword?

Good advice. Problem is, it comes from Constanzo, and I really don't want to follow any kind of orders—Italian or English—coming from him.

Why is he trying to help me out? I have no idea. Why is he speaking Italian? He knows I don't speak Italian. Fucking idiot.

So we just stand there: Constanzo repeating his instructions over and over again in Italian, and me trying to figure out how to conjure up a sword out of thin air so I don't have to follow his recommendation and take Anu's. Honestly, it's kind of ridiculous.

Finally Constanzo loses his temper. "Come *on,* you stupid woman!" he shouts in English. "Go get the damn sword from Anu so that I can kill you honorably!"

Displaying my fangs in a chilly smile, I relax my guard, sheathing the Bowie knife as I make my way cautiously over to Anu's decapitated body. Sunny is now struggling with Nemesio, who appears very skillful with the cup-hilt rapier in his right hand. The Spaniard's athleticism and creativity bear the marks of a born swordsman, who mastered the art before the advent of gunpowder in Western Europe made such skills obsolete. I fear that Nemesio's finesse might just be enough to conquer Sunny's brute strength and speed.

Beyond Sunny and Nemesio, I see Simon's prone form sprawled out on the floor next to a pile of splintered furniture and assume that's the source of the sounds I'd heard before. Alex must have hit him over the head with a chair.

"Come on, Sonia," Constanzo taunts, "you can't delay the inevitable. Pick up the sword and come back to face your doom!"

Face my doom?

Unfortunately, Anu died atop her sword, her sticky gore now drenching the weapon. Sliding it out from under her, I use her sleeve to try to get the hilt clean enough for me to hold in a firm grip. I'm already going to be handicapped enough, having to fight with a *sword*, without the added complications of having the damn thing slipping out of my hand.

Once I've saturated her sleeve, I shuffle over to her legs and use one of her voluminous knit pantaloons to finish the job. As I do this, I scan the room for Alex and Bianca. Alex appears to be nowhere in the room, and I pray to the Powers That Be that he had enough sense to get the hell out of here while he could. Bianca still sits on her throne, watching the battle between Nemesio and Sunny with undisguised pleasure.

Satisfied I've gathered as much intel as I can while cleaning off the sword hilt, I straighten up and make my way back over to Constanzo, swinging his sword around experimentally to gauge its weight and balance. By the time I stand once more before the nasty little Italian, I've reached three conclusions. First, this sword is far too long for me, and not just because I'm trying to treat it like a giant Bowie knife. This weapon had been made for someone considerably taller and heavier than me or Anu. Perhaps it once belonged to her father. Or her brother. Second, this information really doesn't matter much since I have no idea how a sword is supposed to feel in the first place. Even if the damn thing had been made to my personal specifications, I still wouldn't have known the first thing about how to wield it.

And third? There's only one play I have left.

Standing once again in front of Constanzo, I inch forward, praying he doesn't figure out what I'm about to do. Timing is critical, as is speed—I'm slightly older than

Constanzo, and so can move faster. Whether it will be fast enough, I'm about to find out.

Siete spaventato il, mia bella? he says, stretching his smirk into a menacing snarl, "*Dovreste essere.*"

"You know, Constanzo," I say, "you're an idiot. I've always thought so and now you are confirming it. You know damn well I don't speak Italian, so all of your ominous repartee is totally lost on me. If you want to scare me, you're going to have to do it in English. Maybe a little in French. Otherwise, you're totally wasting your time."

"Fine, you uneducated moron. English it is." He then drops the point of his sword, leaving his torso open, as he appears to take a moment to think of something more insulting to say.

It's most likely a ruse. It has to be. But I take the opening anyway. With all the speed I can muster, I drop Anu's sword and grab the Browning from its holster under my arm, and lunge forward so I can fire the gun into Constanzo's face at point blank range.

But it was a ruse. As soon as I move, Constanzo pivots backwards on his right foot while catching the silver bullet just below his temple. He screams in rage as the bullet bursts through the side of his skull in an explosion of bone and brain. He staggers back, then drops to his knees, his weapon clattering to the floor. He is defeated. All of his finesse is no match for a Browning 9mm with silver bullets. I think of Indiana Jones. Stephen Spielberg knew what he was doing.

I holster the gun, and crouch down to pick up Anu's sword. For what I have to do now, it'll make much quicker work of it than a Bowie knife. Constanzo is kneeling on the floor, his head hanging. He is healing, but I cannot allow that. I cannot allow him to be a threat any longer. I move in to make the chop, but something stops me. I crouch down so that I'm face to face with him.

"It didn't have to end—" I start to say.

"Bitch," he hisses.

And with a speed I did not know he possessed, he grabs his blade with one hand, and with the other he grabs me by the hair and drags me down onto his blade that is tilted up at my body at a 45 degree angle. The blade pierces my chest, through my right breast, missing my heart by inches. Constanzo keeps dragging me down upon it until it bursts through my back, making me look like a damn cocktail sausage with a toothpick stuck through it. Constanzo releases me. I fall back on my ass, unable to breathe.

Somewhere from far away I hear Sunny call my name. Then I hear Constanzo's voice, his words filtering down to me through a haze of pain. "What I was asking you earlier," he hisses, "was whether you were frightened." He begins to laugh as if this were the funniest thing in the world. "I suppose," he says through sputters of laughter, "that by now you must be very frightened, indeed."

Sunny calls my name again, his tone laced with hysteria.

But I'm not frightened, which seems odd. Instead, I coolly assess the situation with a sort of detached precision. I have a sword in my chest. Blood is flooding my chest cavity. My right lung is almost certainly collapsed, but my heart is still intact. I cannot heal and I cannot fight until I get this sword out of me.

And then there is Alex.

Alex has not made his escape, as any sound-minded mortal would. He is creeping up along the north wall behind the thrones, and behind Constanzo, with the shotgun in his hands. And with all the noise that Sunny and Nemesio are making, not to mention Constanzo's absorption in the pleasures of killing me, I don't think he's aware of Alex's approach.

This has some possibilities.

Also, Constanzo and I are at a stalemate. He needs his sword if he's going to cut off my head, but I'm not so far gone that I've loosened my grip on Anu's sword. If he moves in to get his gladius, I'm taking his head off. We are at a standstill.

And then the tell-tale sound of the shotgun's slide action rings through the room.

Constanzo freezes. Alex is behind him. And Constanzo has no weapon.

Slowly, I get to my feet, and Constanzo follows suit.

The Italian then slowly brings up his hands in a gesture of surrender.

"Sorry, Constanzo," I say. "But there will be no surrender for you."

I drop down to the floor, and scream, "*Now!*"

Constanzo's head comes apart, the remaining scatter of projectiles screaming overhead as they tear through the space I had just occupied. I cover my head with my hands and tuck into a ball as bits of gore rain down upon me. His body crumples sideways to the floor.

I lay for a moment on my side, not really wanting to move. God, I need to get this sword out of me, but I don't want to open my eyes and face the fact that I have Constanzo's brain matter all over me, though it is a fitting end for that bastard.

I really want to go home.

"Jesus Christ, Sonia." Alex is kneeling next to me, the shotgun now slung onto his back. He touches my hair, smoothing a chunk of gore out of it. "How are you still alive? Holy fuck!"

Suddenly a pair of strong hands hook under my armpits and haul me up to my feet. "She'll be okay once I get this sword out of her," Sunny says. "It takes more than a sword through the chest to kill us. Though this must be annoying as fuck."

Sunny!

I whirl around, whacking the protruding sword against Sunny's chest, and see Nemesio's headless body collapsed in a viscous pool of blood near the stairs where we had first entered. It looks like he is missing some limbs, too.

I turn to Sunny. "How did you—?" I freeze. Sunny's eyes are totally black, the way they were the first time we faced Constanzo and his goons. I take a step back. "Sunny? Your eyes. Are you okay?"

Sunny follows me backwards and grabs Constanzo's sword hilt, and rips the damn thing right out of my chest, the blade scraping against my breast bone.

"Ouch!" I scream.

"Yep," he replies cheerfully. "Never better."

Alex drops down to his haunches, his head in his hands. "Jesus," he says again. "I think I'm going to puke."

"You and me both," I wheeze. I'm doubled over, hands on my knees, dizzy as hell, but still on my feet. I give my head a shake. "Sunny. We need to get you to Neichia."

Sunny holds his hands out if front of him, gazing at them. "I can feel it," he says. "I can feel the creature. It's living inside of me. Crazy, huh? And once it came out, Nemesio was no match. He had no fight left once I tore his right arm off. He could still fight left-handed, but he lost all of his fancy moves."

"Jesus, Sunny. I don't like this."

"Guys?" Alex interjects. "You're not done yet. What about *her*?"

Sunny and I snap our heads up in unison and look at Bianca's now empty throne. I hadn't really forgotten about her. Not exactly. I just sort of assumed that now, with her allies gone and her goons dead, she wouldn't put up much of a fight. Bianca's never been one to get her own hands dirty. She hires others to do that for her.

"There she is." Alex points up to the balcony, where we came in. "She's up there."

Sure enough, there she stands, smiling down upon us almost benignly. Except for the full set of fangs.

The taste of sulfur is thick in the air.

Without warning, every door in the room suddenly slams shut.

Carradhy.

I can feel power throb like a slow heartbeat through the room, the air suddenly charged with static electricity. The tiny hairs on the back of my neck stand up like raised hackles, and goosebumps erupt across my arms. I catch Sunny's eye. He nods, then pulls me closer to where he stands.

Then Bianca vanishes.

Witch.

"You really didn't think I was going to let you three go tonight without a fight," comes the cultured Italian voice behind us. "Not after you spoiled my big 'coming out' party?"

The three of us whirl around. I'm about to say something obnoxious about it not being *that* big of a party, but once I catch sight of Bianca's face, my mouth snaps shut. Instead I take a large step backwards, pulling Sunny and Alex with me.

Bianca has gone through the change, though a different change from any I've ever seen before. Her eyes shine blood red with no pupils or irises, her teeth are all long and fanged like a deep sea creature.

"Bianca," I whisper, "what has happened to you?"

But I already know the answer. The black arts.

Pemulwuy, my Maker's voice, whispers to me again: *Witch*.

The one-time *courtesan* throws her head back and laughs, giving the three of us a good view of all her dreadful fangs. Then she stops, fixing me with an almost coquettish look.

"Why?" she asks. "Don't you like it? Don't you like the vision of your *Basilissa* in all Her glory?"

Sunny is the first to respond. "Bianca," he hisses. "Why would you want this?"

"Why, indeed, *mio amore*? What are the two things most sought after in this world?" She steps towards Sunny, reaching out to catch one of his curls in her clawed hand. "Love and Power." She stalks behind Sunny, trailing a hand across his shoulder. "And you could not give me your love, my golden Adonis. And then you gave it to this Australian slut!" She casts a pointed look my way. "So, I have nothing left to me except for power. Oh, but it is a beautiful power," she adds.

"Sunny," I growl. "Tear her apart."

"Oh, he can't." Bianca smiles at me, again bearing her

terrible fangs. "He has the creature inside him now, and I am that creature's Mistress. He cannot harm me. The interesting thing is that I cannot get him to harm *you*. He is stronger than I thought."

I can feel waves of crackling electricity pulsing from her as I hold her attention.

"It's customary," she continues, "for a monarch to perform an act of justice and an act of mercy on their coronation day. You two..." Her eyes flash to Sunny and me. "...traitors of the realm, would-be assassins of your *basilissa*, I sentence you to death."

No kidding.

"But you, my darling," she declares, turning her attention back to Alex, "I sentence you to the opposite. I shall mercifully free you from death so you may serve me forever." She looks to me, her blood red eyes swirling with fire. "So let it be known to you, Sonia, in your final moments, that since you stole from me, I shall now steal from you!"

Well, so much for Sunny's nice theory that Bianca wouldn't blame me for his love. I was right, he was wrong. If we manage to make it out of this, I will have to remember to tell him so.

"But first," she continues, turning her attention back to Alex as she backs up a few steps, "there is one thing I need for you to do for me, my love. I want you to kneel before me, Alex Chevalier, kneel before me and abjure this Australian whore."

Looking to Alex, I see the strain in his face. His hands balled up into fists, he begins to shake. He closes his eyes, his jaw clenched. Slowly, painfully, one leg buckles, then the other until he's on his knees on the parquetry floor.

"That's right," Bianca breathes in soothing tones, "don't try to fight it. No human can deny me."

One of his shoulders begins pressing down towards the floor, straining under a massive weight, until it forces him to plant one hand on the floor. Then the next shoulder, straining, then buckling until his second hand is on the floor. Beads of sweat trickle down his face.

"Good," Bianca breathes. "That's right, my lover. Now crawl to me, crawl to me and abjure this bitch."

Alex still fights, but the force is too great. If he doesn't move, his arms will snap in half. He begins to shuffle across the floor, each movement forward a triumph of Bianca's power over his self-control.

Halfway across the distance between them an anguished sob escapes Alex's lips.

"That's enough, Bianca!" Sunny shouts. "You've had your fun. You win." As he makes a move towards her, Bianca holds up one hand, freezing him in place.

"You've had your chance, my golden Adonis. Now you will suffer."

As Sunny struggles against his invisible restraints, Alex closes the remaining distance between himself and Bianca.

"Good, good, my lover," Bianca murmurs, running her other hand through his hair. "Now, gaze into my eyes and abjure Sonia forever."

Alex raises his head to look at Bianca's face and a low, gurgling noise escapes his lips.

"What, my darling?" Bianca responds. "I cannot hear you, so you must speak louder."

Another small, gurgling noise.

"Are you still fighting?" Bianca asks, delight in her

voice, "Oh, you and I are going to have a *wonderful* time together." She glances at me. "Sonia, I'm impressed. You do know how to pick your men."

The gurgling noise comes forth once more, though this time with a little added force. Alex is trying to speak.

Bianca hears it, too.

"That's it," she breathes. "You've got one word down, only two more to go."

But in her enthusiasm, Bianca must be relinquishing a little control because what Alex says next rings through the ballroom clear as a bell.

"*Fuck you!*" He stabs her through the foot with the small, serrated-edged, combat knife I thought remained concealed down the back of my pants.

For a moment, Bianca's dreadful face remains frozen in a ghastly mask of disbelief. I take advantage of her momentary shock to lunge forward and yank Alex back out of her immediate reach. Then a black rage clouds her features as she releases Sunny from his paralysis and brings both hands together, spinning a white ball of electric power between them.

"Run!" Sunny yells. As I swing Alex up into my arms, his body nearly broken from exhaustion, I have just enough time to see the electric ball expand to the size of a soccer ball before I turn and sprint for the exit, Sunny falling into step behind me.

We make it halfway across the floor before she releases her energy weapon, overtaking us almost instantly. It first feels warm, then hot, then blistering and excruciating. My body lifts into the air, skin crackling and blistering under the electric fire. More electric fire burns through my veins, channeling towards my heart where it builds up dangerously. Unable to move, unable to breathe, I can no longer bear Alex's weight. Once I release him, he falls to the floor, outside the energy field. The electricity continues to build around my heart. I know that when the electric bubble bursts, I will die. It will blast a hole in my chest too large to heal.

And I feel the electric bubble about to burst. Alex must already be dead. No human would be able to withstand this power.

Even as I realize that I, too, will soon be dead, through the white electricity I see two forms standing in front of me on the recessed balcony.

"Enough!"

The word reverberates through the room, straining my eardrums. Then a giant blue wave, stretching from floor to ceiling like a liquid wall, washes towards us. Once it hits us and passes through us, it neutralizes Bianca's electric field. Sunny and I slam to the floor just below the balcony.

Struggling to hold up my head, I see the figures of Adrienne and the Armenian vampire Siroun float effortlessly down the stairs. As Adrienne moves to stand over Alex's prone body, Siroun's physical form dissolves into a swirling blue mist just as Bianca's does the same into a red sulfurous sludge. The two powers surge towards each other, meeting in the center of the room in a raging whirlwind, shattering the massive iron and glass skylight in a deafening explosion. As deadly glass shards rain down to the ballroom below, Adrienne stands by and watches, protected in some sort of force field that extends down to cover Alex. Her hair and clothes stream behind her, and the last thing I see are her eyes glowing with a strange, green fire.

I smell green things, and freshly tilled soil. Then my eyes dim and the world goes dark.

Sweet, sweet oblivion.

This is how it starts.

The only link to the world around me is the sound of my heartbeat, pounding in my ears. Sound is all I have; sight, smell, touch, and taste do not exist here.

But this is different from before.

The pounding of my heart grows stronger, my pulse faster, beat by beat.

Soon, I've reached a critical point where that little muscle is firing away, pushing me over a threshold—but a threshold to what? To the great divide between the world of life and death?

But no. That's not it. I'm being pushed into a warm light, but not one to dissolve into. It strengthens me, flows through my veins, everything becoming more powerful. There is no failing heart here. There is no terror.

But I'm offered a choice. But is it really a choice? I can either stay as I am, or I can become something more. But what is this more?

I hesitate. Do I take the offer? Do I reach for the hand ready to pull me across the threshold? What will I be?

Time stands still.

I reach for the hand.

Power surges through me and I am blasted into oblivion, but not the one I met before—not the one that serves as the fate for all other vampires. Again, I find myself in limbo, but my sense of self is still intact. I am still Sonia. When I open my eyes, it is once more to a world utterly transformed.

Carradhy, Pemulwuy, my Maker whispers.

Welcome, Witch.

CHAPTER 33

FLUFFY MADE THE NEWS. Channel 4 did a short segment on the pit bull who saved his owner from a man-eating mountain lion while jogging in the San Gabriel mountains. There were some minor discrepancies in the chronology of the account. Fluffy was taken to the emergency vet nearly twelve hours before UCLA Medical Center's emergency room treated Alex for chest pains, severe muscle stress, and skin burns. In the end the combination of Fluffy's and Alex's injuries sold the story. Fluffy was a hero.

Nevertheless, two weeks after Adrienne's palace coup, as the events of that night are now being called, Alex looks nervous as we pull into the parking lot at the Westminster Off-Leash Park in Venice.

I unfasten my seat belt, and turn to face him. "What's the matter?"

Alex frowns. "Maybe this isn't such a good idea."

He watches a lady two car-stalls down unloading her three, immaculately groomed spaniels from the back of her Range Rover. "Pit bulls are generally pretty unpopular in these sorts of places. And just look at him."

We both turn to look at the passenger sprawled out across the back seat of Alex's Cougar. Fluffy, the one-eyed, one-time bait dog, covered from head to tail with scarring from his fighting days, now has four ridged, scarlet scars stretching from his shoulders down to his hip bones. He looks like he's been attacked by a dragon, a fact not lost on the vet who noted that the spacing between claw marks indicated this was the largest mountain lion he'd ever heard of. And the fact that the vet had shaved the entire left side of Fluffy's body didn't help matters. As he solemnly gazes back at us with his one golden brown eye, I can't help thinking he looks like Frankendog.

"Screw 'em," I say. "You've dragged me out past my bedtime, and dammit, we're here to celebrate Fluffy's stitches removal. I'll be damned if I'm going to let a few stupid humans chase me away. Sorry," I add when Alex looks at me sharply. "I meant to say a few stupid *people*."

Then I shake my head, laughing a little.

"What's so funny?" Alex demands. "You'd better not be laughing at Fluffy." He reaches back to stroke the dog's lumpy head in consolation.

"No, you twit, I'm laughing at you," I say between snorts of laughter. "Two weeks ago, you went up against the queen witch/vampire of Los Angeles, and miraculously managed to survive to tell the tale. Yet, here you sit in the parking lot of a dog park all worked up because a couple of wankers in khaki shorts and penny loafers might be rude to you because they don't approve of your non-pedigreed dog."

"Fine," he snaps, jerking his door open, "but if someone

hurts the Fluffster's feelings, it's all your fault." In a much gentler tone, he adds, "Come on, Fluffy." He tips his seat forward so the big dog can squeeze out.

Watching Fluffy's clumsy exit from the car, I realize Alex should probably be driving something more like an SUV rather than the Cougar. I tell him as much as he latches Fluffy's leash to his collar and we begin to make our way over to the no-leash zone.

"You're more right than you know," he answers. "I'm actually thinking of getting another dog. I found one at that rescue center Sunny mentioned. I plan to take Fluffy up there next weekend to meet the dog and see if they're compatible."

"Your apartment is kind of small for two dogs," I point out. "Will you get rid of the Cougar?"

He glances over at me. "No. I think I'm going to buy a house. I need a place with a yard—Fluffy would like a yard—and I need a two-car garage."

I frown, impressed. "Wow, putting down roots. That's a big step."

"Yeah, well, it's time I stopped paying rent. And Los Angeles is as good a place as anywhere, I guess."

As we walk over to the no leash area, I notice that several of the other dog owners have stopped playing with their dogs and are blatantly staring at us. I'm not sure if Alex is aware of this, but I slide my sunglasses on top of my head and return their stares with my darkest scowl. Even so, as Alex stoops to unhook Fluffy's leash, a tall, balding man in cargo shorts and a golf shirt begins walking towards us with a self-important air. I ignore his approach and instead focus on Fluffy as he trots purposely towards a group of dogs on the other side of the park, his straight tail swishing happily from side to side in anticipation of meeting some new doggie friends.

At least I hope that's what he anticipates.

"Uh, Alex?" I ask in a low voice.

"Hmmm?"

"He *is* good with other dogs, right?"

"Yes," he murmurs, "but even if he gets into a fight with one, which would never happen, he doesn't have any teeth, remember?"

"Oh, yeah, I forgot about that."

But I needn't have worried. Fluffy joins the small herd of hounds gamboling through the park in some sort of doggie game, huffing and puffing with his tail straight up in the air, looking for all the world like the fat rhinoceros in Jumanji trying to keep up. By that time, the man in cargo shorts reaches us.

He greets us with a smile. "Howdy, folks. How are you this afternoon?"

"Fine," Alex answers in a clipped tone.

Despite myself, I'm tensed up.

"I was just noticing your dog—" Cargo shorts begins.

"What about him?" I snap before he can finish the thought.

"Was he the dog I saw on the news the other night? The one who chased off P-22?"

Alex responds with a proud smile. "He sure is." He visibly relaxes.

It seems Fluffy is a celebrity. In Los Angeles, whose citizens worship celebrity like a religion, it no longer matters that he's a battle-scarred member of a "dangerous" breed.

When Fluffy's steps begin to slow and his stiff tail lowers

to half mast, we know he's getting tired. Half an hour after we arrive, we have Fluffy back on his leash and are heading up Westminster, past the elementary school, towards the funky shops on Abbot Kinney Boulevard.

"Do you remember the conversation we had that night in my apartment?" Alex begins once we'd turned onto Abbot Kinney. "After we were attacked in the alleyway?"

"Hmmm," I reply, "better remind me. A lot happened that night."

"The one where you said honesty was critical to you and we should always be honest with each other?"

I nod. "Yes. I do remember saying that."

"Well…" He pauses a moment, his face fixed in thought, as if trying to think of the best way to phrase what he wants to say. "I have a question for you, and I want you to promise me you'll give me an honest answer."

I think this over for a moment, then nod again. He saved my life. Fuck the security of the *Koinon*. "Done. What's your question?"

"I was wondering if I have anything to worry about regarding the whole vampire community"

"What do you mean?"

"Well, do I 'know too much' as they say? Now that you guys are organizing, is someone going to bring my name up at some meeting or council as a possible security risk?"

I consider his question for a few moments. "I really don't think so. It's pretty well understood that you're my friend and as such, you're under my protection. Since I'm in good with the new *basilissa*, I think you'll be okay."

"Good," Alex says. "In that case, can I ask another question?"

"Shoot."

"Now that Bianca is dead, whatever happened to the revenant? Is it really living inside Sunny now?"

I shake my head. "That's one hypothesis, yes. Neichia ran bloodwork on Sunny, and found nothing to indicate any presence of a new parasite or anything like that. But Sunny says he can feel it, and there's that weird thing his eyes do now to account for." I shrug. "We searched Bianca's property, and couldn't find any trace of it. And there have been no more suspicious killings of either vampires or humans. Who knows?"

"I see. And now you have a new vampire queen?"

"Well, yes and no. Yes, because Adrienne has proclaimed herself our *basilissa*, and the *Koinon* has accepted her. But the *Synedrion* in Greece will not recognize her until she's officially crowned and anointed by the Athenian *hetaireia*, and they're not cooperating with us. They're sending a delegation from Greece to negotiate with us, and they're doing it soon. Adrienne's position is open to challenge until she becomes a member of the *Synedrion*. We're not out of the woods yet."

I bring us to a stop in front of the faded brick store frontage of Equator Books.

International vampire politics are interesting enough, but I have something more pressing on my mind than our new *basilissa*. "Do you mind if I just pop in here for a minute? I want to see if they've got anything from the Modesty Blaise series. I'd honestly forgotten all about Modesty until you brought her up a few weeks ago."

"Sure," he replies, smiling. "The Fluffster and I will just wait out here."

Pulling open the glass door, I step through the doorway into the bookstore and make my way to the back of the shop, barely registering the bookshelves full of books as I pass them by. I actually already own first editions of the entire Modesty Blaise series. What I'm really looking for in this shop is courage—courage to ask the question that has been on my mind since the night we were attacked in the alleyway off Fairfax.

"Any luck?" he asks me ten minutes later as I exit the store.

"Yes!" I say, triumphantly holding up my plastic bag. "They had *The Silver Mistress*. I've been looking everywhere for this." I plan to gift it to Neichia for her birthday. Her library is mostly limited to scientific stuff, so a good 1970s British spy adventure would be good for her.

We continue our progress down Abbot Kinney. In a remarkably even voice, I say, "Now I have question for you."

"Shoot."

"It's kind of a serious question." We stop again, this time in front of Madley, arguably one of my favorite boutiques in all the world. It's a true testimony to the strong feelings I've developed for the man standing in front of me that I'm not even tempted to peek around him to look at the shop's front window.

But then again, this man can get my blood pumping over and beyond a new party dress any day. As I look up into his face, I let myself get lost for a few moments in the intensity of his eyes. His brows are drawn together ever so slightly in concentration as he looks down at me, his lashes curling thickly. He hasn't shaved in a day or two, giving him a slightly rugged appearance. I notice for the first time that he has a dimple on his chin. Just as I suck in a deep, fortifying breath, the wind blows gently through his hair, rustling the tendrils curling at his collar and stimulating my body with his heady scent.

For just a moment, I feel the familiar throbbing of my canines and I'm struck with the urge to pull him down towards me so I can bury my face into his neck to breathe in the scent of him directly from the source. Somewhere in the back of my mind, a dark little voice wonders what he must taste like.

"What is her name?" I ask softly.

He sighs and looks away, resigned. "Naomi. She was a doctor, working with the tribe I was photographing."

"*Was?*"

"Yes. She's dead."

"Oh." I fidget with the bag in my hand. *C'mon, Sonia. You can do this.*

"Look," he says, "I can tell you want to ask more, but I'm not ready to talk about it. I need to work through some things first."

I tear my eyes away from his face and focus on Fluffy's snoozing form at Alex's feet. "I'm sorry to do this, but I need to ask you about us. The *Koinon* considers you my familiar... *Are* you my familiar?"

He exhales heavily, then looks first one way, then the other, to make sure no one is walking close enough to overhear.

"Am I your familiar?" he repeats.

I nod, trying not to notice how my heartbeat suddenly thunders in my ears.

"The thing is," he begins gently, "I've been through this

before. I loved Naomi. And I don't know if this could work out between us. You're a vampire, I'm a human—one who likes being a human and doesn't want to be a vampire. I'm going to get old and die, and you will stay the way you are forever. How could that possibly work?"

Alex pauses and looks away. No matter how frustrating, I understand his question.

"How can I expect you to stay with me when I'm seventy? Or eighty? I *wouldn't* want that. But at the same time, I don't want to die alone—I want someone I can grow old with and who will grow old with *me*." He takes a deep breath. "Someone whose unchanging face I won't come to hate as I creep closer to death with every passing day."

I nod sadly. Of course, I know he speaks the truth. I've already gone through this with Owen. The only difference was that Owen and I had already been married for several years before I became a vampire. We had no choice. How could I expect anyone to *choose* this?

"There are other reasons, too," he says softly. "I want someone I can take home to meet my family. You know what I mean. I want someone who will help my sister over-cook the turkey on Thanksgiving and pitch a softball during the Fourth of July family softball game." Again, he pauses before he whispers, "Someone I can have a family of my own with someday."

With every reason he fires at me, I continue to nod. Looking down at my shoes, I feel the dangerous beginning of tears catch at the back of my throat. So I start walking again, pulling away from him so he won't see me struggling.

How could I have been so stupid to have thought this might work?

How could I have been so selfish?

"But the problem is," he says, catching me by the hand and pulling me gently back to where he stands, "despite all these good reasons, I can't get you out of my head. The best thing for me to do, the *smartest* thing for me to do, would be to just cut off contact with you. Maybe move to another city if I have to. But I just can't."

Pulling my hand out of his, I turn and begin to walk down the sidewalk again as a tear escapes and trickles slowly down my cheek.

"When I wake up in the morning," he calls after me, "the first thing I think about is you. I wonder how your night was and what you did. And when I go to bed at night, your face is the last thing I see before I fall asleep."

I stop and hear him jogging to catch up to where I stand. Once again, he catches me by the hand and pulls me back to face him. And then he pulls me closer, taking advantage of my upturned face to kiss me firmly, but tenderly on the mouth. At first, I'm too surprised to pull away, and as his kiss mingles with my few escaped tears, the heat of his nearness temporarily eclipses the pain in my heart. I become overwhelmed by my naked need for him and abruptly pull away.

"Then what are you saying?" I turn my back on him once more so he can't see my face.

"I need some time, Sonia, to figure some things out. To think of a way to—somehow—make this work. Impossible as it seems, I want to see if there's a way for us to be together without hurting each other."

I don't know what to say. He's said it all already. I can't give him any of the things a normal human woman could, a normal, healthy, natural relationship. But then again, what is normal or healthy—what is a natural relationship? Does such a thing even exist?

Part of me wants to simply make the break, cut him off, make the decision for him and tell myself it's for his own good. But is that playing the martyr? What do *I* want? I'd asked myself that question so infrequently in the past, I can't help but feel that I'm due. I've denied myself companionship for a century, so don't I deserve to be happy, too? Is it alright to be selfish? Just this one time?

I face him once again. "Okay, I'll give you your time, Alex Chevalier. I admit, I also need time to work some things out." I allow myself a small smile as I warn, "But don't make me wait forever. I may have eternity, but you don't. And I've already been alone for too long."

"I won't." Sincerity, passion, and perhaps a little something more dangerous roils together like a tempest in his gray eyes. "I won't make you wait forever. I promise."

I smile up at him, wiping the few errant tears from my face.

Clear tears, by the way. Anne Rice got that wrong.

I go up to my tiptoes to kiss him on the cheek, then walk past him to retrace my steps back to Madley.

Maybe I need a new party dress after all.

The End

Sonia and The Vampires of Los Angeles shall return...

ACKNOWLDGMENTS

It is only very rarely that a novel is born entirely alone. I am most thankful to:

Terry Carter, my beautiful husband and the inspiration for the character Sunny. Without you, this novel would never have been born.

Laura Taylor, my editor, my mentor, my friend. Thank you for your constant encouragement and advice. Without you, dear Laura, this book would not be in print.

Virginia McCollough, my content editor and fellow Early Bird. Thank you for your support for this project, and your opinion that this book is something special.

Catherine Matthews, my dear friend and fellow Early Bird. Thank you for reading the entire manuscript and providing priceless commentary and edits.

L.A. Myles and Julia Bennet, my two beta readers. Thank you for taking a look at my manuscript, and allowing me to test the waters with you. Your encouragement has helped bring this story to the light of day.

Professor David Phillips, PhD. Thank you for helping me come up with the Greek terminology for my vampire world. I will always remember fondly the time I spent sitting in your office talking of vampires and department politics. You were a light in my graduate school days.

Kathy Piller, PhD. Thank you to my dear Latin tutor for creating the glossary of Greek terms at the front of the book. You almost made learning Latin fun... almost.

ABOUT THE AUTHOR

Heather Ewen-Foster is a native of Southern California who calls both Los Angeles and San Diego home. She is a huge fan of Los Angeles noir stories, and everything spooky and mystical. When not writing, Heather is either reading Stephen King, playing her flute or ukulele, or chasing her young twins through their busy schedules. Heather lives with her musician inamorato husband, two precocious children, elderly snake, and Labrador Retriever puppy (who eats everything).